THE AUTHOR: Satoko Kizaki was born in 1939 in Shinkyo in Japanese-occupied Manchuria. At the age of five, she moved to Japan's Toyama Prefecture, a place that was later to become the setting for "The Phoenix Tree." Graduating from college with a degree in English, she married and lived in France and the United States for fifteen years with her husband. Her first story, "Barefoot," written when she returned to Japan in 1979, received *Bungakukai*'s annual Award for New Authors and was nominated for the coveted Akutagawa Prize in 1980. After three stories received consecutive yearly nominations for the prize (one of these was "Flame Trees"), "The Phoenix Tree" was awarded the Akutagawa Prize in 1985. The stories in this volume are selected from the three short-story collections Kizaki has published in Japanese.

THE TRANSLATOR: Carol A. Flath is an assistant professor of Russian language and literature at Duke University. She began her study of Japanese in 1983, and in 1988 her translations of Satoko Kizaki's "Barefoot" and "The Phoenix Tree" won the Japan–U.S. Friendship Commission Prize for the Translation of Japanese Literature awarded by the Donald Keene Center of Japanese Culture at Columbia University.

SATOKO KIZAKI

THE
PHOENIX TREE

and
Other Stories

Translated by
Carol A. Flath

KODANSHA INTERNATIONAL
Tokyo • New York • London

Each story was originally published by Bungeishunju-sha under the titles "Rasoku," "Kaenboku," "Mei howa ru," and "Aogiri" respectively.

Distributed in the United States by Kodansha America, Inc., 114 Fifth Avenue, New York, New York 10011, and in the United Kingdom and continental Europe by Kodansha Europe Ltd., Gillingham House, 38-44 Gillingham Street, London SW1V 1HU. Published by Kodansha International Ltd., 17-14 Otowa 1-chome, Bunkyo-ku, Tokyo 112, and Kodansha America, Inc. Copyright © 1990 by Kodansha International Ltd. All rights reserved. Printed in Japan.

First edition, 1990   ISBN 4-7700-1790-1
First paperback edition, 1993

93 94 95 10 9 8 7 6 5 4 3 2 1

Contents

BAREFOOT

It is evening now. The onset of twilight can be felt even here in-side this old one-story house, sunk deep in its narrow gully be-tween the tall buildings. An eight-mat room with a veranda and a six-mat living room look out onto a small garden; it is in this garden that the sun retreating from Tokyo leaves its first shadows. But even with the windows closed, the sensation of dusk reaches into the tiny three-mat room adjoining the front vestibule. My uncle told me to feel free to use any of the rooms—after all, I'd be living by myself—but it is here, with my head resting against the wall of this room that was allotted to me as a young girl, that I feel most at home. And I don't need a lot of space. Leaning against the wall I toy with the melancholy frag-ments of my memory, as a hand might idly spread and mix a deck of playing cards lying within reach. I pick one up at random between my thumb and finger and scrutinize it. There are plenty of fragments; I can spend all day and not get tired of it. At times I am suddenly startled to find myself sitting up formally, in the very depths of this house that is itself submerged deep in the twilight. I don't get bored, but when evening falls I start to feel hungry. Peeling myself away from under the twilight, with its scat-tered fragments of memory, I go into the kitchen. The kitchen is cramped and old, but when the lights are turned on, I can feel the still vivid presence of my aunt Tokie. During the two months be-tween my return from France and Tokie's sudden death we used to prepare dinner together.

I take some green onions out of the vegetable basket. There comes a shrieking sound, and, holding the onions in my hands, I strain my ears. Someone is proclaiming: "Koito Takio, Koito Takio." A woman's voice: "Koito Takiooo!" The woman's ampli-

9

fied voice strikes against the walls of the buildings, echoing again and again, and finally strays into this old, worn-out house; then, as if finding a foothold in the little garden, it bounces up and dissipates in the sky like a flock of birds breaking out of a cage and noisily fluttering away. For a moment the sky is filled with the sound "Koito Takio." From the kitchen I can't see outside, but I can visualize the staccato sounds, released in a single burst and sparkling briefly in the dark blue of the evening sky.

I turn on the faucet and water gushes out. My uncle said that making improvements on such an old house was like throwing money away, but for Tokie's sake he had completely replaced the water pipes. The old iron ones had gotten clogged with rust. It cost over 150,000 yen. I had wondered when the new ones would rust out, but he said they wouldn't; they were made of plastic. He was of the older generation and believed all women were backward in their thinking. When he spoke about the pipes, something like a smile stirred in his wrinkled face. That's when I realized that using iron pipes for plumbing was old-fashioned.

He'd gone and spent 150,000 yen on the new pipes, but shortly afterward Tokie died of a heart attack. Left behind by his second wife at the age of eighty-one, my uncle moved to Urawa to live with his son and daughter-in-law. The pipes were left to me—a gift for the caretaker. It's a good memento; the gushing water reminds me of the diligent movements of my aunt's hands. I peel a layer of white skin from the onion, and feel the slime on my hands. The onion is so clean it really doesn't need washing. Those round onions you buy in the French markets—no matter how many layers you peel off, there's still dirt inside. Henri used to say that it's when onions keep building up the layers of dirt this way that they get mushy. Henri grew up on a farm, so he knew all about it.

I turn off the water, and from far away come the faint echoes: "Please . . ." Most of the scattered fragments of the name "Koito

Takio" are diluted now in the evening sky.

I take a pot from the shelf under the sink and fill it with water. My aunt Tokie had been a careful housekeeper, but the bottom of the pot is all black. French women scour their pots and pans until they shine, and sometimes a spasmodic urge comes over me and I, too, get out the cleanser and set to scrubbing, my torso shaking like a mad dog's.

I put the pot on the stove and light the burner. The blue flame flares up. Suddenly: "Narashima Yumiko!" The words drop from the sky, from right over my head. "Narashima Yumiko! For your district, Narashima Yumiko at your service. Narashima Yumiko at your service, Narashima Yumiko . . ." The campaign car must have stopped on the street right in front of the house. Were they addressing me directly? They couldn't be. It must be my uncle; his name is on the name plate. Waiting for the water to boil, I realize: The buildings on both sides of the house and across the street are all apartment houses. I don't know how many families live in them, but there must be quite a large number of people. Of course they wouldn't know about the woman whose husband had committed suicide, who had come back from France and was living here alone in this little old leftover house. . . . Certainly Narashima Yumiko doesn't know.

The water is boiling now; I put in a bunch of udon. Spaghetti is yellow and half-transparent. When you put it in boiling water it stays stiff for a long time, and no matter how roughly you stir it, it just bends a little, it won't break. But udon is opaque and whitish like flour, and it soon turns soft and clouds the water. If you accidentally stick your chopsticks in too soon, the noodles will break. So I'm careful. I stir gently, and when the water starts to simmer, I add some cold water and turn down the heat. Then I steal into the front hall and crack open the door. I want to see what Narashima Yumiko looks like. A white car is stopped in front of the house. On its roof is a large signboard announcing:

"Narashima Yumiko: the Communist Party Candidate." I'd expected to see a truck carrying a lot of people, but here is this ordinary sedan with just one young man and two young women inside. The women are wearing matching white blouses and blue skirts, like a uniform, and they have white sashes across their chests. Both of them, the one gripping the microphone and the one with her hands resting on the steering wheel, are looking towards the large apartment building across the street. From my front vestibule, which is slightly elevated from the street, I can see the whole interior of the car. The man's head is bowed; he's writing something on a large piece of paper that's resting on his knees. I don't know what sort of person this Narashima Yumiko is, but evidently she's not one of these two women. The young one at the wheel starts the engine and the white car drives off, so I close the front door. I lock it, too, and peer out through the peephole. Light shines from almost all the windows of the apartment house; in some of them television screens glow through the glass. The sliver of sky visible above the apartment house is strangely reddish, as if reflecting the color of the building's brick walls. The area around the railroad tracks that Henri had jumped onto had been that color for a while. The engineer who ran over him had been a friend of his the whole time he'd worked for the National Railroad; it must have been a nasty experience for him—for the friend, I mean. There's no way of knowing whether, before he jumped, it had crossed Henri's mind that the man driving the oncoming train was his friend, but of course afterwards *he* couldn't have felt disgusted at the sight—he was dead.

I remember the udon and hurry back to the kitchen. I had made a point of putting in plenty of water, but it has boiled down, and the udon is making an ugly squishy noise. The half-transparent white liquid has boiled over and spilled onto the stove around the burner. It is sticky and has started to thicken, and the part closest to the burner is scorched and blackened. The air smells burnt. But it's not a bad smell; it smells like burnt rice stuck to the bottom of a kettle. I take the handles of the pot, one in each hand, and hurriedly—it's hot—dump out the noodles into the sink under the tap. The slimy white liquid continues simmering, and the thick strands of the udon twist around themselves. It's disgusting, like long white worms swarming and swimming in a thick paste. This wouldn't happen with spaghetti. Even if you leave it in the boiling water too long and it gets soft, the strands stay separate. I figure the udon is ruined, but hesitate. It's not that I regret having to throw it away, I just don't know what to do with it. Finally I put it in a colander. If I treat it like a liquid and try to wash it down the drain, the udon that is still solid will clog up the drain. But it's too slimy and wet just to dump into the garbage. Even in the colander, the congealed broth plugs up the holes, and when I try shaking it, the whole mass just quivers and nothing drains out. I turn on the faucet, and the water gushes out right into the colander. To my surprise, it washes the noodles clean. The white strands of the udon are strange-looking, ragged along the sides, but at least the slime is gone. I pick up one noodle and taste it, but it's too tough to eat. I drain off the water and empty the colander into the garbage can.

The sky echoes with a high-pitched whistling sound, like several sirens blowing together in a short burst, but I realize that it's the campaign car again, the microphone. It sounds like whistling. A woman's voice. Like screaming. I suddenly picture Narashima Yumiko, her hair disheveled, shrieking in a shrill voice, rushing barefoot between the tall buildings. Her long hair waves in the wind like Esmeralda's and the hem of her skirt is ripped. The concrete scrapes at her bare feet, and blood trickles out. Her face is gruesome, distorted like that of a witch mounted on a broom. Screaming her name, she begs, "Vote for me, cast your ballot for me!" and rushes on through the streets under the russet-colored sky. The torment is unimaginable; no wonder the voice is shrieking.

Maybe the wind has changed, or it may have something to do with the configuration of the buildings: Suddenly the whistling is clear and distinct. I strain my ears and distinguish the words "Aikawa Masaru." A man's name. Not Narashima Yumiko. Is it his wife who's shouting out his name? Once, long ago in a distant land, a man's wife mounted a horse and rode out into the streets naked, to save the citizens from her husband's violence. Her long hair completely covered her body, and she paraded through the streets like the grand duchess she was. The people, not wanting to embarrass their kindhearted duchess, retreated into their houses and shuttered the windows. One man peeked out of his window, hoping to catch a glimpse of her naked body, and got his just punishment: He was struck blind. And if I encounter Aikawa Masaru's wife in her shrieking car, I will lower my eyes so as not to see.

It's been raining all day. The rainy season. Here I am back in Japan for the rainy season, after six years away. A puddle has formed in the hall outside the bathroom. A leak in the roof. I toss a rag on the puddle. The walls and the tatami floors in the three-mat room are starting to get damp. I guess I ought to gather up all those scattered fragments of memory from there and move over into the living room.

The phone rings, startling me. I'm still not used to hearing the phone ringing in my home. Of course there was a phone in the Maruichi Shoji office in Paris, but Henri hadn't allowed one in the little house where we lived in F–. I had wanted to have a phone in case Henri should go into convulsions, but he didn't like it when people called. He was unsociable to begin with, but mainly he couldn't stand the sound of a ringing phone. Even when I suggested we could adjust the noise level of a phone so it would ring at the lowest possible setting, Henri still didn't want to get one. When I looked at his snow-white hair and his red face, I realized how much it bothered him, and I gave up. I guess people with such delicate skin pigmentation are sensitive to all kinds of stimulation. That's why he had to get drunk all the time.

Henri's parents still farmed the land and lived in the house in the Brittany countryside where he had grown up. The only time I visited I was surprised to learn that they didn't even have gas or electricity, much less a telephone. The little house, built with mortar and pieces of stone from the nearby mountains, was divided into three parts: one for the animals, one for storing their fodder, and one for the people to live in. The smell of pigs, goats, and chickens that permeated the house was so intense that it overwhelmed the other smells—the oil lamps and the smoke from the fireplace. Henri's parents' home was insulated from the irritations of human progress and civilization, but that didn't mean that Henri was content there. Even when he was with his aged, placid parents, all he did was sit and drink in silence. But the French National Railroad betrayed an overly casual attitude when it hired this man who, though seemingly calm, was frightened by the ringing of a telephone. And Henri was epileptic and an alcoholic to boot. It may have been just a small suburban town that saw only one train an hour, but still, they ought to have been concerned.

The phone keeps ringing. I have no choice but to get up and answer it.

"Hello?"

"Oh, you're in after all. Seiko? It's me."

"Uncle."

"I'll be coming by tomorrow."

"All right."

"It's election day. The registration came, didn't it?"

"Some kind of postcard?"

"That's it. I'll stop by your place to pick it up before I go to vote."

" 'Your place.' It's your house, you know."

"As long as you're living there it's your place. But now that you mention it, are you registered as a resident yet?"

"Well . . ."

"Did you get a form?"

"There were a couple of forms, but I didn't really look at them. They were both addressed to Kubota, so I figured they were for you and Aunt Tokie."

"That's ridiculous; she's dead. Once you die you lose the right to vote."

Funny: "You lose the right to vote"—as if you still keep your other rights. Are there some rights that you keep after death? Maybe the right to be resurrected suddenly in the mind of another person . . .

"One of them must have been addressed to Kubota Seiko."

"I guess so."

That was just like Tokie; methodical as usual, she would have notified the office when I came back from France.

"The polling place is the N– elementary school. You come along with me."

"But I don't know who to vote for."

"That's right, you've been out of the country for so long. Anyone but Narashima Yumiko is all right."

"What's wrong with her?"

"She's a woman, and a Communist too. And she's one of the front runners. It's a close race, the only one that's not already decided, so at least vote against the Communists."

"What time will you be here?"

"Some time in the morning."

"All right, I'll make some lunch."

"You will? Well then, I'll be your guest. Harumi needs a break sometimes." Harumi is his daughter-in-law, his second son's wife.

I put my wallet, a handkerchief, and the keys into my shopping bag, slip my sandals on my bare feet, and go out to get some food. In F–, even for a quick errand, I used to wear street shoes and take a handbag. The handbag was for my alien registration card; no one there wore sandals. The rain is really coming down. The toes of my vinyl sandals squish through the water flowing down the dark surface of the pavement.

Jacqueline had been delighted when Henri and I got together. Back when she worked as a cleaning lady at Maruichi Shoji in Paris, she often used to tell me about her brother's fits. She told me she was relieved that I would be there with him in case he should go into convulsions; and when I said that I wasn't with him during the day, she answered that his co-workers at the station could take care of him then. It was as if the National Railroad had offered its staff at F– Station as custodians for Henri. Of course the entire "staff," including Henri and the stationmaster, consisted of only four men.

We lived in a small house on a hill about ten minutes' walk from F– Station. F– was some forty minutes by train from Montparnasse Station in Paris, and many Parisians owned weekend cottages there; there were several on that hill. When one of the owners died, leaving his house vacant, we rented it. We were never legally married. I figured it was too much trouble to register our marriage because of my alien status, and Henri didn't have long to live anyway. But we still were husband and wife. Everyone considered us a married couple: Jacqueline, the staff at the station, the proprietor of the café. Jacqueline was delighted with our "marriage," and soon afterward—though not because of it—she got divorced, quit her job as a cleaning woman at Maruichi Shoji, and moved with her children into an apartment house next to the F– church. Her ex-husband was an alcoholic too, but unlike Henri he got terribly abusive when he was drunk. Before her divorce she had shown me the dark maroon and purple-colored bruises that covered her white, swollen body. She had laughed at the time, but I had been shocked. Jacqueline wasn't an epileptic like her younger brother, but she had kidney problems, and I noticed how exhausted she seemed when she mopped the linoleum floors at the office. The men who worked at Maruichi Shoji commented that "that white lady" might have heart disease. The ones who pointedly called her the "white lady" had worked in the New York or Los Angeles branches, where all the cleaning women had been black. But none of them ever stopped to help her carry her bucket. To make it easier for her I used to put the chairs back into place after the men had moved them, and gradually we became friends. Jacqueline was always saying that she had to get Henri to stop drinking, but she never actually did anything about it. As for me, since he was quiet and good-natured, I didn't mind his alcoholism. The only thing that bothered me was that when he didn't drink he fell into a profound depression. He was all right again if he could just have a drink. Alcohol was cheap, and he could drink as much as he wanted on his salary, so I didn't worry about it.

My street dead-ends onto the main street where the buses run. At the entrance to the building on the corner a little boy, about three years old, is riding a tricycle. He is imitating the campaign cars: "Please vote for Koito Takiooo." He circles around and around in the tiny space at the building's entrance. Round and round like a top in that little space. I cross the street at the traffic light. On this side there's a wall lined with campaign posters. I look at each one as I walk past them. The rain has wrinkled the paper, and the fine lines gleam with a strange light. The flat, oversized faces all look alike. Maybe it is because I am used to French people that all Japanese faces look the same to me. Or maybe it's because people running for political office all put on the same kind of expression. All of them wear a forced smile; their eyes have assumed an aggressive self-confidence. None of them looks normal. Of course, I suppose no one could look normal with his face magnified to such huge proportions and made into a poster like this. I continue walking along the wall, thinking that, rather than wearing those forced smiles, it would be more natural for the faces to be strained and sober, and suddenly I see a fairly ordinary expression on one of them. It's a woman's face. She reminds me of a junior high-school teacher. Her hair is short and permed, and there is no smile on her unremarkable, round face. At the same time, she hasn't tried to create an impression of authority. The picture has captured her normal, everyday look. The natural expression in the picture is striking, so I look at the name: Narashima Yumiko. On the basis of the name alone, I had pictured a thin woman with large eyes. There is no such Esmeralda here. So now I start looking at the names on the posters as well as the faces. Koito Takio, Aikawa Masaru—both of them have squarish, plump faces, and their smiles look as if they have been coached onto their faces by someone. The fat, swollen grins make me uncomfortable.

To get away from the posters, I go straight back across the street, and the uncomfortable feeling reminds me ... Henri hadn't liked big cities; or rather, he seemed to be afraid of them. Although he could ride the trains for free, he rarely went into Paris. I also preferred to spend my days off in F–, so we hardly ever went to the city together. I do remember, though, one walk we took in Paris. It was before we got "married." We met at Montparnasse Station and, arm in arm, strolled down the Boulevard de Rennes. It was in July, and the sky was a clear blue. The shops lining both sides of the street were lively with the colors of summer. I pointed out one creamy-white art-deco shop that was mirrored vividly in the glazed-glass walls of the adjoining modern-style building. Henri, because of his delicate complexion, was dazzled by the light, and, our arms linked, I dragged him along like a blind man. In no time he broke out in an oily sweat, and my arm was soon soaking wet too. Within ten minutes Henri sheepishly suggested we stop somewhere for a drink. We stood in the corner of a café that doubled as a tobacco shop and Henri had some Pernod. It's a kind of liqueur with a strong taste of fennel. I drank a soda. Even in his usual café in F–, Henri would go into a far corner and drink, standing, with his back to the wall. It was a position from which he could keep an eye on the whole interior of the café, while he himself remained unobserved. Henri held his glass, filled with the golden Pernod, and from the corner, itself even darker than the rest of the dimly lit cafe, his snow-white hair and his red face gleamed. It was like an old Dutch painting. With the meager light of the café reflecting on Henri's white hair and red skin, his life's spirit radiated out. I loved seeing Henri like that, allowing his life its own enjoyment. And it meant that his thin, wrinkled mother out in Brittany, whose son resembled her only in his small, gray eyes, had not borne him in vain.

We continued walking to the cathedral, stopping in cafés about every fifteen minutes. Even in the café behind the cathedral, Henri stood in the corner with his back to the wall, drinking Pernod. The position had its advantages for me, too. Since I stood with my elbows on the high table and my back to the chairs, the people who passed behind didn't notice me—that there was a Japanese woman here, too.

"What's the matter with that guy? I thought he was an old man, but look how young he is. It's weird."

A high voice speaking in Japanese. I restrained the urge to turn around.

"He's an albino."

"So there are European albinos, too. Oh, he's drinking wine. That's disgusting."

That was all. I cast a quick sidelong glance and saw a row of young Japanese men and women about to sit down at one of the tables. Of course I knew how strange-looking Henri was. But never, from the time I first met him at Jacqueline's house, had he disgusted me. I suppose you are only disgusted by something you don't truly understand. Like when you see a snake. Not seeing the soft part, the fragile part, of a person's heart, you suspect he's plotting against you. You feel that any minute now he might do something unpredictable.

Henri was albino, epileptic, and alcoholic (could these three things have some connection?), but he had a gentle heart. You could tell at a glance that this man was incapable of plotting against anyone. Caucasian babies have a pinker complexion than Japanese babies, and usually their heads are nearly bald, with tufts of downy whitish hair. Henri was like one of those babies, one who had grown up without changing in appearance. Right then I decided to stay and live with him until he died; it wouldn't be that long anyway. If you are upset by someone like Henri and not by those grinning faces of Koito Takio or Aikawa Masaru on the posters, mightn't it be because in them the upsetting part is hidden inside?

Finally, after crossing the main street, I find a fish stand that is open. It's four o'clock in the afternoon. This shop is only open in the evening, and they sell very high-quality fish in small portions, just enough for sashimi. Their main business seems to be selling it already cut and arranged in the aluminum foil plates that are lined up on the counter. I suppose it's for the young housewives who live in the high-rises and don't clean and cut their own fish. Or maybe the shop is patronized mainly by the owners of the small eateries in the area. I stop in front of the shop and try to decide what to serve my uncle tomorrow. In those two months I had lived with her before she died, I ought to have noticed what kinds of side dishes Aunt Tokie had made for him every night, but now I can't remember. She used to meticulously prepare several different kinds of food and arrange it—or rather, set it out—onto small plates for him. My uncle would chat with her, drinking two or three small flasks of sake with his food; it was more like appetizers than a meal. As I watched him drinking and eating contentedly, I recalled Henri in the corner of the dark café in F–, his red face shining, the glass of Pernod in his hand. The townspeople knew Henri, they knew about the epilepsy and the Japanese woman, and they were especially aware of his shyness. When they noticed him drinking his Pernod, they would simply signal their greetings to him with a silent nod and leave him alone. And Henri was satisfied with that. Many French cafés keep as a mascot a large dog who wanders among the tables or sprawls out on the floor, nestling at the feet of some customer. Maybe the people at the F– café considered Henri a kind of mascot.

Maruichi Shoji was close to the Opera House. I used to have to take the subway as far as Montparnasse Station, then cross all the way over to the other side of the station to catch the suburban train. It was exhausting. Last year they increased the number of trains, so that one ran every fifteen minutes during the rush hours, but before that if I missed my train I used to have to wait a long time. I would finally arrive at F– Station around eight o'clock. In the summer it would still be light outside, but beginning in the fall I would hurry from the station toward the café, alternately rising up into the brightness of each isolated streetlight then sinking back down again into the darkness. I'd reach the café, push open the little door with its layers of paint hardened here and there into globs, and peer through the cigarette smoke, beyond the faces of the men turned toward me, looking for Henri. When he'd see me his red face would light up even more. He used to come to meet me at the station, but I made him stop. I preferred seeing him radiating his red light in the dim corner of the café rather than loitering at the deserted station, a focus for the jokes of his bored co-worker on the night shift. The proprietor of the café would signal me a silent greeting with his chin and bring me a glass of red wine. He would never let me pay for it. After the wine, I finished off one or two glasses of Dubonnet or Ambassador, pried Henri's Pernod from his hand and put it on the counter, then took his arm and led him home. There were no street lights at all on the way to our house, so it was completely dark, but even in winter Henri's body was warm and damp, and just being beside him made me feel warm. I never felt afraid in the darkness; Henri's hair was so white it reflected even the faintest starlight. Light shone orange from the windows of the little house, and when I opened the door I smelled meat cooking with garlic. After work Henri would come home and start preparing dinner before heading for the café to wait for me.

I look over the fish in front of the shop but can't decide what to buy, so I give up and start toward the P– supermarket.

Aikawa Masaru's campaign car passes by—it's just a normal sedan. It's going slowly. When I stop to look inside, a middleaged woman in a lace blouse nods to me. I return her bow, and a man in a business suit waves a white-gloved hand. I don't know if it's Aikawa Masaru himself—I've already forgotten the face on the poster. It's strange; thanks to the election I have some acquaintances here in Japan.

At the supermarket I buy some salted mackerel, pickles, tofu, and green beans. A big supermarket had opened outside F–, too, but Henri didn't like shopping at that kind of store. He wasn't satisfied unless the food came from the market that was open two mornings a week in the park. Even when his alcoholism got worse and he started feeling sick most of the time, he would still stagger out to the market and bring back some vegetables or meat. One of the days the market was open was Sunday; I could go with him then. One time when they had fresh *dorade*, we bought a large one whole. I steamed half of it in white wine with champignons for Henri and cut the other half into sashimi for myself. Henri stared at me, his little eyes incredulous, as I gobbled up the pale, pink pieces of raw fish. His face was all red; only his small eyes, fringed in white lashes, were a clear, pale gray.

I go home, make myself a cup of tea, and drink it alone. I start stripping the strings off the beans, and again a voice wails, "Pleease . . . for the last time Koito Takio is requesting your vote. Vote tomorrow for Koito Takio, Koito Takio. Please vote for Koito Takio, Koito Takiooo. . . ." The pitch keeps rising and getting more strident. It sounds as though the car, which has been circling the area at a distance, has turned inward and is coming closer. Koito's requesting "for the last time" sounds like his "last request." Do all these people think that they might die tomorrow? I begin to feel surrounded, cornered. Then, one by one, the faces on the posters start coming back to me. None of them looks capable of shrieking this way, like a wild animal that has been tearing about the desolate streets in the rainy twilight and is now trapped. It really is weird.

I wake up at 7:30 and open the shutters. A nice day. The earth in the tiny back garden is dark with the water accumulated from yesterday's long rain. The aojiso leaves have grown out. The lower leaves are laced with holes where the caterpillars have eaten them. Had my uncle planted the seeds before he moved out? Had Tokie saved the seeds from last year, not suspecting that she would be dead by spring? When it gets hot this afternoon, I'll chill the tofu and garnish it with aojiso. I don't know how long I'll be staying here taking care of this old house, but even if it's just one morning, at least it is a morning like this.

I cook two cups of rice. Henri hadn't eaten much rice. He said he preferred potatoes. Occasionally I would measure out a small cupful of rice and fix it for myself. Sometimes Henri would make some. As soon as it was cooked he dumped it out into a colander, put it under the faucet, and rinsed it with water. Like me yester-

day with the udon. He rinsed the stickiness off, leaving the
smooth grains, then mixed in some dressing and made it into a
salad. It wasn't bad at all. What if I had put some dressing on
yesterday's udon? Probably wouldn't have been any good because
of the toughness.

I put the lid on the electric kettle. A quiet morning. It reminds
me of the quiet mornings in F–. Then I realize it's because there
aren't any more campaign cars. In French election campaigns
they don't ride around in cars with loudspeakers, but election day
itself has a festival air. The polling place in F– was the town hall,
which was located in the middle of the park. The back yard of the
office opened right out onto the park's broad expanse of lawn. In
the center of the park was a pond with a nude female statue, and
in the lawn a massive oak tree loomed, spreading its roots. An
elementary school stood on the opposite side of the pond, and
pastures and fields extended into the distance beyond. The farmers' market was located at one end of the park. In France, too,
election day is on Sunday, and people come to vote straight from
church, dressed in their Sunday best. It's like a holiday. The
people in their brightly colored clothes stand on the porch of
the town office, which is festooned with tricolor flags, or on the
stone steps of the war monument, and talk with one another
about whom they voted for or are going to vote for. Unlike the
Japanese, who sit inside for their conversations, the French like to
socialize out in the open air.

In France the men, as well as the women, enjoy making casual
conversation. But Henri was different; he hardly ever said anything. Maybe he had grown that short, half-transparent whitish
moustache to draw attention away from his taciturnity. His thin
lips were red, but then, so was his whole face, so if the moustache hadn't been there, you wouldn't be able to tell at all where
his mouth was. Even when he did mumble something, moving
his thin lips under the sparse moustache, either you couldn't

hear his voice, or, even if you could hear it, you couldn't make out what he was saying. He spoke with a heavy accent. People from Brittany in general don't move their lips much when they speak; they form the words inside their mouths. I wonder if Henri ever voted. I can't remember. Once, I don't recall which election it was, I went to the market with him. We stood in the park, the shopping basket hanging from my shoulder, and watched the people on their way to vote. Farmers came to the market with live rabbits or chickens to sell, and held them, packed two or three to a basket, one basket under each arm, as they went into the town office. The chickens fluttered their wings loudly in the baskets, but no one seemed to mind.

My uncle arrives just before noon. Complaining of the heat, he totters to the stoop and drops down on it to take off his shoes. From where I am standing, above him, I look straight down onto the top of his head. It is slightly pointed and there's almost no hair. The hair that's left is completely white. Little drops of sweat cover the crown of his bald head with its brown spots. Like transparent fish eggs. In spite of his complaints of the heat, he's wearing a shirt and tie under a suit jacket. I take the jacket from him and put it on a hanger. He goes into the living room, loosening his tie and rolling up his long sleeves. To my surprise he's also wearing a long-sleeved jersey undershirt underneath. Maybe Harumi made him put it on. Or perhaps he's just kept the habit of wearing long-sleeved shirts from the winter, when Tokie was still alive.

He sits down cross-legged in the living room and asks for a cool washcloth. I'm flustered; I'd completely forgotten about that custom. It's a shame I hadn't kept some cloths in the refrigerator for Henri, who wore short-sleeved shirts even in winter and was always sweating and complaining of the heat. I'm confused; I don't even know where the washcloths are kept, so he says he can do without one, and wipes the top of his head with his handkerchief. I soak an ordinary towel and bring it to him.

"At last the weather has cleared."

"Uh-huh, a nice day."

I bring him some cold barley tea. He looks tired, and is staring vacantly out at the garden. Suddenly he speaks:

"Did they send you the campaign bulletin?"

"The what?"

"It's like a newspaper with the names and short biographies of the candidates."

Now I remember. It came about ten days ago in the mail. I get it from the pile of old newspapers and bring it to him.

"Aikawa Masaru is doing fine. He's going to be elected." He has the bulletin spread out in front of him and continues to skim it as he speaks. I look over his shoulder.

"Koito Takio is in trouble. I'll vote for him. You too."

His hand is just like a dead branch. The skin with its brown age spots stretches over the bones. It's a yellowish-white, hardened claw, made of some unidentifiable material—maybe tough, maybe brittle. In front of it I see the name Narashima Yumiko.

"Look, Narashima Yumiko graduated from Tokyo University!" My voice shrieks. She went there after graduating from one of the city's prestigious private girls' high schools. Of course Tokyo University has no Esmeralda among its alumni.

"Really? There are a lot of highly educated people in the Communist Party leadership."

"That's true in France, too. The people who run the party are rich intellectuals." I'm repeating what I heard from Henri's friend, the train engineer—the one who ran over him. A thin man with dark hair who liked to talk. The complete opposite of Henri.

"Is that so? France, too, huh?"

He looks through his glasses at my face. It's as though he's just remembered about my time spent in France. Unlike most Japanese he has clearly defined features. As he's gotten older all the fat has left his face, his eyebrows have fallen out, and the hair that covered his broad forehead is gone; his face looks like the death mask of some foreigner. The bone in the ridge of his nose is so prominent that you feel like tracing its slight indentations with your finger.

"Why don't you like the Communist Party?"

"It's not that I don't like it. But I'm thinking about Kuniaki's and Tomoji's companies."

When I hear Kuniaki's name, something stirs in my chest and I tentatively touch my stomach just below the breastbone. It doesn't really come as a shock.

"Oh, that's right. Big business. Both Kuniaki's and Tomoji's companies."

"It's that or something else. Tokie was a fool—she used to go on and on about how the Communists would confiscate this land for the government if they ever got into power." My uncle laughs, his mouth with its missing teeth wide open, and I realize how important the land under this house in the center of Tokyo had been to Tokie. She was his second wife; the first one had died childless. Both Kuniaki and Tomoji had been born when their father was almost fifty, and he had spoiled them. And he isn't much better himself, rattling off Kuniaki's name like that in front of me. I look at his face, but he is gazing dully out at the garden again. Maybe in his second childhood he's forgotten everything that happened.

The money I had been given at the time of his older son's wedding must have been from my uncle. Certainly Kuniaki couldn't have had that much money, and even if he had, he wouldn't have given it to me. It was right at that time that one of his drinking buddies from Maruichi Shoji told us that they were looking for a woman to work in their Paris office. So I took the job and used the money for the trip to Paris. It was a scheme they had dreamed up together.

I'm just like a prostitute, aren't I? I get the sudden urge to say the words aloud as I sit here gazing at the ridge of his nose. Even though the patrons had just been Maruichi Shoji employees. What would my uncle do if I just came out and said it? Would he turn to me with some response?

Kuniaki had forced himself on me when I was fifteen. It may be offensive to put it that way, but I can't think of any better words. I mean, I was a freshman in high school. When I think about it now, I realize I didn't have any sense. I had figured at the time that, since my uncle was taking care of my mother and me, I had no right to object to what his son did to me. But for seven or eight years after that, as he continued to use me as a convenient outlet for his lust, it still didn't dawn on me that it was unfair; I must have been pretty dull-witted and insensitive. Not only that, I didn't realize until his engagement that he had just been using me; before that I had simply assumed we would eventually wed.

The guy from Maruichi Shoji must have been pleased when he heard the whole story from Kuniaki, that I was someone you could use as you pleased, that I was an orphan and that my foster father was an old man, that I used to be Kuniaki's mistress but now it was all over. This was such a convenient way of settling affairs. I'm getting upset; I almost told my uncle what was on my mind just now but realized how ridiculous it is—he's over eighty. At times my mother had gotten hysterical about the situation, but she got a stomach ulcer and died. And I wound up believing that if you complain about something that you can't change, you get an ulcer. But then I remember overhearing Tokie, early on, reproaching her son and trying to get him to marry me. Maybe it was because of this temperament of hers that she, too, had a heart attack and died.

"What do you want to do first, vote or have lunch?"

He grunts and, grabbing onto the tea table, tries to stand. I offer my hand and help him up.

"Let's get the voting over with. Are you coming too, Seiko?"

"Me? I'll do it later. I'll set the table while you're gone. Take care."

He's quite tall when he stands up. Even now, unsteady as he is, he looms over me. I watch him tottering off in the direction of the main road and wonder if I shouldn't have gone along with him. But he made it all the way here from Urawa by himself. It should be easy for him to get to the elementary school.

I had rarely seen Henri off to work. I was always the first to leave. Whether because of his illness or the alcoholism, he hardly ever worked the night shift anymore, so for a railroad employee he had a pretty good life. But still he always used to get up before me and bring me breakfast in bed: a tray with a croissant and café au lait in a large round cup, yellow on the outside and white on the inside. The steaming café au lait filled the cup to the brim, and every morning without fail I would drink it dry.

At the Maruichi Shoji office in Paris, except for the commute my work was limited to working hours. A lot of the Japanese employees were there with their families, and those who came alone knew their way around Paris, so here too my "affairs were settled." It was convenient for me, too, because it was about that time that I moved in with Henri. My broken French gradually improved as a result of my conversations with Jacqueline. I got so that I could answer the phone without too much trouble, and continued on at Maruichi Shoji as a regular clerk. In the morning as I was leaving for work, the thought would cross my mind that Henri might go into convulsions while I was out, but then I reminded myself that he was going to die soon anyway. From the very first I knew that, as an alcoholic albino epileptic, he didn't have long to live. And I realized that if he hadn't known his days were limited he wouldn't have possessed that unique gentleness—that miserable, transparent affection of a dog who, knowing he is going to die, still wags his tail at his master. Knowing

his death was near, I too was able to be kind, and living with
him that way, I was able to forget about Kuniaki. It was a wonderful feeling of liberation. Somehow it was just not in my nature to
dwell on Kuniaki's cruelty and resent his taking advantage of me,
or to feel sorry for myself for growing up without a father who
could have prevented it. Not only that, it wasn't logical. Like turning myself, my whole life, into pickles soaking in a barrel, where,
pressed under the heavy stone lid and covered with rice bran, I
would just weep my whole life away. It wasn't right. I realized this
without particularly reasoning it out: Henri's way was much better. Rather than moping and bearing grudges, he just stood there
in his dark corner of the café, a glass of Pernod in his hand, his red
aura glowing. And as long as I was with him, I myself could be a
tender and affectionate woman.

I set the food out in little plates and bowls: green beans with
sesame, cold tofu with the aojiso, grilled mackerel, green onion
salad. There's something wrong. When I look down at the plates
trying to figure out what the problem is, I realize that, rather than
the food, it's my own state of mind that's not right. I pour the
sake out into the flask but the whole time I feel the words in my
mouth, "No, not like this." Aunt Tokie used to do it this way—
she'd arrange the food neatly on these little dishes and set them
out on the tea table, then sit down beside him and serve him
while he ate. Tomoji's wife Harumi would never serve him this
way, in the traditional style, but after being abroad so long, I
wanted to please him as an old-fashioned Japanese wife would.
But here I've got everything set out on the tray, and somehow
things aren't going as planned. There's a heaviness in my throat.
Never again will I have a meal like those Henri and I shared. We
sat opposite each other, facing coarse chipped plates piled high
with fried potatoes, and as I ate thick sausage with mustard, the
tension left my body and I was truly happy. We ate like a pair of
dogs, hardly saying a word, but before that time I had never real-

ized what a wonderful, simple pleasure eating could be.

Jacqueline had found a large, sturdy table at a used furniture store and bought it for us. The table shone darkly with the oil that permeated the oak wood. When we sat facing each other across that table, I felt that both of us had found a place for ourselves in the long history of mankind and were living in it, and that there was a simple virtue in that.

My uncle comes back, all sweaty again. My uneven state of mind doesn't change, but I bring him some sake and sit down beside him.

"This looks great." He contentedly surveys the food set out on the tea table. Maybe he's just flattering me. "Here you were gone so long, and you can still prepare something like this."

"What does Harumi fix?"

"The children are still small—frozen hamburger or rice with instant curry sauce."

"It's because we don't have good potatoes or cheese in Japan. They're easy to fix, and good for children, too."

"But Japanese don't eat that kind of thing. We have rice and miso."

"That's right, but still . . ."

I stop myself; I realize that Harumi's frozen hamburger meat and curry sauce with their unknown ingredients are just what you would expect her and the children to eat. Like Tomoji's business suit. He always dresses neatly in a well-fitting suit, but you can never tell what it's made of. And the clothes Harumi wears are the same—bearing no trace of animal origin and made of light-weight synthetic material. The sweaters that Jacqueline used to wear always reminded me of the sheep whose bodies their wool had once covered; she herself seemed to take on their animal smell. Jacqueline's odor was always present in the thin cotton dresses she wore in the summer, even though she washed them constantly. Henri's oily odor was even stronger in those thick cotton sheets he used. Even after they'd been to the cleaners, they were permeated with the oil that had soaked into the cloth from the bodies of his parents and grandparents.

Tomoji had been a well-adjusted boy, popular with girls from the time he was in middle school. He showed very little interest in my affair with his older brother. As though he thought you didn't have to understand everything 100 percent. As long as you got most of it, it was better not to look too closely into the rest. Like frozen hamburger. I am like that myself. Jacqueline had been surprised that I had no body odor, even though I never used cologne. She asked whether it was because I was Japanese. Toward the end, Henri's odor completely filled the little house; it probably soaked into me as well. It was the smell of alcohol.

"I guess Tomoji and Harumi will be voting today too."

"Yes, there's more at stake in Saitama Prefecture because they're electing a governor."

"Though there's not that much at stake for the people who are voting."

His hand holding the small sieved ladle with the chilled tofu hangs suspended in the air; he can't decide which plate to put it on. I pour out some soy sauce into a small dish with a blue pattern. "Spices," he says, and I take a little grated ginger and shredded onion and serve them to him, one at a time. Aunt Tokie used to sprinkle his condiments hurriedly, her eyes downcast. I guess I'm just no good at it. In France I was the one who got served. Henri used to peel my apples and put the mustard or salt on my food for me. And he didn't do it silently like Tokie used to. He would ask me every time, mumbling from under his thin moustache, "Would you like some salt, do you need any mustard?" Tired after my day in Paris, I would just answer yes to everything.

"By the way...," my uncle began, setting his sake cup down and turning serious.

"What?"

He hunched his back, his eyes distant, and rested his hands on his knees, as if what he was about to say was not going to be easy.

"I got a letter from Taiwan."

"From Kuniaki?"

"That's right. And he didn't even come back for his mother's funeral."

He sounds irritated. Not at me, of course, at his son, but I get the irrational sense that it's because of me.

"I wrote him and told him that since Tokie died I was going to move to Tomoji's house right away and also that . . . you had just come back in time to take care of the house."

I let him go on.

"Well, for a long time he's been saying that this old house is more trouble than it's worth and that we should tear it down and put up apartments or condominiums. So I wrote him and said that there was no point in leaving it vacant until that time, so I would ask you to live here."

"And then?" I was surprised; this was the first time I had ever heard of Kuniaki saying anything about me, even indirectly.

"Then I told him that if we built some apartment building here, we could ask you to stay on as a manager."

"Me?"

"If you don't want to, that's another thing, but Kuniaki and Kumiko have a house in Mitaka that they're renting out while they're in Taiwan. Even when they come back they won't live here. And you need an income and someplace to live. You could manage the place and still work somewhere, and at least you wouldn't have to worry about living expenses. I told him in my letter that, if possible, he should give you the deed to a small apartment."

"What was his answer?"

"He's just hopeless. It's either him or Kumiko, one of them is no good."

"But Kumiko doesn't have anything to do with it, does she?"

I recalled Kuniaki's wife; I'd only met her once. I'd heard that her father was an executive of a subsidiary of Kuniaki's company. She wasn't that bad-looking. Her face had classical features quite unlike Harumi's. Naturally Kumiko would be upset if she knew about me and Kuniaki, but then, she probably didn't know.

"That's right, she has nothing to do with it. But her opinion . . ."

He stopped again. If it's hard for him to say it he doesn't have to, I think, but then again I wouldn't mind hearing it.

"He told me to get you to draw up a document and notarize it."

"A what?"

"A document."

"Saying what?"

"That you will vacate this house immediately if they tell you to." He spoke irritably. As if he was angry with me, not Kuniaki or Kumiko.

"But they don't need some document. . . ." Anger wells up in me, burning me up inside.

"That's right. I've asked you to stay and take care of the house. I can even pay you. It doesn't make any sense. There's no cure for an idiot like him."

"Well then, I'll get right out."

He lifts his cup expectantly. I'm not about to pour his sake for him, so he does it himself.

"Of course you're upset. But . . ." His pallid, wrinkled lower lip stretches out to touch the cup.

"You are upset, aren't you?"

I say nothing.

"No parents or family, not even a husband. And I'm going to die soon. There's only Kuniaki and Tomoji for you to turn to.

And Tomoji figures you're his brother's problem; no matter what I say, he just smirks and won't listen. When Kuniaki comes back I'll give him a good talking-to, but you'd better be prepared for the worst. Kuniaki and Kumiko are not the kind of people you can depend on—they're completely irresponsible."

"But, like you said, this has nothing to do with Kumiko."

"You're right, nothing to do with her." A vacant look suddenly comes over his face and his eyes stare blankly out toward the garden. He sits motionless.

"Uncle?"

"Huh?"

"So you were about to say?"

"What?"

"Finish what you started to say."

"Say what?"

Shocked, I peer into his face, and a cold shudder runs through me. His eyes are absolutely vacant. At this moment his heart and mind are an utter void. I know because this is what Henri's face looked like before one of his fits. A person whose entire content has been completely extinguished, leaving only blank space, a person devoid of expression. Could senility and epilepsy be the same thing? I stare speechless at his face.

His eyes are green. The green of the trees in the garden is reflected in the void of his eyes. Eyes like mirrors.

I call his name. I shout it out, as if he's run far away and I'm trying to get him to come back. Those times with Henri, I hadn't called so loud; I figured that if he was going to die anyway I would let him go quietly. You shouldn't yell at people going over into the other world. My mother told me that if you try to get them to come back, you confuse their spirits and they will be stuck in a limbo between the two worlds, unable to enter the other world but incapable of returning here as well. Of course, the first time I had panicked anyway and cried out to him.

I call to my uncle again, urgently.

"What's all this noise? What are you yelling about?" I guess he's suddenly come to. What a relief. His face is irritable, as before—he's not going to die on me right here. That's Tomoji's and Harumi's department.

"You're cruel, worse than Kuniaki."

"What do you mean, cruel?"

He waves the empty sake flask as he talks.

"All of a sudden turning into someone completely different."

"When did I turn into someone different?"

He waves the flask as if to say, Look, it's empty.

"Just now. What were you thinking about just now?"

"When? I wasn't thinking about anything. Is the sake all gone or what?"

"That's what I mean, you're being cruel."

"You're the cruel one, not giving me the sake when you know there's more."

Suddenly I know that that's what's really cruel, or, more precisely, inconsiderate: to become suddenly someone else, or, rather, to become something not human at all. Both Henri and my uncle. My uncle for an instant; with Henri it had been longer. They had lost their humanity. And when Henri finally died, his inhumanity became eternal.

"How about that sake?"

"There is some, but I'm not going to give you any more. I'll really catch it from Tomoji if you have a stroke and die here."

"Not Tomoji. Who cares what Tomoji thinks?"

"Oh, come on. You know that you're totally dependent on Tomoji and Harumi, now that Aunt Tokie is gone."

"Think so? Maybe so. It really is miserable getting old."

He nods submissively. He doesn't look so pathetic.

That is the last I hear about being the manager of the apartment house or about the notarized document. And I say no more about leaving the apartment. Maruichi Shoji gave me some severance pay when I left, and Jacqueline turned over to me the pension money that the French National Railroad paid when Henri died; the combination will tide me over for the present. I don't want to go to work yet, and I don't mind not worrying about the rent.

It was a dark morning. It was December, almost Christmas, and at eight in the morning it was still dark as night outside. It's not that I chose that morning. It just approached quietly from outside and stopped abruptly before us. Or appeared to us suddenly right when Henri and I, enveloped in a deep fog, had gotten mired in the sediment of the river we had been floating down. If I had to say when, it would be six months ago, but there are mornings and evenings that don't yield to that kind of measurement. Such a "morning" or "evening" or "night" floats gently in some distant space unconnected with the earth's rotation; then it suddenly appears to a certain person at a "certain moment." This kind of "morning" or "night" is usually connected with death. In our case this was clear.

Maybe the alarm clock rang and I didn't hear it, or maybe it didn't ring at all; whatever the reason, I overslept. The other bed was cold, undisturbed. Henri had not slept in it for several nights. I dragged myself out of bed; I was an hour late. Henri had stopped bringing me my café au lait a long time before. Since the beginning of autumn his condition had steadily deteriorated. The days grew shorter, and with the lengthening of the nights Henri started spending all his time drinking. The whole house smelled like alcohol, and when I came back, exhausted, from work, it would nauseate me. He was continually drunk, but I stopped drinking altogether, and I found my head clearing steadily with the onset of the bitter winter cold. In November Henri stopped going to work. I think he continued going to the café while I was out, but he stopped waiting for me there. The railroad told us he needed a medical statement in order to keep getting his salary, so I dragged him, against his will, to the doctor. Henri's fear was so pathetic that I almost decided it wasn't worth it, that we could do without the salary. There was a doctor in F– named Rimbaud, like the poet. He was a former military doctor with a reputation for unceremonious treatments. He took one look at Henri's face and twisted the corners of his handsome lips condescendingly as if to say, Oo la la! This is one you don't even have to ask about. He went through the motions of examining Henri, then turned to me. "Madame," he said, "it is your urgent patriotic duty to get Monsieur immediately into a hospital." He spoke solemnly, as if he were offering me his condolences. Then he turned to his desk to write out the diagnosis and emitted a curse in a quiet but terrifying voice. I couldn't tell what effect the curse had on Henri; his face was always red and his hands always trembled. But, thanks to the medical certificate, Henri was able to continue on as a station employee until that day.

I got out of bed and threw on my robe. My head was spinning; the air in the tiny house was thick with the smell of alcohol. The kitchen door was closed, and light leaked through the crack. I touched the door, steadied my breathing, and opened it. Henri was hunched over the kitchen table, leaning on his elbows, but his eyes were open. On the table stood a silent forest of empty cognac and wine bottles. He'd been sitting there drinking nonstop for three days. During that time I had ventured into the kitchen only to get myself milk or sausages from the refrigerator.

Of course by then he wasn't really alive. Or at least he wasn't a human being. He was just a creature who took in alcohol in liquid form, then converted it to vapor and exhaled it through his nose and mouth and the pores of his skin. Now he really was a gruesome sight. I realized that the time had come to squeeze out the last drops of the tenderness that I had borne for Henri, or that he had inspired in me.

"Henri, it's morning." I spoke gently, fighting the nausea as I drew near to the huge mass of red meat. He turned his face toward me, but his dull gray eyes were as blank to me as the sea spread out under an overcast sky.

"Henri, it's eight in the morning. It's still dark outside, but the sun will be up soon." I spoke slowly, peering down into his face from above, and, miraculously, a thin light ignited in his pupils.

"Go on and die."

I whispered, mustering all the strength in my body and addressing that thin light. "Go on and die, for your mother, for Jacqueline, for me, die." A voice inside my chest added, And most of all for your own life.

Henri stared up at me as if he didn't understand who or what I was. It looked as though the light was about to fade out of his eyes again, so I raised my voice. "You do understand, don't you? If it's now, the National Railroad will pay some condolence money. But if you wait, they might dismiss you and then there won't be anything." Right up to the end I was taking advantage of his kind nature, groping for something that would appeal to this side of him. "You must realize that I want to go back to Japan. But I can't if you're here. Can you go back with me? You know you can't." Then I added, in spite of myself: "Listen, can you hear all those telephones?"

I really did hear what sounded like a lot of telephones blaring all together—not ringing exactly, but honking. Instinctively I covered my ears.

"You have to ride an airplane, a jet, you know. They make an awful noise. It's terrifying." I cringed; the words I had chosen to coerce Henri were frightening me as well. I could hardly stand it.

"I wouldn't mind dying too, but I just want to go back to Japan and see Aunt Tokie." I blurted out the words without thinking.

"You're strong enough to die by yourself. You really are, you know."

I couldn't tell whether he was listening or not. He turned his eyes away from me and looked down at the forest of empty bottles. His fat red thumbs twitched spasmodically. This twitching of the thumbs, is this what life is? I guessed it was, and realized I couldn't raise my own hands against him. Of course I didn't want to be arrested by the police, but more than that, I thought that Henri himself, in the last dim remnants of his consciousness, should be the one to do it. It was because of his handicaps that Henri had been a good man, but, broken by them, he had become this freak. He was ruining the glowing, gentle, pure life that he himself had created. But if he still had any awareness left . . .

Then I went into the bathroom, washed my face, combed my hair, and got dressed for work. As I was about to go out the front door I turned and looked back. The kitchen door was still open the way I had left it, and the bright light shone down on Henri, still hunched over in that same position. His white hair had thinned considerably, revealing the red skin of his scalp.

"You understand, don't you, Henri?" I said it again, gently, just to make sure, and walked out the door. A white mist had rolled in, so thick you could almost hear it. It resisted me as, lifting the collar of my coat, I ran down the hill from our little house to the station. Then, pressing my forehead against the train window, I gazed at the red glow of the cold winter sun as it rose, shining through the pure white mist.

It was Jacqueline who informed me of Henri's death that afternoon. It was about three o'clock, and I was at Maruichi Shoji, typing. Henri's co-worker at the station didn't know where I worked, so he had run to the laundry where Jacqueline worked to tell her.

"Henri's dead." Jacqueline's voice, though choked with tears, was calm and even bright. I was relieved; it must have been hard for Jacqueline, too, to see the gentle Henri reduced to that animal condition. She said he had gone into convulsions at the station and had fallen onto the tracks. As bad luck would have it, there was a train coming. I answered simply, "oui," and hung up. Without saying anything to the men at the company, I put on my coat and, my handbag under my arm, left work. As I rode down the old-fashioned black iron-clad elevator, I thought, "Bravo, Henri," and even clapped my hands. I hadn't gone so far as to figure out what method he might use, but Henri had chosen the station by himself, without my help. He hadn't tormented himself trying to get something he didn't have—sleeping pills or a pistol—but had chosen the most certain method. For one splendid moment his mind, desecrated by alcohol and epilepsy, had cleared, and he had subdued the clouded part of his life. He had been a human being after all.

I had to wait a terribly long time at Montparnasse Station. And just as the suburban train started off, I suddenly remembered that Henri used to call me *"mon ange,"* his angel. For all his awkwardness, he had been a true Frenchman. That morning, when he had looked up at me with those pale gray eyes in their border of white eyelashes, might I not have seemed an angel to him? Mightn't he have thought that it was an angel, in the form of a smallish Asian woman with black hair and yellow skin, who had descended as a messenger of death? Or maybe what he had seen had been just another animal reflected in an animal's eyes.

I murdered my husband. Where would I go from there, walking the blue-black abyss of days, alone? All I could see from the train window were the dead fields under the gray winter sky. Beyond them was a Japanese automobile plant, but that day it did not reflect in my eyes.

Jacqueline and Henri's co-workers were waiting at F– Station. They swept me up and quickly drove me away, so I wasn't able to go see the track where he had jumped. I heard later that there had been two men on duty at the time, but one was in the ticket booth and the other was working the signals, so no one noticed Henri going up onto the platform. Henri had probably avoided the station building by climbing over the fence alongside. The black-haired man driving the oncoming train must have been horrified to see Henri standing there. He said he'd wanted to use the emergency brakes. But just because Henri was standing there didn't mean the emergency brakes could be used; and there wasn't enough time anyway. So the train had entered the station normally, at its usual speed, and had run over Henri. Everyone repeated to me that he had been standing right at the very edge of the platform, the way railroad workers do; that even if he hadn't gone into convulsions, his drunkenness was enough to make him fall. The next day I went to see the track where he had jumped. There was a blackish-red bloodstain. I didn't see his body. I didn't want an image of his dead body to block out the red glow of Henri's face, smiling slightly under the short, transparent moustache. Of course a dead body is a dead body; it's not Henri, but if the face had looked the same I might have gotten confused.

Except for weekday mornings and afternoons, when the children pass by in their matching blue caps, shouting loudly to one another, the street leading to the N– elementary school is a particularly quiet one. All you see on Sundays is an occasional car with a foreign child or two. But today it is flooded with people. The election has brought out a special atmosphere; each flat face conceals some secret satisfaction. But hardly anyone talks. Even the ones coming back after voting are silent. There is no loud discussion, say, about who they voted for. Maybe they're just more restrained than the French, more secretive.

I came out without cleaning up. Before he left, while putting on his shoes, my uncle had reminded me again to vote. When I checked the registration card from the Board of Elections, sure enough, it was for a Miss Kubota Seiko. I got the sense that some other woman had been living in this house while I had been in France, and that I had usurped her right to this card that had come addressed to her. Could Miss Kubota Seiko be the same as the woman who had, on that dark winter morning, urged that man, helpless as a baby, to die, to go on and die? Had it been to remind me that I was this other Kubota Seiko that my uncle had kept telling me to go out and vote? Probably not. Maybe, remembering how he had blanked out into that void, he had figured that going to vote was a way for me to guard against it myself.

The people streaming on toward the polling place under the late afternoon sky do not greet one another, though they must be neighbors. I guess they are all strangers, residents of these new apartment buildings that keep cropping up.

At the front gate to the N– elementary school, someone has posted a large, plain sign with "ENTRANCE" written in black ink. There's no sign of color; this is no festival. But at the same time it's not a solemn occasion either. Instead, it's a mood like that of those swollen, smiling faces in the posters.

I follow the people into the voting hall. When I hesitate, a young man sitting behind a small desk snatches the voting card out of my hand. He marks one corner with a red pencil. A woman sitting next to him hands me a ballot and says politely, "for the Diet." It takes me a few seconds to realize that she means the Lower House. I recall the newspapers making a big fuss over the fact that this year, 1980, is unusual because both houses are up for election at the same time. They point toward the voting booths, and I go to a vacant one and take a pencil. The people on both sides of me are looking up, so automatically I look up too. There are the names I've come to know: Koito Takio, Narashima Yumiko, and the others, all posted in a neat row. I'm about to write Narashima Yumiko, but somehow that flat face with the short perm is just wrong, and I give up. I hesitate a moment, but sense someone waiting behind me, so I leave the ballot blank and go on to the ballot box. I try to slip the blank ballot through the slot, but it's too big. A man is bracing the box between his knees, his arms around it, and he orders me to fold my ballot in two.

I'm handed the variously colored ballots one by one: National Candidates for the House of Councillors, Prefectural Candidates for the House of Councillors . . . I leave them all blank, fold them in two, and slip them into the boxes. I leave through the gate posted with the paper "EXIT" sign. As I come out onto the street again, I realize that this is the first time I've ever voted. I'd been in Japan several years after I'd turned twenty, and there must have been some elections, but I have no recollection of any. Had I been that wrapped up in my problems with Kuniaki, or had I really been that oblivious to the outside world?

The phonetically typed name "Miss Kubota Seiko" rises up before my eyes. The life beyond that name has no red, glowing aura, but at the same time there is no red-black abyss, either. The procession of days, lifeless like the phonetic type, will continue to pass. As I turn the corner into the alley, I suddenly recall the moment they handed me the ballot printed with the names of the candidates for the Supreme Court. Of course I had turned the ballot in without marking it. But as I ran my eyes momentarily over the names, I had suddenly realized that these people were the judges. What an absurd irony. Here a woman who had snuffed out the life's breath of her husband was evaluating the judges. I've never inside a courtroom, but suddenly I wonder where the Supreme Court is. I'll take off my shoes right here, and barefoot I'll tear off through the evening streets to the court, burst in and lodge a complaint: Kubota Seiko murdered her husband. Please judge the case of Kubota Seiko.

The judge, in a black robe, will ask, "And who are you?"

"I'm . . ." On the stone floor to which she has fallen after bursting in, trailing blood from her bare feet, the woman suddenly tosses her head. It shines with a red aura: the red light that shone from Henri's face. At the moment it reflects the glow, the woman's face is completely blank. The judge, pointing his finger, says "You—" then breaks off; at that instant his face, too, is utterly blank.

I unlock the front door, and something soft brushes against my leg. My whole body stiffens in fright. It's a large dog with shaggy yellow fur. I've never seen a stray dog in this neighborhood, but Aunt Tokie had told me about them; she had felt sorry for those dogs that had been pets in the old neighborhood. As the old houses were torn down and replaced by apartment buildings, the dogs and cats were abandoned in the streets and went wild. Tokie said that almost all of the poor things wound up at the pound. This dog must be one of them. He sniffs forlornly at my legs.

I close the door gently in his face and, remembering, go into the kitchen. There's some mackerel skin left on one of the plates in the sink—just a tiny piece. I pick it up between my fingertips and take it out to the front door. I open the door and toss the mackerel skin out to the dog, who has just started to run away. The dog unceremoniously downs it in one gulp. This time he eagerly comes right up to me, and I slam the door in his face. For a moment I stand behind the door without stirring. Then I peek out the peephole and see that the yellow dog has made his way dejectedly over toward the brick-colored apartment building and is standing at the door, about to enter.

FLAME TREES

I

On the lawn, sparkling and expansive as the waves of the sea, stood a woman. She was so tall, she might have been supporting the sun with her head. Makiko thought of the female figures that adorn ships' prows.

"This is my wife," said Professor Novozhilov. The blue eyes of the large woman looked straight into Makiko's eyes, and Makiko was seized with a sudden tension. She entrusted her right hand to the white hand thrust out toward her and said, "How do you do, Mrs. Novozhilov?" Her voice rasped and her left hand moved instinctively to cover her abdomen.

"Don't call me Mrs. Novozhilov. Just call me Lyudmilla. Everyone in America uses first names. What's yours?" The tall woman spoke English slowly, with an accent, but fluently. She looked steadily down at Makiko. Makiko's throat had stiffened and she couldn't get her voice to work. Motoo's glasses flashed suspiciously in Makiko's direction, but she still couldn't speak, and he gave her name for her.

"Makiko seems tired; let's sit in the shade of the eucalyptus and talk." Professor Novozhilov, growling in his ponderous, accented English, grasped Makiko's elbow. Makiko suppressed a wary, instinctive urge to pull her elbow away. She looked out into space and the scenery froze, motionless like a film when the projector has broken. The intense sunlight of the Southern California noon set the tree, the people, and the picnic tables in distinct relief against the lawn. All shadow was lost under the clear blue, dry sky. Makiko halted and tried to make herself, too, into an object. A stone figure in a stone landscape. She had to freeze the flow of time, like the sorceress who bewitched the sleeping princess. If she didn't, the film would run backwards at an incredible speed and cross the gap of sixteen or seventeen years and ten thousand miles in a single leap. From a place in the past long sealed under a thick stony lid, blue Slavic eyes stare at Makiko.

The fat fingers tightened their grip on her elbow. "Are you all right?" Professor Novozhilov's monotonous, heavy voice filled the air above her. "Yes," she said softly, and lurched forward again, walking stiffly, like a marionette.

The film began moving in the right direction. The noonday sun radiated white light, and the landscape clothed itself in the dry heat. In the center of the broad campus lawn a large eucalyptus tree stood, spreading its long, hanging branches over its thick shadow. Steadied but constrained by Professor Novozhilov's hand on her elbow, Makiko crossed the twenty or so meters to the tree.

Motoo was walking with the professor's wife, a few paces in front of them. Although Professor Novozhilov noticed Makiko's pallor and was solicitous, her own husband didn't even glance back at her. Next to the tall Lyudmilla he seemed small and thin. Makiko glared reproachfully at his familiar shirt with its checked pattern, as if the effort could free her from the middleaged professor's oppressive grip on her arm and the shock inflicted on her by his wife's blue eyes.

Mixed groups of men and women sat around several tables in the eucalyptus shade. They were taking cold chicken and ham out of coolers and setting them out on the tables, opening beer and soda bottles. Their chatter paused briefly and a cheerful voice called out to the Novozhilovs, "Hi!" Someone at one of the tables drew up a couple of chairs for them.

Suddenly the drooping branches parted, and a well-built youth appeared under the tree. His German heritage showed unmistakably in his face. He smiled broadly. "How are you today, Anton?" He spoke to the professor first, then, addressing Lyudmilla, repeated the casual greeting.

Motoo, speaking English even to her, introduced the young man to Makiko as Conrad Lange from the neighboring lab. As she offered him her right hand, her eyes were drawn to the small face of a woman who was standing nestled against his broad shoulders. The shadow of the eucalyptus leaves unexpectedly brought out the glow in the woman's deep brown eyes, and Makiko smiled at her. Somehow she felt this woman could help her. "This is my wife, Helga," said Conrad, putting his arm around the woman's shoulders. They shook hands, and Helga Lange asked the usual question, "When did you arrive in Pasadena?" Her German accent was so strong that Makiko felt she could touch it with her finger.

"We just got here three days ago."

"Did you come straight from Japan?"

"No, the Hatas came from France," contributed Conrad.

"Really? Where in France?"

"G–, it's a suburb of Paris."

Helga tilted her head to one side, trying to recognize the name. Conrad again helped out. "That's the place with the huge phytotron that the great Charles DeGaulle poured all that money into, part of his campaign to restore France's glory, even though the war in Algeria was already costing him so much. That's the lab Motoo Hata came from. He didn't even think of dropping in at his home in Japan to catch his breath, just crossed over the Atlantic and our own New York."

"Conrad, it's not *our* New York, even if you're just joking. But what's a phytotron?"

Helga's brown eyes opened wide, filling her small, triangular face, and she looked up at her strong, handsome husband. The sun's rays filtering through the eucalyptus leaves touched her long, curved eyelashes, then scattered.

"Isn't that inexcusable, Motoo? Imagine a plant physiologist who gets married without even explaining to his wife what a phytotron is," Professor Novozhilov interrupted bluntly.

"I can't help excusing it. I didn't tell Makiko either." The three men laughed together.

But Makiko remembered asking that same question at their first formal meeting, when she had been introduced to Motoo as a prospective bride. He had answered seriously, explaining that a phytotron was a facility used to create a contained plant environment. Neither the sound of the words nor the way they were written called up any image in her mind. After their marriage, when they went to France, she visited the one in G–. The phytotron was made up of a large, unattended engine room and an enclosed upper chamber made of glass and metal. It was filled with artificial light that penetrated into every corner. In the large, bright, but completely sealed space, a wide variety of plants were living, lined up in rows. Makiko imagined the breathing of these confined plants and looked at the substance that supported their roots. "It's not earth, is it?" she asked. She touched it with her fingertip; it glittered and was strangely weightless. "It's made by fusing crushed fiberglass with mica," answered Motoo. Makiko looked up at him curiously. What were these men trying to grasp, isolating these plants from nature, testing their strange subsistence as experimental objects in this artificial enclosure? Even if the plants, dismembered down to their individual cells, did hand over a grain of their life's secret to them, life itself was not something that scientists could scoop up in their hands.

"You future moms should sit down," Mrs. Novozhilov said, wrapping her arms around Helga's and Makiko's shoulders and guiding them over toward the chairs. Hearing the words, Helga met Makiko's eyes and asked, "Oh, you too?" They both looked down simultaneously to gauge each other's waists. Helga's abdomen swelled noticeably beneath her loose dress.

"This year the Novozhilov troops are especially productive." Mrs. Novozhilov glanced at the men, who were still standing and talking. Then she drew up a chair for herself. Her head touched one of the hanging branches of the eucalyptus tree; the small oval leaves rustled, showing their undersides and brushing their powdery whiteness against the silver of her hair. Even the thick shade of the huge tree couldn't cloud the rich, creamy whiteness of her skin.

"You're right; there's Katie and Rose too." Helga counted, her right hand pressing down the outstretched fingers of her left, one by one.

"And Kamini, too."

"Who's that?"

"She's coming from India."

"So Lyudmilla, hurry up; don't miss out on the trend!"

"Hey, I've already got three boys—take a look at them! Besides, having babies under the bright California sun is the prerogative of the wives of our university's post-doctoral fellows. We are too old."

She spoke seriously. When she pronounced the words "we are too old," her blue eyes looked straight at Makiko. Makiko avoided her glance. She reached out and plucked one of the eucalyptus leaves. She rubbed its underside, but the white powder didn't come off on her finger. A bitter, bilious taste welled up from the pit of her stomach and filled her mouth. She swallowed the saliva, but the taste wouldn't go away. It was probably just another symptom, if you could call it that, of early pregnancy. From the beginning, when her pregnancy had been confirmed by the doctor in G–, she hadn't felt particularly nauseated. She hadn't been aware of any of the usual minor conditions of the first trimester—changes in taste or smell—but was constantly tired. Her eyes had sunk in their sockets and her complexion, never very healthy, had turned sallow.

Maybe her oversensitive nerves and feelings of vulnerability were another symptom of her pregnancy. That's probably why, when she was introduced to Lyudmilla Novozhilov, she had been so shocked by those blue, owl-like, Slavic eyes. In Paris, too, there must have been Slavs among the people she saw on the street, or even among those who came to visit the lab. But could it be that Lyudmilla Novozhilov was somehow related to that blue-eyed soldier, and that's why she stood out from the rest; that that was what was in her eyes that had terrified Makiko so much just now? Then again, it must be a chance resemblance—how could she trust her memories from when she was a five-year-old girl?

Here she was in the middle of this typical American social event, this picnic on a college campus, and what was she doing? At the slightest provocation she had closed herself off and sat silent, looking deep within. Makiko started and swung her head up.

The dry Pasadena sky wove shining blue lace through the broad sweep of the hanging eucalyptus leaves. Makiko, the middleaged Russian woman, and the young pregnant German were sealed off together inside a transparent green jar. Inside the green jar, light and time flowed backwards together.

"Makiko, have you found a doctor yet?" Mrs. Novozhilov peered into Makiko's face.

"No, not yet . . ."

"Since you've just made a long trip, you ought to go soon. If you'd like, I can introduce you to my doctor." Helga's small, triangular face was turned to Makiko. She, too, seemed to want to make Makiko the center of their conversation.

"Thank you, but I think that our Japanese friends, who have a farm here, will be introducing me to a second-generation Japanese doctor. Though I myself would like to get an American doctor; it would help me get to know American society better." Makiko's words tumbled over each other.

Mrs. Novozhilov raised her index finger. "But, Makiko, if he's second generation, he *is* an American, you know."

Makiko reddened.

"Me, I'm Russian by blood and birth. But I'm an American, right?" She opened her blue eyes wide and nodded at Helga, seeking confirmation.

"My husband would be delighted to hear you say that, Lyudmilla. How do I know Conrad hasn't bought you off?"

"Well, no matter what, you will become the mothers of Americans. You know that, don't you, that all children born in this country become Americans, automatically. . . ." Mrs. Novozhilov spoke calmly but emphatically to the two younger women.

"Ah, what would my grandma say: American great-grandchildren! My grandmother turned our attic in Tübingen upside down looking for baby clothes to send us—clothes she herself had worn!"

"Worn by your grandmother when she was a baby!" Makiko was impressed, but Mrs. Novozhilov just nodded as if there were nothing unusual in it.

"I'll show you next time, Makiko. They're hand-knit from cotton, so they're really durable. You can wash them in hot water a hundred times, and they won't tear; they just keep getting whiter and softer. My grandmother wore them, then my father wore them, then I did. . . ." Helga pressed her abdomen through her dress.

Lyudmilla Novozhilov shook her white cheeks solemnly, then added, just to make her point: "Soon it'll be a little American baby wearing them."

"You two are good in English, so it's all right for you to have American children, but my English is bad. . . ." Makiko blurted out the words. Her Japanese accent was inevitably present, whether she spoke French or English. She realized that she should speak slowly to make sure she reached her listeners, but, self-conscious in front of others, she mumbled and spoke too rapidly in spite of herself.

"Your English is good. But you should have more self-confidence and practice until you really feel comfortable using the language. For your own sake . . ."

Mrs. Novozhilov clipped the syllables, "your own sake," giving special emphasis to each one; her blue eyes stared into Makiko's eyes, driving home her message. Makiko's hand rose involuntarily and pressed against her throat.

"You can become fluent in English. But you can't lose your foreign accent." Professor Novozhilov's thick voice sounded over her head. The men, each holding two soft drink cups, were standing behind their wives, looking down at them. Makiko took a cup from Motoo's hand. With this movement, she managed to camouflage the fear that had been aroused again by Lyudmilla Novozhilov's blue eyes.

"People who speak English with a foreign accent are respected here. This may be one of America's most famous universities, but all its best professors are from other countries," the professor said stiffly.

Conrad's cheerful voice overlapped the professor's monotonous drone. "Well, Motoo, at least we have one thing people can respect."

In spite of his words, Makiko hardly noticed any accent in Conrad's English. Motoo grinned wryly and, in his accented English, changed the subject to the huge eucalyptus tree. Motoo had been a student at Stanford before going to France, and he was well acquainted with the plants and trees of California. His long fingers gently stroked the big tree's trunk, whose light brown bark had peeled, exposing white patches of tree underneath. Although his specialty was plant physiology, Motoo knew a great deal about garden plants as well; whenever he went to a party he always brought up the topic, engaging like-minded people in comparisons of Eastern and Western plants.

"Plants like the aucuba, the yatsude, and the spindle tree grow everywhere in Japan; you can find them in any garden, but here in California they're planted in expensive pots and displayed on people's porches." He addressed Mrs. Novozhilov blandly, without expression, and his voice was lost when Conrad started talking:

"Motoo, have you heard about Professor B-? He found that you could extract valuable florigen pollen from Washington palm tree blossoms. The distinguished professor took a ladder out to one of the trees in Pasadena—you know how many of them there are along the streets—and made quite a scene pulling himself up the ladder. But you know how hard it is to get florigen . . . he made such a fool of himself! Everyone was talking about it." Conrad laughed aloud.

Makiko had met this elderly scholar at a party at the lab in France. He was a real, authentic American type. How many generations of your family have to live in this country before you can be considered a real American? It struck Makiko that maybe Conrad was picking on Professor B- in particular because he was so authentically "American," just to gain Professor Novozhilov's favor. From her time in France Makiko knew that plant physiologists were generally straightforward people, but she noticed a fleshiness in Conrad's face that reminded her of German sausage. It was not physical; it was rather a kind of spiritual fat. Her eyes shifted to his wife's small face. Young and pregnant, Helga rested her back against the thick trunk of the eucalyptus tree and gazed up with large, sparkling brown eyes at her splendidly built husband.

Professor Novozhilov just smiled and paid no attention to what the young German was saying.

When they left the campus, the western sky was red beyond

the rows of Washington palms. The black silhouettes of the palm trees engraved themselves in a line dividing the scorched sky from the dried-out earth. This red evening sky, too, is different, thought Makiko, resting next to Motoo in the front seat. Motoo whistled as he drove. The theme to *Shane*. That's it, it's the blazing sunset of a Western movie; that's why it's different. Those sunsets had given the settlers the strength to hope for tomorrow, even after Indian raids. But in that ruined, or rather, that false country that had never existed even at its very beginning—Manchuria—the sunsets had blazed as if the end of each day were the end of the world itself.

"Look, that's jacaranda, that's hibiscus. . . ." Once they left the tree-lined avenue behind, Motoo started pointing out the gardens of the houses along the street. Makiko laughed. He'd started in again. Things she just wouldn't learn. "Thanks anyway."

"I have to try; you can't even tell the difference between a potato and an eggplant."

"Well, there can't be that many people who can identify a plant just by looking at the leaves."

"I'm not joking. They're completely different; anybody knows that. Anyway, Pasadena is famous for its beautiful flowers. Even you will learn their names after you've lived here a year."

"It's not the names that are important; it's the impression they make. As far as I'm concerned, the only flowers . . ."

". . . are cherry blossoms and roses?"

"No! *Tanpopo* and *nadeshiko* . . ."

Motoo laughed. Ever since she had seen the Japanese flowers that bore the same names as the flowers she remembered from her childhood in Manchuria, she had lost all interest in the words. The names were the same, but how different the flowers were. . . .

In the spring the thick ice melted, revealing the black earth. If you peered into it, you could find a grass sprout. The children, hardly breathing, would gaze at the young blade of grass. They made a circle around it with pebbles to protect the tiny, freshly sprouted life. But the moment passed quickly. Before you could take a breath, a great mass of deep, green lives would press up, transforming the fields completely. And among the coarse weeds bright yellow dandelions would appear, big, vivid flowers. How could these be the same as those fluffy, soft little yellow blossoms that peeped out from underneath Japanese hedges? They had a different density, these lives that blazed into bloom after the severe winter with its extreme sub-zero temperatures. The passionate voices of the flowers, resurrected from their death under the thick ice, filled the fields and echoed even in Makiko's little ears, but the only name for them in her memory was the Japanese word *tanpopo*, dandelions. And then *nadeshiko*, pinks. The dyed indigo flowers that had blossomed on the robe that had covered her mother's dead body.

". . . That's a boxwood; those are camellias." Motoo pointed to a hedge through the car window.

"Even I know that much."

"Is that so? Well, all the same it's in my nature to be thorough in whatever I do. I'll be repeating the names of flowers to you my whole life. Once I decide on something, I will never change my mind. It's your destiny." He was only half joking.

"If you're going to make a decision, how about deciding on something that I would appreciate a little more?"

"It depends on what you have in mind. What kind of thing?"

"Something like deciding to protect me my whole life through?" The words slipped out, and she looked out the window. Beyond the camellias and boxwood bushes, on beautifully trimmed lawns, large, one-storied wooden houses stood, shining white in the evening sun. Red hibiscus blossoms tossed back the twilight that was starting to descend.

"Protect you your whole life? I wouldn't go that far. We never know what's ahead of us; I could lose my job and not even be able to feed myself."

"Clothing, food, shelter . . . that's not the kind of protection I mean."

"Well, then, protection against what?"

Makiko hesitated, trying to find the right words. "Protection against my fear of the unknown . . ."

"Shouldn't you try to figure out what you're afraid of? The unknown—you mean ghosts?"

"That's it . . . I'm afraid of ghosts."

"That kind of talk is too abstract for me; I don't understand it. You have to catch your ghost and get a good look at it."

"Well, then, catch it."

"You can't catch something that doesn't exist. You first have to observe nature carefully."

"Observe with eyes full of fear?"

"No, objectively."

"Only people who can face the reality of nature and let themselves become pure, transparent instruments of observation—only they can become natural scientists. 'Objective' means without self. But if there's no subject, doesn't that mean that the act of observation, too, is impossible?"

"The subject exists at the point where the act of viewing becomes part of nature."

"Something's wrong with that idea; there's some mistake."

"Not at all." Motoo spoke without emotion, and pointed to the western sky.

"Look at the half-sun over there."

Makiko strained to hear. He must mean the setting sun. But I can't call this a sunset. A sunset is something terrifying. . . .

"Is it going down or coming up?"

"Don't be silly."

"You think it's a setting sun because you know what time it is, and that we're facing west. But if we took a picture of it, we wouldn't know whether it was morning or evening. Isn't it because you understand where you are in time and space that you can identify which it is?"

"What are you getting at?"

"With your ghost, too, you have to first of all set your coordinates for the place and time you see it. And unfortunately you can't establish that, I suppose."

Makiko said nothing. She'd started out wrong, asking for protection.

The car passed through the Ides' gate, circled around to the back of the big house, and stopped in front of the garage.

Bob Ide, a second-generation Japanese-American farmer, had been Motoo's sponsor on his first trip to America. Motoo had spent all his university vacations with the Ides in Pasadena, helping them on the farm. For Motoo, a foreign student on scholarship with a love of gardening, it was a wonderful way to spend his free time. On the recommendation of a French professor at the university, Motoo had moved to France to fill a research position at the French national laboratory, but now he was back to spend a year at the university in Pasadena. The Ides were delighted at the coincidence that had brought him back, this time with his young wife. Bob Ide was a farmer, but he had graduated from law school, and if it hadn't been for the war he would have become a lawyer; it was his wife, born in the U.S. but raised in a farming family in Hiroshima, who took the most pride in Motoo's success, bragging about him in her circle of second-generation Japanese friends.

Vicky, a collie with a luxuriant coat of dark brown and white fur, bounded out the kitchen door to meet them. When she saw the Hatas, she stopped short, her body stiffened, and she turned warily and walked back into the house. The evening sun brought out the brilliance of the bougainvillea, in full bloom against the white, Spanish-style walls.

"That really shows off the beauty of the flowers."

Makiko touched one crimson-purple blossom with her hand. It felt like thin, dried paper brushing against her dry fingertips.

"That's not a flower. Too bad."

"What do you call it, fruit?"

"The thing you thought was a flower is called a 'bract.' The flower is, look here . . ." Motoo peered at the plant and pointed gingerly. Inside the brilliant purple husk nestled a pale yellow dot, so tiny it might have been left by the tip of a fine paintbrush.

"That's a flower?"

"You can hardly see the petals; those are the pistils and stamens."

Makiko nodded. You can't see the petals. . . .

A white Ford station wagon slid to a stop behind them. Vicky bounded out from the kitchen a second time. Mrs. Ide, her sunburnt face all smiles, stepped out of the car.

Mrs. Ide's Japanese farming heritage showed itself in her broad face, short arms and legs, and her sturdy, short body, but her long years of living in America were evident in the easy fit of her longsleeved blouse and slacks. Her stout, firmly muscled body gave no indication that she was nearing sixty.

The collie, standing on her hind legs, was as tall as her mistress. Mrs. Ide buried her face in Vicky's fleecy white mane, saying, "Oh, good girl, good girl," then raised her head and burst into loud laughter. "When Ken was a little boy he used to come out and jump on me like this. Now that he doesn't come out to meet me any more, Vicky has taken his place."

"Is Papa still out in the field?" asked Motoo. Motoo had adopted the Ides' friends' custom of calling them Mama and Papa. For Motoo, who called his parents Father and Mother, this was natural, but Makiko had decided to call them Papa Ide and

Mama Ide. She called her foster parents in Hokuriku Mama and Papa.

"He's busy with the November chrysanthemum exhibit; the Mexicans won't help him."

"Tomorrow the university is closed, so I can do some watering or trimming. Maybe I can be a bigger help than the Mexicans."

"What, you with your Ph.D.? You're not a boy anymore; you don't have to go around watering plants. A Ph.D. . . ." Mrs. Ide left her canvas shoes at the kitchen door.

"Hello, boy!" squawked a parrot inside a cage hanging in one corner of the large kitchen. The brilliantly colored bird, caricaturing a human voice, repeated the same greeting all day long. "Hello, boy," replied Mrs. Ide gaily.

"I may have a Ph.D., but there are too many of us these days, and pretty soon it will be difficult to find jobs. I'd better at least learn how to trim chrysanthemums, just in case."

When she heard Motoo's self-deprecating words, Mrs. Ide turned solemn. "Even doctors of physics?"

Motoo dodged: "No, physicists are doing all right; unlike biologists and botanists, they have a place in the sun." The Ides' only son Ken was still in school at the age of thirty; he had been studying physics, transferring from one Eastern university to another, but eventually he probably would get his Ph.D. Would he be edged out by young researchers pressing in from abroad? Not only that; at the rate things were going, the war in Vietnam could escalate and he could even be sent away as a soldier. The possibility must have crossed Bob Ide's mind.

Motoo changed the subject. He looked at the guest house that was joined to the garage, noticed that the door was closed, and asked, "Is Julia out today?"

"It's her day off. She said she was going shopping in L.A and would meet her husband for lunch. They're newlyweds, you know."

"You must be kidding. What does her husband do in Los Angeles?"

"He's a shoe repairman. But the problem is, he married Julia for her bank account. There's something fishy about someone so young marrying her."

Makiko recalled the huge Mexican woman, shapeless as a laundry bag, and asked, "How old is she?"

"Same age as me, fifty-eight."

"And her husband?"

Mrs. Ide answered Motoo's question deadpan, her face tight: "I'm not sure, but probably under thirty."

"What?" Motoo was amazed.

"Julia would spend all her money if we'd let her, so we took out part of each week's salary and built up a savings account for her. And she lives in this guest house for free. . . . But now that she's gone and taken up with that guy it's all over," said Mrs. Ide, putting on her apron. Resignation sounded in her voice. From the oven came the smell of a roast. She must have set the timer before she had gone out into the field. Makiko realized that she ought to take some responsibility for dinner, since it was Julia's day off, but she just felt lost in the huge kitchen, with all its electric appliances.

After dinner, Mrs. Ide loaded the dishes into the dishwasher and went upstairs. Shortly afterward she came down in a snug-fitting black bathing suit.

"Motoo, would you like to take a swim? Makiko, too. I have a bathing suit for you—it's one of mine, though; it might be too big for you."

Makiko, flustered, declined. She couldn't imagine swimming while she was pregnant.

Behind the garage was a twenty-five meter pool, surrounded by a privet hedge. The water stood motionless and black, but Mrs.

Ide turned on a switch, so that when you looked at the bottom, it appeared greenish.

Makiko reclined on a deck chair and gazed up at the night sky. The trees were strikingly tall; at the black tips of their uppermost branches not a star was to be seen. The faint pink had also faded from the sky beyond the palm trees. Makiko watched as the plump, stocky woman swam across the expanse of dark water, her arms and legs splashing. She swam with her grand crawl stroke, practiced and perfected in the sea off Hiroshima. Motoo floated upright in the pool, treading water. He kept his head out of the water; he didn't want to get his glasses wet.

A transparent, floating instrument for observation, thought Makiko. Were all those scientists who had been at today's picnic also transparent observation instruments, just like Motoo? In a country like America, where humanity bloomed in its fullest variety, they could put all their energy into their research, not distracted by the loss of their homelands. Unlike Lyudmilla Novozhilov, who kept stressing her American identity, Helga was constantly repeating "in my country," drawing the conversation back to her Tübingen. Was it only women who were obsessed with their homelands? In Paris, too, whenever the Japanese wives got together, they would always talk about Japanese food and about how they wanted to go home as soon as possible. Some of them said they'd go out of their minds if they couldn't call their mothers in Japan every month. Makiko would tell Motoo how lucky he was that *his* wife wasn't like that. She had understood when she married him that she might never go back to Japan. "Was there any other woman who never said she wanted to go home?" Makiko would ask him, putting him in her debt. Motoo would get the upper hand: "But you haven't got a homeland, so you have no place to return to." She had first been introduced to Motoo as a prospective bride in Japan, where he had returned for an extended vacation from his work in France. Later he had remembered and taken advantage of the words she had murmured then, "My homeland is a country that no longer exists; I'll go anywhere in the world. . . ." Even now, Makiko didn't know how much of her desperation at that moment had been communicated to the young scientist who had been living abroad for so long. Maybe the words themselves, "lost homeland," were just an abstract fabrication to him, like the ghosts.

Do I really have no homeland? Makiko peered under the lid that rose from deep within her. It was like a house of ice, in which time was frozen, motionless. When she had seen the Russian woman's blue eyes glittering inside the ice house that noon, Makiko had slammed down the lid. Hadn't those eyes been asking, Where is your homeland?

The light hit the water splashed up by Mrs. Ide, and a shining drop grazed Makiko's eye. The tiny glitter flashed across the night and was gone. For a moment Makiko's eyes were caught up in the light.

Suddenly she muttered the words, "That's not the way it is." Through all her school years in Japan, right up through her graduation from high school, the words would come to her constantly, "That's not the way it is." And even after her marriage, living in France, they had sounded in her chest. Now in America, pregnant, the same words rose to her lips.

If she had been asked what she meant by "it," she would have answered, "life." But if it wasn't like that, then what was it like? Her answer would come: something like a crimson flame blazing up. . . . But there was no one to hear Makiko's mumbling and ask her about it directly, and so she didn't give voice to her words. If she spoke them aloud, she herself would have to recognize the contradiction in them: How can there be life inside a flame? Life can only exist if the temperature is right.

Inside a flame there is only death. But strangely, death itself is cold and blue. Makiko had contemplated this contradiction from her earliest days. The face suddenly becomes blue and falls to the pillow, as if separated from the neck. The eyelids close, and suddenly the person is no more. The flames crackle loudly and burn her body. Inside the giant kiln of the setting sun, a person disappears.

Against the background of the night, Motoo rose up, scattering shining drops of water.

Stealthy footsteps echoed in the hall. Makiko strained her eyes in the darkness. The door creaked quietly. There was no doubt about it; someone was in the room. Even here, in the Ides' cold, formal guest room with its dusty, grand furniture immersed in darkness, something had sneaked in and was lurking among the bulky black shadows. Suddenly Makiko was overcome with the terror of a cornered animal cub. Her whole body turned hollow, and the base of her ears tensed up. The door continued its quiet creaking. Makiko watched, terrified, as the blue eyes of a predatory bird pressed in on her. Translucent eyes, thick as ice. Eyes that, though their pale centers seemed as blind as the whites, had nevertheless sought out the hidden prey.

The Soviet soldier stood at the ready, his gun pointed at her father. But for some reason his eyes aimed directly at the little five-year-old girl, gripped tightly in her father's hands. Makiko turned her whole body to ice and took in his blue gaze. If she let his eyes go, he would shoot her father.

She had lost her mother the year before. This time, too, she would be left behind. In the back of her mind Makiko wanted to be killed. Already, at four years of age, her experience watching her mother die had planted in her the illusion that her fears would be extinguished only with her own death.

The door kept creaking. The footsteps continued in the hall. Makiko pictured the kitchen door, left open even at night. An intruder had stepped in from the broad, dark fields that surrounded the Ides' big farmhouse and the pool with its black hedge.

From a point inside her terror, Makiko let go of her resistance and was swept away. Her frozen eyes were fixed on the door, and her overwrought mind directed her to spring up as soon as the door opened, so that she would be killed first, before Motoo. No amount of fear could make her awaken Motoo, sleeping peacefully at her side. The murderer would undoubtedly kill the person who got up and stared directly at him. By turning her own body into a shield to protect her husband, Makiko would protect herself from her own fear of being left behind.

The door swung open and Makiko sprang up in the darkness. Against the glow from the nightlight in the hall, the collie's bushy tail glistened. Vicky's black eyes flashed, she took a look at Makiko sitting bolt upright on the bed, and, blowing a puff of air out her nose, she calmly turned and retreated down the hall.

Next to Makiko Motoo's lips moved indistinctly, and he turned over in his sleep. Makiko quietly lowered her body, still tense. Probably Motoo, after spending all his college vacations at the Ides', felt right at home in this room; he must have known that the door didn't close well, and that Vicky was likely to stop in during the night. He could have thought to mention the possibility to her; if he had, she wouldn't have felt the way she did just then— that her body had peeled away, leaving only her heart.

Motoo didn't know the Makiko who could feel such terror. As much as she could, Makiko concealed it from people. She had since childhood. She herself didn't know why. Was it that she considered the fear a bad thing? That she was ashamed of it? She didn't know, but the fear continued to oppress her solitude. It had become much more intense with her pregnancy.

Makiko tried to make herself fall asleep, but her overwrought nerves would not let sleep come. She reached over softly and

touched Motoo's arm. The transparent observation instrument
had taken the data it had observed and processed it in its brain,
and now had fallen into a deep, blank sleep. But the eyes filled
with terror could not sleep peacefully without assurance of protection.

... But every protector is just a living body that can die and
disappear at any moment. That's all right; I will be left behind
only until my own death, and then the fear will be extinguished.
It's all right to die. Makiko kept repeating the words like a spell.

On that other morning when she had opened her eyes, dense
blossoms of ice had formed on the glass of the double-paned windows. The morning light glittered, reflecting the ice that blan-
keted the world outside, and shone through the icy flowers on
the window glass. Makiko, still in her pajamas, clambered up onto the sill of the bay window and touched the glass. With the ra-
diators on it was warm inside the room, but the bitter cold pierced
her small fingertip and penetrated her sleepy body. She felt a keen
pleasure. The faint warmth of her fingertip didn't have the slightest effect on the thick flowers of ice that covered the glass; they
just continued their hard glittering. But still, every morning she
would press her little finger against the icy flowers of the glass,
and every morning she would be grabbed, dragged down from
the window sill, and reprimanded: "Are you at it again? You'll
catch a cold." The frostbite never left her finger, and even her
cheek was marked with a red spot.

Towards noon Neiya, her nanny, answered the phone, then
silently dressed Makiko in her *shuba* and fur hat. How did they
get to the hospital? Makiko remembered that there were a lot of
people standing around in the room. On the white bed in the middle of the room her mother lay with her eyes closed. Her face was
ashen. Neiya called to her tearfully, "Mother, Miss Makiko is

here," but she said nothing, and her eyes stayed closed. Then, in a choked voice her father called her mother's name. He sounded angry. Four-year-old Makiko stared fixedly from her father's embrace.

Her young mother's ashen face, the eyes still closed, suddenly became suffused with blue, shuddered, and fell to the pillow. It was as if it had been resting on something above the large, white pillow and then had slipped off. Makiko would take that moment, no more than a few seconds, and rewind it slowly, like a film in slow motion. This was the actual moment when her mother's life—which, for Makiko, had already begun to ebb away while she was making her way to the hospital—had ended once and for all. And that was the way it should have been. Immediately after her mother's death came a time of stillness, when Makiko found some peace of mind. But then, later, when Neiya had said that about her mother . . .

There were a lot of people in that room, too. Their alternate murmuring and hush gave the room an unsettled atmosphere. Where was her father? Makiko played by herself in front of the *pechka*, the Russian stove in the corner. Her back was hot from the fire. When she raised her eyes, it was to ask Neiya some trifle. But Neiya misunderstood, and bursting into tears, she clutched at Makiko's small shoulders. "Miss Makiko, now your mommy's body is being burned. Oh, Miss Makiko, did you know we put your drawing in the coffin? Your mommy is holding it in her arms, and when she's all burned up, there will be nothing left, and she will rise up into the sky. Her spirit . . ." But then someone called her and she got up and left.

Makiko turned and stared blankly at the fire in the *pechka*. She saw the shape of a young woman blazing up in the crimson flames. She had been forbidden to look inside the coffin, but she had seen the maids pick out her mother's favorite yukata, a pink one with an indigo pattern, and gently arrange it inside the coffin. Makiko's picture was a crayon drawing of a little girl with a round, cropped head. Was it supposed to be herself? Makiko couldn't remember. But her mother, wearing the pink yukata, had burst into flames and disappeared, transparent, into the February sky of Shinkyo. In February, the sky, trees, and earth of Shinkyo were all frozen. Makiko thought that the flame that had blazed up from the white, frozen earth to the blue, frozen sky was beautiful. Though what she had actually seen was only a fire in the corner *pechka* of the crematorium waiting room.

Was that all there was to death? To turn pale and cold and simply end? Isn't there something that begins after that in the blazing of the red flames? No, nothing begins. The whole body, flesh and bones, is simply discarded in the enormous fire. The living body has ceased to exist and is left without sensation; it feels neither heat nor pain. It just disappears in the crackling flames.

But this aroused a painful yearning inside Makiko. The place that was consumed by the red flames—that was Makiko's homeland.

"I mustn't . . . I must go to sleep," Makiko reproached herself. Though her pregnancy wasn't yet noticeable, she felt pressure in her chest and couldn't catch her breath. She could harm her baby, getting so overwrought. Makiko thought of the thing inside her womb. What if there were something wrong with it? Makiko speculated ominously about the hollow that was the inside of her womb. She couldn't see anything. What if the baby were handicapped? A lifeless baby, a baby transparent like a jellyfish . . .

Well, if so, I can die. Faced with all the dangers and fears that presented themselves in her imagination, Makiko sought a solution in the idea of her own death. Thrusting this response like a mask at the mirror, she could escape from the vision of her own face, ugly and distorted with terror. The idea of death was her almighty trump card. Clutching this card like a charm, Makiko closed her eyes.

Motoo parted the full, gathered lace curtains and opened the window. The Pasadena sky was again dry and blue. It rarely rained here, and the earth was as dry as in the desert. Makiko got up, blinking. After her sleepless night the morning sun hurt her eyes. The night's terror had vanished, but the fatigue remained.

As they descended the broad staircase, Makiko whispered, "Don't you think there's something weird about this house? All these luxurious things thrown together—it's not like the Ides at all."

Motoo looked like he'd had a good night's sleep. He lowered his voice and told her that some time ago, the state had bought up some of the Ides' farmland to build a highway or something. Papa Ide, drawing on his knowledge of the law, had acquired ownership of this big house in compensation. The previous owner died soon afterward, before he had a chance to move out, and the Ides were left with all the original furnishings of the house. "A typical example of American generosity," said Motoo, laughing. Makiko, lighthearted now that it was morning, speculated that maybe the thing that had been lurking in the shadows of the furniture last night was that man's spirit.

The hosts of this strange mansion had already finished breakfast in the dining area off the kitchen. Bob Ide, in clean, neat working clothes, was reading the paper, and his wife was opening a can of dog food for Vicky.

"Well good morning!" Bob smiled at the Hatas. Bob was sixty, but the large eyes sparkling under his graying eyebrows were the clear, bright eyes of a much younger man. Motoo often described Papa Ide as an eternal youth, a dreamer. Makiko couldn't guess what kinds of dreams this little old man could have. Maybe about creating marvellous, miraculous flowers unknown to the earth.

Makiko's father, if he were alive, would be the same age as Bob Ide. When she had decided to marry Motoo, who was ready to go anywhere in the world for the sake of his research, perhaps she held a hint of a childish hope that somewhere in the world her father was still alive, lost in the crowds of some city, and that by marrying Motoo she was increasing her chances, however small, of finding him. Her father had been unusually tall. His smile was gentle and kind. Could these traits be enough to identify a man after twenty years? Makiko thought that she would surely recognize him if she met him again.

"You said the university is closed today?" Bob Ide's Japanese was flawless, though he spoke with slightly excessive emphasis. His speech was typically male, though. Makiko had often heard that second-generation Japanese men, since they were taught Japanese by their mothers, spoke like women.

"That's right, so I thought we could look for an apartment sometime this afternoon," answered Motoo guardedly. He expected to meet resistance from Mrs. Ide, and he was not mistaken. She stopped opening the can.

"There's no need to hurry; I can take you out myself later," she said.

"But we don't want to be always troubling you for things." Makiko quickly came to Motoo's aid. She wanted to hurry up and find a little nest for this one year and settle in. It was not only the fetus that she was carrying inside, she thought. She wanted to contemplate it. . . .

Mrs. Ide wouldn't give up. "Why don't you stay in our house a little longer?"

"We'd love to have you stay here the whole time. But if you did, you wouldn't have a truly American experience, right? The best way to do that is to rent an apartment for just the two of you." Bob Ide helped them out, speaking formally.

"The apartment can wait, but you have to get to a doctor soon.

So let's go today." Makiko was intimidated by Mrs. Ide's insistence on taking over all their arrangements.

She did everything: the accounting for the farm, the management of the Mexican laborers, the mail order business; she even worked in the fields. Makiko didn't want to add to her work, but Mrs. Ide paid no attention when Makiko said she could at least go by herself to the doctor.

"Good morning everybody!" A high, nasal voice echoed in the kitchen, and Julia, her huge body shaking like a big shapeless bag, appeared in the dinette. A mirthful look appeared in Bob Ide's clear eyes.

Even on her trip to Germany, where there were a lot of fat women, Makiko had never seen such a huge quantity of surplus flesh as on this Mexican woman's body. Her baggy double chin melted into the flesh that swelled up from her chest, and her enormous breasts sagged, resting on her protruding stomach. Flesh called up flesh, and melted into waves of flesh. All that flesh was supported by ankles that were as delicate as a young Parisian girl's; it was a strange sight.

Makiko couldn't finish her bacon and eggs. Julia stood next to her with her hands on her hips and laughed through her nose.

"Mrs. Hata, when is your baby coming?" she asked, speaking in her nasal voice, high as a young girl's. Julia's eyes looked caressingly at Makiko's thin waist.

"When is *your* baby coming, Julia?" Bob Ide teased the woman who had just married a man thirty years her junior. Julia snickered, spreading wrinkles on both sides of her nose.

"Mrs. Hata, if you don't eat more and make your stomach big, your baby will look like a mouse." Julia's large gray eyes opened wide like a fish's.

Mrs. Ide joined in: "That's right. Makiko, you have to eat some more. Have some melon."

Bob Ide came to the embarrassed Makiko's aid. "But you know, recently they've been saying that pregnant women should watch their weight, too. It was in *Time* magazine."

"Well, that's just for white women; Japanese are different," Mrs. Ide said. "I ate a lot before Ken was born. No matter how much I ate, I was always hungry."

Then, with a hearty laugh, she added, "Anyway, while he was in the womb, I fed Ken so well that after he was born, even while we were in Nevada, he never got sick."

"Oh, you mean when you were in the camp, right?" Motoo chimed in. During the war, Americans of Japanese birth were interned in camps. Motoo had told Makiko that Mrs. Ide felt guilty because of Ken. It must have been a painful experience for the boy to be parted from his school friends. At the time Makiko had said that the parents' fate was the same as the child's, and that Ken's parents weren't responsible. What if the parents die? Then there's no way they can be held responsible.

Motoo had laughed easily and said, "If Ken had met his parents' expectations, there wouldn't have been a problem." Even when the Ides worked in the fields, their skins completely blackened from the sun, not only did their only son never help out; he would bring girlfriends home and swim with them in the pool or play the guitar, like a spoiled child. Julia said under her breath that Mr. Hata, who took it on himself to do the watering, was a much more appropriate son for the Ides than Ken. But Julia herself, though she "came out to work" every morning from the guest house next to the garage, would just haul her big, baglike body around the house all day; she didn't seem to do any more work than the collie, Vicky. So many people were borne on the shoulders of the middle-aged, diminutive Ides. Makiko suddenly wondered what Mrs. Ide, who was now trying to take on the burden of her care as well, wanted for herself in life.

"Well, shall I try to call the doctor?" Mrs. Ide stood up and left the room. Her Hiroshima dialect, mixed with English words, echoed vigorously from the kitchen telephone; soon she came back in, a discouraged expression on her face.

"I thought that, since birth is a natural process, Doctor Yoshino could take care of it, but he just said he would refer us to a white obstetrician."

"It's better that way. If something should go wrong . . . I mean, it won't, but nevertheless, it's better to go to a specialist." Bob's clear eyes, accurately catching the young couple's fears, spoke for them.

"Maybe so, but all of us go to second-generation Japanese doctors. . . . I guess it's all right. Shall we go this afternoon to see a white doctor, Makiko?"

"I'm sorry to cause you all this trouble." Makiko bowed her head. From the kitchen the weird voice of the parrot called, repeating over and over, "Hello, boy!"

From where she lay on the examining table, her gaze fell naturally on a speaker, set in the sterile white wall. A Bach chorale flowed quietly out of the black box. Like inside an airplane, thought Makiko. Passengers enclosed in a chamber, flying through the air, entrusting their bodies to fate. The sound quality was the same as the music they played just before the plane took off, to relieve stress. Psychologists had determined that quiet sound, calm music, was effective in soothing nervous excitement. A year ago, in the plane leaving Tokyo for Paris, they had played a Japanese lullaby. Now, in the obstetrical examining room, a chorale praising God.

The silver-haired middle-aged nurse spoke in a low voice, like a machine, "Good girl; don't be afraid," and lowered a curtain from above so that it hung over Makiko's abdomen, just below her chest. The upper part of her body, its head filled with Bach, was cut off from the lower half, which lay exposed, defenseless, to the space of the examining room; the two halves were like two separate living beings.

The doctor mumbled something on the other side of the curtain, and metal instruments clinked together. Makiko stared at the curtain and reddened, recalling her first gynecological exam in G–, outside of Paris.

The doctor had barely listened to her faltering explanation in French, that she thought she might be pregnant. He said, "*Voulez-vous bien vous deshabiller?*" and pointed to a screen standing in the corner of the examining room. Taking the words literally, Makiko understood he wanted her to undress, and she went behind the screen and started to take off her clothes. But then she got confused; could he really mean for her to be completely naked? She left her chemise and panties on and appeared self-consciously from behind the screen. A surprised, quizzical expression flashed momentarily on the doctor's face and he lifted the hem of her chemise with his fingers. Then he said in an affected tone, as if he were trying to amuse the baby at the same time, "Excuse me, but I'll just take these off." and touched her panties. Later, whenever Makiko recalled the lightly ironic smile of the doctor, so typically French, she would get angry at herself. Why hadn't she realized the simple fact that panties were really all you had to take off for a gynecological exam? The only things that stirred her feelings were abstract like death; blindness to concrete realities was her fatal flaw. She told herself that her embarrassment was a just punishment and that she'd better just face it. Her self-reproach was like a slap on the cheek, but still the inexpressible misery and embarrassment remained. Afterwards, whenever she met the doctor driving his car in G–, she imagined he was grinning that way at her and she would lower her eyes.

Someone must have thought up the idea of using a curtain to divide the body into halves. On the one hand, it was a clever thought, but Makiko felt that the examination room in G–, where the doctor saw the body as a whole and tried to understand it in its natural shape, was more appropriate. After all, the lower half of the body, ugly as it may be, is a part of life. Here, the psychological tactic of the piped-in background music was quintessentially American. The metal instruments were inserted, and when their sound reached her head, Makiko instinctively stiffened and arched her back. Could it really be that, inside the dark cavity now invaded by these metal instruments, an egg was glowing, clothed in life? Or rather, that what used to be an abstract thing, a glowing egg, had already grown into a strange-looking fetus? Once, when she was a little girl, Makiko had seen a fetus. Why is it that when I was a child I saw only things a child shouldn't see? Resisting the sharp pain, Makiko tensed her knees. The nurse's voice sounded quietly, "Oh, no, it's because you're tense that it hurts. Just relax and take it easy."

During the war she had lost her mother to tuberculosis; then, after the war, the Soviet security police, the G.P.U., had taken her father off with them. Makiko was left an orphan, and she and Neiya were taken in by the neighbors. The Japanese had no concrete plans, and spent their days in anguished suspense under Soviet occupation, facing the alternating attacks of the troops of Chiang Kai-shek and Mao's Eighth Army, until finally the decision was made to evacuate. One day Mihoko, the daughter of a local doctor, announced to Makiko that when the day was set for their return to Japan, all the children who were an extra burden would be killed. One child was allowed for each adult. All the children left over would be killed. Mihoko, who was three years older than Makiko, looked at her with wide, clever eyes and said, "What are you going to do, Maki-chan?" When Makiko mumbled, "But I have Neiya," it was just a defense against Mihoko's air of smug superiority. But inside she was convinced that Mihoko was right. It was only natural. Neiya didn't pay much attention to Makiko even during the day, and early in the evening she would fall into a deep sleep. Lying beside her, Makiko suffered from her nameless fear, and her nightmares revealed to the unconscious mind of the six-year-old the boundaries of life. "I'll be all right," said Makiko. When Mihoko saw Makiko's wide eyes, the whites showing, looking up at her, she must have thought Makiko didn't believe her. She took Makiko's hand. "If you think I'm lying, I'll show you something good. But don't tell anyone." Mihoko pulled her by the hand and they sneaked into her father's examining room.

In the empty room, the unfamiliar instruments looked like an assortment of massive, strangely shaped rocks, sunk under the sea. On the window sill stood a row of various-sized bottles. A weird object floated in one of them. Makiko took a closer look, and saw that it was shaped like a little baby with a huge head. The little "child" had no eyes, and floated upside-down in the space inside the jar. Its little hands were crossed over its chest, as if it were praying. Mihoko whispered, "This baby was a burden, so they killed it."

Makiko stared at it. Isolated, blind, the child would float forever upside-down inside the pale blue jar. . . . With a rush of nausea, Makiko felt a sudden kinship with this child. She didn't notice that her nausea resulted from an excess of fear. "It's the Moris' baby. They already have two children, one for the mother and one for the father. So they couldn't take any more back with them to Japan." Later, during the evacuation, holding Neiya's hand, Makiko had occasionally fixed her eyes on Mrs. Mori, who was in their unit. All the adults had the same pale, expressionless faces; Mrs. Mori didn't stand out as someone who could have abandoned her baby.

Now Makiko doubted that the fetus had actually been Mrs. Mori's baby. Even if, under the pressure of the upcoming evacuation, she had undergone an abortion, it would have been very strange if the Moris had preserved the fetus in alcohol and then kept it in the doctor's examination room. It must have been only a specimen that belonged to Mihoko's father. The story about the

Moris was undoubtedly something Mihoko pieced together from adult conversations she had overheard. After Japan's defeat, researchers, including Makiko's father, had taken specimens and medicines home from the universities and institutes that had been closed. And even if that wasn't the case, it would not have been unusual for a doctor to have methyl alcohol. . . .

The metal tool slipped out with a gentle flow of lukewarm water.

"Everything is fine. The baby is growing well." The doctor spoke from the other side of the curtain and gently patted Makiko's stomach. Makiko let the tension leave her body. She noticed that the music had changed to Vivaldi's "The Four Seasons." It was the "spring" section. An eighteenth-century Italian composer's impressions of spring had given a young Asian woman in twentieth-century America a sudden glimpse of the life inside her, about to be born. The faint inkling of life, as ephemeral as the memory of the pale smile that Makiko had once seen rise to her young mother's face, disappeared into empty space.

While Makiko was arranging her clothes, the bald, slightly aging doctor called Mrs. Ide in. He must have thought she was her mother; he told her to watch Makiko's calorie intake and to make sure she didn't gain more than twenty pounds. After speaking to Mrs. Ide, who looked irked at his advice, he smiled and, patting Makiko's cheek, added, "You'll have to give up sweets for a while."

II

In an area where the seasons never change, time seems to stop. It was strange to think that the baby due to be born in March was actually growing. Nevertheless, Makiko's abdomen gradually swelled and protruded, and whenever she visited the Ides, Julia would tease her about it.

Motoo and Makiko had taken a year's lease and settled down in a furnished apartment about ten minutes' drive from the Ides'. It was a classic California-style apartment in a two-story wooden building constructed around a rectangular patio. Though Mrs. Ide had been reluctant to let them leave her house, once she accepted the idea she went all out. She took the Hatas around to see nearby apartments, and hammered out the contract herself in her broken English, forcefully rejecting Motoo's efforts to help. The Italian woman who managed the apartment was a good match for her, but Mrs. Ide drove a hard bargain. When the manager asked, in her own accented English, "You have your own business, don't you?" Mrs. Ide laughed with delight, and on the way home in the car, she repeated the words gleefully.

Their place was near the boundary between Pasadena and San Marino. After dinner Motoo and Makiko, with ever renewed interest, would take walks along the streets of San Marino. San Marino, an even more exclusive residential district than Pasadena, was a Los Angeles suburb with trim, lovely streets that recalled Southern Europe. It was said that not only blacks and Mexicans, but also Japanese and Jews as well, were excluded from living there. In the front gardens, enclosed by low hedges, well-tended tropical plants faced the outside world, but as for the houses themselves, the doors and windows were shut, and the psychology of the "propertied owners," who were terrified of intruders, seeped through the cracks. When the Hatas passed by, unseen dogs would bark at them. "Even the dogs reject the Japanese," laughed Motoo. Even racial discrimination could become a phenomenon of nature for him to observe with his neutral gaze.

At Helga's invitation, Makiko attended exercise classes for pregnant women and tea parties given by the university's Junior Women's Club. The aging wives of professors took it on themselves to pour tea for the younger ones and invite them to church suppers. Mrs. Novozhilov did not make her appearance at this kind of event, where sociable, middle-aged women, dressed in brightly colored suits, entertained the younger wives. All of them had typically American faces, and none spoke with a foreign accent; undoubtedly the wives of foreign professors, even if they had American citizenship, didn't feel like participating in this sort of typical American "charity work."

"If you come to these parties often, people will lend you baby things, like cribs or scales. There's no point in buying this sort of thing yourself; they grow out of them so fast." Helga's brown eyes gleamed shrewdly.

At their doctor's recommendation, Motoo and Makiko enrolled in a three-month class for future parents. They attended every Friday evening at the Catholic hospital. The main teacher was a nun in a white habit. She was a physician who combined a high degree of medical knowledge with an enthusiasm for her task. Using charts, she explained first the physiology of pregnancy from conception to birth, then the early development of the baby. Makiko wondered again at the nature of the passion that arose within this middleaged nun and shone on her pink cheeks. Makiko's inborn curiosity about the origins of people's passions had intensified since she had left Japan.

One evening, the nun mentioned the word "circumcision." Makiko asked Motoo what it meant. Motoo didn't understand either, and he whispered the question to the prim American woman sitting next to him. "It's something they do to boy babies," she answered curtly. It was an operation done at birth to cut the foreskin, which normally opens naturally when boys reach puberty. The nun explained that the law required prior permission from the parents, both for circumcision and for anesthetizing the lower half of the woman's body during labor. "What should we do?" Motoo consulted Makiko, but Makiko, for whom the very existence of the baby, not to mention its sex, was in doubt, couldn't begin to answer. She just suggested vaguely that they should ask Helga.

Every three days or so, Helga would drop in on Makiko. The two of them would sit side-by-side on the red sofa and work on their knitting. Helga did most of the talking, enthusiastically imparting to Makiko the knowledge she had gained about the American hospital system, obstetrical practices, and infant care. She was due in January. "I'm first, so I'll tell you all about it when it's over," she promised. Makiko assented. Helga, who had graduated with a pharmacy degree from Tübingen University, was probably a good observer. When she wasn't talking about childbirth, Helga would bring up her memories of her homeland. She talked about the scenery and customs of Tübingen, about her mother and father, who was a Lutheran pastor, and about her grandmother, who had gotten her old baby clothes down from the attic and sent them to her. When she got carried away with her memories, her German accent grew so strong that Makiko thought it would infect her as well. Makiko herself, on her trip to Germany, had sat on a bench by the Neckar river, basking in the sunlight filtering through the trees on the riverbank and watching Tübingen students sailing boats on the river. Helga never tired of hearing Makiko tell about that time. She would exclaim, "*Ja!*" and her mouth would open wide as if she were about to bite someone. Makiko thought this expression spoiled her pretty face, and she was embarrassed by the intensity of Helga's fervent love for her hometown.

"But then again, I too . . . ," thought Makiko, as she wove the white yarn on her knitting needles. Suppose I were to tell someone about the huge, blood-red, burning evening sky in my homeland, or rather, that my homeland was that gruesome sunset itself—wouldn't I scream louder than Helga is doing now? Though no one forbade her, Makiko never spoke about Manchuria.

Suddenly, in the middle of one excited conversation, Helga's knitting stopped and her large eyes stared blankly into space. Her eyes called to mind some small forest animal, its ears attuned to the distant sound of a lumberjack's axe.

"The baby's moving, isn't it?" Makiko had felt the same sensation herself. The brown in Helga's eyes deepened, and nodding vigorously, she answered, "*Ja!*"

In November the young President, who was from a family of Irish immigrants, was assassinated in Dallas. When Motoo came home from the university, he suggested that they go to the Ides' to watch the reports on television. The Hatas didn't have a TV.

When they got out of the car in the Ides' backyard, Vicky shuffled slowly out through the kitchen door, which had been left open. When she saw the Hatas, she opened her mouth wide in a bored yawn. The light was on in Julia's apartment, too, and the light and shadow of the television screen flickered through her window. Makiko pictured the enormous, sixty-year-old Mexican woman sitting next to her husband, thirty years her junior, the two of them watching the President who had been killed during his parade.

They went into the Ides' big living room. "Well," said Bob Ide, sunk into an armchair, a solemn expression on his usually smiling face. On the TV screen, the young wife was shown from behind, collapsed onto the President's body. She was the first President's wife to have a baby in the White House, but it had died.

The TV showed a retrospective of the President's life. "Retrospective," referring to the life of the man who had been killed suddenly in broad daylight in front of all those people, was a strange, haunting word. The announcers gave their commentary in dry voices, as if they had swallowed that inappropriate word too quickly and were now trying to digest it. Listening to the expressionless English words, slipping out too fast, the memory of her loss throbbed up within Makiko. No matter how sudden the President's death had been, still his dead body remained to prove that it had happened. At least his wife had something to cling to, to embrace and to weep over. Makiko's father had suddenly disappeared in broad daylight, right in front of her. It couldn't be called a shock; and it had left only a strange, blank void in her. No matter how she tried, she couldn't digest it. Her mother had gone gradually. She had seen the moment of her death. But her father—one moment he had been standing on the road, and the next, he was gone. She was sure of only one thing: that he had been surrounded suddenly by three or four G.P.U. men.

Her father, a researcher in physiology, had kept bottles of methyl alcohol among the medicines in the cabinet in his study. The case was locked, but a young, alcoholic soldier had broken the glass, taken a bottle down, and drunk it dry on the spot. It was clear from a glance that this red-haired soldier was an uneducated country boy. He must have mistaken the medicine case for a liquor cabinet, or thought that the methyl alcohol was actually ethyl alcohol. Her father had jumped up and tried to stop him, but another soldier poked him with his rifle. The only thing that Makiko, who had been standing beside her father, remembered clearly was the soldier's blue eyes and gun, in that hushed moment in the brightly lit room when time stopped. Everything else she learned later. The Soviet soldiers were always tramping into the Japanese houses with their shoes on, wreaking disorder and plundering whatever they laid their hands on, meeting no resistance from the Japanese residents. For form's sake the G.P.U. would be present to supervise. When suddenly, two or three days after this incident, the G.P.U. came and took her father away, the neighbors surmised that it was because the young soldier who had drunk the methyl alcohol had died, or perhaps gone blind. In an instant her father had been surrounded by G.P.U. uniforms, and if he had looked back at Makiko, she hadn't seen it.

For Makiko, with the vision alive inside her for some sixteen years, her mother's death was clearly a completed event, but her father's disappearance had left only a vague emptiness, and even now it wouldn't settle in her mind. The emptiness was shadowed by the thought that somewhere in the world he might still be alive.

Unconsciously, following the rhythm of the dry English words, Makiko traced the emptiness inside her with her fingertip. Suddenly something knocked gently in response. From inside her womb, a movement came like a tiny signal touching her finger. At the moment the announcer's precise manner of speaking was pierced by this tiny signal, Makiko's vision shattered, and she was suddenly convinced. It could have been the inevitable result of fatigue from all that time spent pondering the possibility of her father's life, a possibility that was no more than a fantasy. But it was the death of the young President—a complete stranger—in broad daylight, together with the slight movement of her unborn baby, that finally convinced Makiko that her father was really gone. The vision collapsed, rustling slightly. Her father, too, had been sucked up into the blazing red evening sky and burned away. He had probably been taken to Siberia. What color was the sunset in Siberia? But it was in Manchuria that he had disappeared. Makiko again found her homeland in an extinguished country, and in death itself.

Makiko addressed Mrs. Ide, who was sitting flat on the rug, her eyes fixed on the television. "Mama Ide, would you like a backrub?" It had become customary for her to ask.

"No, you're the one who must be tired." Mrs. Ide refused at first, but finally she spread a mattress on top of the carpet and lay flat on it. Giving her a massage had become for Makiko an unex-

pected opportunity—her only opportunity—to show her thanks
to Mrs. Ide. She had decided to keep it up until her stomach got
so big that it became painful for her.

Her fingers felt hard lumps in the tense muscles of Mrs. Ide's
thick back. When she concentrated on massaging them, Mrs.
Ide's pleasure showed in her comments, first that it would lower
her blood pressure, then that her blood pressure actually had
gone down. Makiko kept it up for a whole hour, until her own
back started hurting, but Mrs. Ide seemed to have fallen asleep,
and might never tell her to stop. This woman who was so hard on
herself now showed her only weakness. Once in a while Bob Ide
would say in his formal Japanese, "That's enough; you must be
tired too." Makiko concentrated all her strength in her fingers,
and, while scrutinizing the patterns in the folds of the splendid,
chrysanthemum-patterned silk brocade curtains that reached
from the high ceiling to the floor, she massaged the hardness out
of the lumps on Mrs. Ide's back.

All at once the thought came to her that, rather than
smoothing over these lumps with massage, it might be advisable
for Mrs. Ide to have them checked out in a thorough medical examination. It suddenly felt wrong to be massaging them. Makiko
tried to soothe herself with the thought that these small lumps on
the muscular back of the woman who had worked her way
through a half century were simply the outward mark of her
fatigue. But the next moment, the words "no, it's resentment"
welled up into her throat, frightening her. Mrs. Ide lay before her,
her muscular, sunburned neck exposed, and Makiko remembered
the anger in her small Oriental eyes when she had spoken to her
earlier: "Men are no good—they never give a thought to the
children"; "Men go through menopause, too. Make sure you
remember that. It's a lot worse than women's menopause, it's really terrible"; "Don't rely on men—they have no sense of honor
and they're a lot weaker than women." Makiko had heard all this

while helping out in the kitchen. Looking at the broad face which so plainly displayed its farmer's heritage, she had been confused by its expression of utter resentment. She had asked, "What? When you have such an ideal husband?"

Mrs. Ide's reply was blunt. "You can't understand yet what 'ideal' is." Motoo had told Makiko what he had heard about the hardships the Ides had suffered even after their release from the Japanese-American internment camp, how they had worked together as hired laborers for strangers, their failed attempt at running a small grocery store. Makiko actually thought it was funny that Mrs. Ide could spit out such words about her aging husband, when those difficult days should have bound them even more closely together, and she even laughed about it with Motoo: "talking that way about dear old Papa Ide . . ." But now there were these little hardened knots, this thing that could be called a lifetime's built-up resentment communicating itself directly to Makiko through her fingers. This thing that Makiko, who had lost her parents, wished so fervently to resist and, fearing to lose an important part of her life because of it, had subconsciously been striving to thrust aside and isolate—even going so far as creating a false bottom for it in her own heart—this thing, this resentment, could it be something that shows its countenance from a person's back? Without that person realizing it?

Makiko raised her eyes and looked at Bob. The aging man was absorbed in the TV, his clear eyes opened wide. Motoo sat next to him, looking in the same direction, his usual transparent expression on his face. Makiko flashed a glance at him, then lowered her eyes again. The women, their bodies bent, gathered up the grains blown from the hands of the men by the wind sweeping across the field. Perhaps all this time even Mama Ide, biting her lip, had just been picking up the many grains of life that Bob, the idealist, had let slip from his body.

Athough her father had differed in character from those

resolute, ambitious men who had come to build the country of
Manchuria, he, too, must have dreamed of the freedom and
creativity that work in the new laboratory would allow. When her
mother was lying in her sickbed, had her young breast, already
beset by consumption, been beset again by the thought, If only
we hadn't come to Manchuria . . . ? Makiko didn't want to think
so.

Vicky stretched out her neck without getting up and ran her
tongue over Mrs. Ide's sunburnt neck. There was no luster in the
short hair that barely reached Mrs. Ide's neck, hair bleached by
the intense sun that shone on the fields. The abundant white hair
gleamed coarsely.

"But it must be tough for Presidents. They tried to kill the
French President, too, didn't they?" Mrs. Ide spoke from where
she lay.

Makiko pictured the old general, his chest exposed above the
open car that was making its way slowly down the Champs-
Elysées during the Bastille Day parade that summer. They had
chanced into tickets for seats right along the main street and gotten a close-up view of the old general's aquiline nose, his thin,
closed lips, and his chest, still majestic in the military uniform. It
seemed to Makiko that his eyes, gleaming sharply from under
their sagging lids, were staring right through the masses of people
that covered the sidewalks, gazing at the course of his own life.
And that for him the cheering masses, too, were nothing more
than countless eyes fixed on the glass box that was his "life." But
shortly afterwards he had been shot at in the Paris suburb of Petit
Clamart. It was after the Algerian war. Had the old man, over
seventy, been prepared for the gun aimed at him from the dense
shade of the chestnut trees, or from an upper window of the
stone buildings that lined the street? Could there exist such a
thing as a politician whose life was not at risk? In her agitated
mood the involuntary thought came to Makiko that in the body

of a true politician the shadow of a bitter death, like a wild beast roaming the fields, should be visible through the flesh.

Inside the plane flying from Dallas to Washington, the man who until today had been the Vice-President took the oath of office to become the new President. The TV showed a close-up of his face. The brows of the middleaged man were knit, his eyes downcast, and a terrible sorrow showed on his face. Rather than sadness at the loss of his superior, the sorrow that overcame him was opaque, one whose reasons were unclear.

"But what's going to happen to the country now? There's Vietnam, the racial problems ... If only something terrible doesn't happen," said Motoo. Makiko emerged abruptly from her over-stimulated mental state and once again she felt the thing that was not quite anxiety, not quite terror, quiver and rise from deep inside her. Bob Ide sensed the overwhelming emotion that had arisen and filled Makiko, and, opening his mouth quietly, he caught and suppressed it before it could color her eyes with terror:

"It's all right. Even though it's the President it's still only one man. America's the kind of country where fundamental changes don't come about just because of the death of a single man. The structure of the country is much too stable for that."

Testifying as someone who had been born and raised in America, Mr. Ide spoke with conviction. Mrs. Ide, who had melted, as though into mud, under Makiko's massage, suddenly raised her head.

"Recently I read something strange in a Japanese magazine. About what *sutamina* is. And things like how to relieve it."

Makiko, speechless, exchanged a glance with Motoo.

"No, wait. It can't be how to relieve stamina; it must be how to increase it."

"But stamina is an English word, isn't it?" Motoo asked Bob Ide.

Mr. Ide looked as though he had missed the point, and just made a strange face. Then, when Motoo spelled the English letters, he looked surprised: "You mean they use that word in Japan?"

Someone turned off the lights in the parlor. Everyone sat hushed for a moment in the darkness. One by one, the lights on the tall Christmas tree were lit by the Novozhilov boys. The dim, yellow circle of light gradually increased and brightened.

Real candles on a real silver fir. Makiko guessed that of all the people who had come to the Novozhilovs' party, probably the most delighted was Helga.

Occasionally, on their way back from the exercise class, Helga would invite Makiko to go shopping. Once, when the stores had started decorating for Christmas, Helga stopped in front of an artificial tree adorned with miniature light bulbs. Her lips distorted into a grimace, and she startled Makiko by shouting in her strong German accent, "I hate it! How can they call them Christmas decorations when the tree and candles aren't real?" A nearby clerk with lavender-tinted hair soothed her: "You're right, but of course business comes first."

Helga sat in the semi-darkness and gazed up at the Christmas tree, countless tiny flames flickering in her large brown eyes. Makiko felt the beauty in the sudden flush of her small triangular face, whose air of dreamlike enchantment was illuminated by the light of the candles. The Christmas celebrations of her childhood, when the family had gathered around the brightly lit fir tree to sing Lutheran hymns and she and her father had said the prayers together, welled up inside Helga, and Makiko thought she could see them inside her. She didn't know what the Novozhilovs' religion was, but since they celebrated Christmas it must be a branch of Christianity. But perhaps out of consideration for their Japanese and Indian guests, or because they thought it was childish, they didn't sing any carols.

"You all came here by car, right? Are your engines in good shape?" Mrs. Novozhilov checked, looking around the room. Several of the guests caught her meaning and laughed. Rose, from Switzerland, Katie, the American . . . and when you added in Helga and Makiko, there were four women in maternity clothes. Kamini's body was swelling, too, under her sari. Rose, whose due date had already passed, sat collapsed in an armchair cradling her abdomen, which looked as though it were about to slip down even further. Her gray-green eyes gaped wide open behind her glasses, but they showed no reaction, even to the candle flames. She looked utterly exhausted and bewildered. Makiko whispered to Motoo, "Even in that condition she comes to a party. I can't imagine it happening in Japan."

"And they say Katie has been swimming."

"It's true; I couldn't believe it. She puts on a special maternity bathing suit and swims in an open-air pool. This may be Pasadena, but the water looks awfully cold."

Makiko realized that it was rude for them to be whispering to each other in Japanese, but she was too tired to want to talk to people in English. The director of the laboratory in G–, too, was constantly giving dinners with his wife. The guest list was always the same, so the topics of conversation were fairly predictable. But still they would talk through the night until one in the morning. Motoo, who usually went to bed early, would start yawning and finally would doze off, his eyes half-closed with the whites showing. It made Makiko nervous. She wanted to pinch him or kick him to get him to open his eyes, but since they weren't sitting together, neither her hands nor her feet would reach. But still, they both always went and forced themselves to stay right until the party broke up.

"Makiko, have you gotten everything ready for the baby?" Mrs.

Novozhilov came up with a cocktail glass in her hand.

"Well, my due date isn't until March." Makiko's answer was am-
biguous. Ensnared by Helga, she had bought some baby clothes,
but she couldn't imagine that a person small enough to wear a
shirt the size of her hands pressed together could actually exist.
In America, clothes for newborns had the same styles as adult
clothes, just cut down to size. It confused Makiko, who had only
seen the shapeless baby clothes used in Japan.

"Makiko, are your parents coming from Japan to see the
baby?" Lyudmilla Novozhilov's blue, owl-like eyes, reflecting the
candlelight, came right up next to Makiko's.

Makiko instinctively turned her face away and answered weakly, "No." She noticed that her empty left hand was covering her
abdomen. During their first meeting, when Lyudmilla Novozhilov's eyes had struck deep within her own eyes . . . that time,
without realizing it, I lifted my hand to my stomach. Though
I didn't feel the pregnancy then the way I do now, I must have
been protecting the baby. Could it be? . . .

An awkward silence fell between the two women, one middle-
aged, one young. They both turned their eyes away at the same
time and gazed at the fir tree, shining with lights. Someone must
have opened a door; the candle flames wavered and swayed. On
the other side of the blurred light, Makiko saw Helga leave the
room. Without knowing why, she followed her with her eyes;
Mrs. Novozhilov stood up inconspicuously and followed Helga
out.

Staring into the candle flames, Makiko repeated in the back of
her mind the question about whether her parents were coming
from Japan. She had given the wrong answer. They were coming.
For some reason, when she heard Mrs. Novozhilov pronounce
the English word "parents," she had thought of the father and
mother she had lost. Her foster parents had written that they

would come at the beginning of Motoo's summer vacation, taking the opportunity to visit the baby and go on an American tour at the same time.

Even this weak candlelight could hurt your eyes if you stared at it. After Mrs. Novozhilov stood up, her husband came over. Makiko tensed; she always had trouble understanding his growling English. What could she have to talk about with this middle-aged professor?

Fortunately Kamini's husband went up to him and, bourbon glasses in hand, the two men started talking about their work. Makiko was already familiar with the lucid conversation of plant physiologists; their discussions always had a clearly organized structure, like that of the cells of the plants they studied.

On her left, Katie was rattling on in her Western accent to Rose, whose due date had already passed, about the benefits of painless delivery.

"In California, up to ninety-nine percent of the women have painless delivery using epidural anaesthesia. You're really behind the times talking about natural childbirth ... plus, you'll have enough to go through just with the fatigue."

Rose, who was already exhausted enough without even getting to her natural childbirth, just nodded and mumbled her assent.

Makiko pretended to be absorbed with the small cocktail glass she gripped in her hand, and kept staring at the candle flames. When will I manage to conquer those blue, Slavic, owl-like eyes? The truck with the Soviet soldiers had advanced right up to the house, and they loaded up the furniture, even carting off the piano. They especially valued watches, and the first things they took were her father's pocket watch and the wristwatch her mother had left behind. Makiko had a vivid memory of a soldier's clumsy fingers overwinding her mother's delicate watch and breaking its golden mainspring. When they took the electric clock down from the wall in the dining room, the cord writhed like a living snake and twisted around one of the soldier's tall boots. The soldier clicked his tongue, and his thick finger wrenching off the cord branded itself in the little girl's brain, leaving a scar that she couldn't erase. The soldier had probably come from some place in the country where there was no electricity. Or did he simply not realize that the clock was electric? They even made off with the red leather knapsack that had been put aside for Makiko's upcoming entrance into school in the spring. In some far-off corner of that huge country, the Soviet Union, were those watches still keeping time? Was there a child who carried that red leather knapsack, now old and worn, on her back?

Even so, the children weren't too frightened when the soldiers came during the day. But at night the rumbling of the truck would shake the earth through the darkness. At which house would it stop? From behind their tightly shut doors and windows, the Japanese held their breath, frozen stares fixed on the dark fields. Within the tension, tight as a drawn bowstring, that filled the whole neighborhood, Neiya would grip Makiko's hand in a stranglehold. Even Makiko realized that it was not to protect her; rather she was clinging to Makiko's father through Makiko's little body. Makiko would climb up onto her father's lap. He would pat her on the back, a somber expression on his face. Neiya had closely cropped hair and wore black pants. Fearing they might catch the eyes of the Soviet soldiers, the girls cut their hair short and disguised their sex with loose clothes.

Rumbling in the earth, the truck approached through the darkness; its heavy growl stopped . . . our house. A heavy pounding sounded on the thick door in the front entrance. "Open up!" someone shouted over and over. It was a deep, muffled shout, like the roar of a wild animal in winter. "*Akero*! Open up!" It was the only Japanese they knew. While his comrades kicked at the front door and bumped against it with their bodies, one of the soldiers went around to the kitchen. The big, red-haired man with blue eyes climbed up the wall like a spider to the double windows, then started yelling. When she heard the sound, in which she couldn't make out any words, Makiko felt that she herself had become a blind, wild beast that would tear through the dark fields howling in terror. Her father lifted her down from his lap and stood up slowly. There was no change in his breathing, and only a hard line in his eyelids showed the anger he was suppressing as he went to open the back door. If the windows or doors were broken, they wouldn't be able to survive the Manchurian winter, whose temperatures would go down as low as minus thirty.

These nights repeated themselves, but the children still slept. They would wake in the middle of the night to see a soldier's boots pacing around their beds. The cracked, hard leather, caked with reddish mud, would be right next to their hair.

But at least Father was there. If only there hadn't been that moment when the blue-eyed soldier pointed his gun at her father, Makiko wouldn't have felt such fear when Lyudmilla Novozhilov looked at her with her blue eyes. The eyes that, together with the gun, pressed in on her, were trying to snatch Makiko's father away from her. They would thrust Makiko out into the primeval darkness and leave her there alone. How could a five-year-old child see it as just an idle threat? Makiko had tried to take a step forward. Only now did she realize that she had been unconsciously trying to make the soldier shoot her.

At that moment the red-haired soldier who had drunk the bottle of methyl alcohol sprang howling out of the kitchen, and the one holding the gun, distracted, hurried out after him.

Makiko and her father were both safe. But at the time Makiko thought that something had been broken inside her, that the soldier really had shot something deep inside the little girl. Even now she didn't know what that something was, but she suspected it was something essential to life itself.

"Makiko, won't you have some turkey?" Lyudmilla Novozhilov

had brought over a plate with a slice of turkey and some cran-
berry sauce, and was standing behind her.

The food was arranged on a table on one side of the room, and
Professor Novozhilov, brandishing a large silver knife, was carving
the turkey. The foil drumstick ornament had fallen off, and it lay
in the center of the table sending up silver sparks. The boys added a paper napkin to the a knife and fork on each plate, and handed the plates to the guests standing in line. "It's a real Christmas
party, isn't it?" said Makiko, standing up. She felt slightly dizzy.
The thing she had been contemplating a moment before and the
things she was seeing now in this room seemed to have exposed
her single body to two different kinds of atmospheric pressure,
two different realities. Mrs. Novozhilov whispered into Makiko's
ear:

"You should be careful beginning with the new year. Helga just
left for the hospital."

"What?" Makiko looked around the parlor. Conrad was gone
too.

"But Helga's due date was in mid-January."

"That's right, but you can't rely too much on the due date. The
baby spends so much time in a dark place, when outside the
Southern California sun is shining, and he can't wait any longer.
He wants to hurry up and get out into the bright outside world."

A smile played on Lyudmilla Novozhilov's white cheeks.

Someone asked loudly from a corner of the room: "Professor
Novozhilov, what do you think of the Beatles?"

This Christmas the stores were making huge profits selling wigs
inspired by the long, shaggy hairstyle of the British singing group.
The professor must have made some clever answer in his growling, monotonous English: Laughter filled the room, but Makiko
realized that she hadn't been listening.

The pain started right after Motoo suggested it was time to go

to bed. It was completely different from the pain she had imagined. It started deep in her abdomen and radiated quickly through
her body, then was gone before she knew it. A white pain that illuminated the evening sky like a searchlight, then disappeared instantly. After it had repeated itself a few times, she told Motoo,
"It may have started, but I'm not sure." Motoo was nervous. He
said, "Whether or not you're sure, we should get going to the
hospital," and he picked up the suitcase that Makiko had packed
beforehand.

Makiko suddenly didn't want to go; she wanted to stay at least
until dawn. The evacuation from Shinkyo, too, had begun at
dawn. Six-year-old Makiko and Neiya had joined the evacuation
together with the neighboring family. The night before, Neiya
packed Makiko's knapsack and put it by her pillow. She made a
threatening face and told Makiko, "We're starting out early
tomorrow for Japan; you'd better be able to keep up with the
group, and you'd better not complain or cry. If you start going on
about the knapsack being heavy, they'll leave you behind in the
sorghum fields."

Makiko had no sense of what Japan was. All she had ever
known were desolate fields that stretched on forever. She pulled
the quilt, with its familiar smell, over her head. All she wanted
was to be able to keep this quilt with her.

Now, wishing only for one night's sleep in a safe bed and a cup
of tea in the morning before setting off, Makiko recalled that
morning of the evacuation seventeen years before. Even the realization that she was exaggerating had no effect on her irrational
fear. Like a child, she insisted stubbornly that she wouldn't go and
burrowed into bed. But within an hour she was up again. The
slight, white pain had changed into a dull, heavy pressure in
her abdomen. Without waiting for Makiko's answer, Motoo said,
"No more dawdling, let's get going," loaded the suitcase in the
car, and started the engine.

Makiko irresolutely called the doctor on duty at the hospital. It is hard for a woman having her first baby to describe the labor pains, even in her native language. The doctor, without even listening to Makiko's faltering description, instructed her in a sleepy voice to come right away to the hospital.

White light filled the main entrance hall of the hospital. Makiko imagined she could see everything right through to the very center of the building, as though through a huge display window. It was so bright that she distinctly pictured the groans of the women, the wailing of the newborn babies . . . even the very back recesses where the miscarried fetuses were quietly disposed of. But in all that brightness there was not another human shadow.

Motoo, one hand holding the suitcase, the other supporting Makiko's arm, stood at the entrance. The automatic glass doors swept open, and, as if by magic, a black nurse appeared on the other side with a wheelchair. The black woman in her white uniform pushed Makiko into the wheelchair without a word and covered her neatly, waist down, with a white blanket. She silently pointed out a counter in one far corner of the room. Behind the counter sat a man, evidently a clerk. Motoo, his face strained, hurriedly crossed the room.

Makiko looked up at the highdomed ceiling and tried to prepare herself.

Once she entered the hospital, she would no longer be a human being. She would change into an object that the doctor would manipulate at his own will. It was better that way. . . . When she lost her "self," she would also lose the anxiety and terror. The exercise teacher had taught the members of the class how to regulate their breathing like a machine. But how could she herself control her breathing if her "self" no longer existed? . . . Maybe the body that was called Makiko would do it passively, by itself. If she wrapped up her ego tightly, maybe she could rid herself of the fear.

She was wheeled up to a room on the second floor.

The black nurse spoke for the first time when Motoo finished the paperwork and came up to the room. The thick lips commanded, "When the pain gets worse, I'll start the anaesthetic. You, hold her hand tightly."

Motoo hastily took Makiko's hand.

After the nurse had left, Makiko whispered, "I might as well be a terminal case the way she's treating me." Mrs. Ide had said offhandedly that childbirth was a natural thing, and that even if nothing was done to help the mother, the baby would be born anyway, by itself, but you wouldn't expect that attitude from a modern American hospital. Yet Makiko, who had already become a passive object, felt she couldn't do anything without a doctor's help. Though the uterus, which was continuing to contract, was a part of Makiko's body, and inside it a new, separate life was struggling, pushing its way through the narrow passage, none of this was real to her. Only the pain was real, and she frowned. Motoo, troubled, asked what the pain was like. From beneath his confusion flashed the observant eyes of the natural scientist, and he peered at her. Makiko was angry at him for that, but during the pains she clutched his hand.

Gauging the interval between contractions, Motoo brought up the question of circumcision again, and told her he had agreed to it. Makiko nodded vaguely. Helga's baby had been a boy. Helga had said that he would have to explain it if they went back to Germany and the other boys asked why he was different, but that it was more hygienic this way. She hadn't sounded too sure of herself. Motoo missed the point when she reported this conversation to him; he just answered that Conrad had told him he wanted to become a naturalized American, and that it would be hard for him to persuade Helga. Maybe he was using Conrad as an example of a German who circumcised his son in order to become a member of the country he was adopting. If so, then might it mean that Motoo, too, was considering becoming a naturalized citizen? The question of why she was leaving such an important decision up to him came to her, but at the same time it was pushed aside by a rising wave of pain. It's all right; the baby is a girl anyway, so we don't have to think about it. Makiko rode the wave of pain and thrust aside the pang of guilty conscience.

It went on for twenty-four hours. When she felt too much pain they gave her more anaesthetic, and she would doze off. Like a doll made of mud, enduring the dripping of the water torture, she lost her true shape. It seemed to her that Motoo had been beside her the whole time, but then it seemed that he had been gone for a long time. In her half-conscious state, now and then the boundless fields would suddenly spread out before her. From the *pechka* in the crematory waiting room in Shinkyo, the flames blazed up and spread, scorching the entire plain, then became the blood-red sun and sank behind the horizon. With all her dissolved consciousness, Makiko gazed at it.

The house in Shinkyo had large, double-paned windows, but since they couldn't be opened completely in the middle of winter, there were other, smaller windows set inside them. In the coldest part of winter, even these were difficult to open all the way, but at other times of the year these "windows inside windows" were very special to Makiko. After her mother left her sickbed for the hospital, Neiya and the others were always busy, and with her father away until night, there was no one to pay attention to her. Late afternoon, when women are busy preparing the evening meal, is a lonely time for children. Makiko would concentrate her strength in her little arms, climb up onto the shelf of the bay window, and survey the outside world through the "window inside the window." The window faced west. Makiko gazed across the low elm hedge, across the sorghum fields, and stared at the enormous sunset sky above the broad plain that stretched out beyond.

How many evenings had she spent staring at the sunset? If a

child spent every evening that way, gazing so intently at the
bloody setting sun, it was inevitable that she would take in
something that would affect the course of her whole life. If
Makiko should chance to see in the eyes of a child, even a child
she didn't know, the reflection of that sunset, she would reach
out with her hand and try to shade the child's eyes. To keep it
from scorching the young child's brain. That color must not be allowed. The young body of the being who saw that setting sun at
the beginning of her life would be stained blood-red; forgetting
even to touch the ground with her feet, she would rush off fran-
tically to the very edge of the earth and, blackened and scorched,
would plunge into the very heart of the burning sunset.

. . . Makiko alternately slipped off into a doze, then awoke to
the pain. She noticed that her arm had been bound and fitted
with an I.V. She didn't have time to wonder why it was there.
Motoo had apparently gone off somewhere, leaving the bedrail
lowered, and now the nurse was scolding him.

"There's your wife semi-conscious; she could fall on the floor,
just like that. Be more careful!"

Makiko, seeing Motoo's guilty expression, tried to speak to
him, but the words wouldn't rise to her lips, and instead were absorbed into the semi-conscious bog at the back of her head and
disappeared. Only the nurse's voice, saying "fall," rose again from
the depths of the bog.

The delivery room was even more brightly illuminated with
blinding white light. Makiko was aware of the strange brightness
even while her whole body was pierced through with pain. Then
a voice said, "It hurts, doesn't it," and she saw the round, smiling
face of the doctor beside her. It was the first time she had seen
him since entering the hospital. In the dark brown eyes that
peered into Makiko's eyes she saw a flash of compassion, and at
the same moment an intense wave of pain welled up and overcame her.

The wave abated, leaving behind a portentous emptiness, as broad and white as a clear sandy beach. Into the empty expanse of her brain popped the realization that they'd hooked up the epidural anaesthetic.

Helga had brought her baby to Makiko's apartment and, in an especially strong German accent, had given her a complete, detailed account of the birth. She sprawled across the red sofa, acting it out. Afterwards Makiko had told Motoo about it, laughing, "At least she was wearing slacks." Helga had started out with an endearing desire to prepare Makiko for the experience—she had given birth in the same hospital where Makiko would be going—then her German rationality and desire to illustrate took over.

"But once they put you under the anaesthetic, you're not in control anymore, right?" Makiko had asked.

"Of course, after that it's all up to the doctor." Helga's brown eyes flashed. "There's a huge mirror in front of the bed that shows everything. You can see your own baby being born! What a wonderful idea!"

"Did you see it?" Makiko didn't know what to think.

"I did! Actually Conrad wanted to be there too. California is in the process of adopting a law that will allow the husbands to be present, but it wasn't passed in time. Too bad for us! It's so wonderful to see a new life being born out of your own body. It was really moving. And it's only possible because of the anaesthetic. Without it, even if the mirror were there, you wouldn't be able to watch; the pain would be too much for you." Helga impulsively lifted her baby and pressed his cheek to hers.

Now this mirror hung in front of Makiko. If she opened her eyes, she would certainly be able to witness that moving moment that Helga had told her about. But she didn't want to see it. She didn't want to see that bloodstained thing.

Her eyes closed, she tried to separate her lower half—from which all feeling had vanished—from her conscious upper half.

The deep, dull pain that she thought she felt must be a hallucination. "They cut you, you know," Helga had said. "During natural childbirth sometimes you get torn, but if they cut you while you're under the anaesthetic you heal much faster; you're in better shape afterwards." Her pharmacologist's frankness sounded in her tone. The dull howl of the cut flesh echoed in Makiko's head.

Suddenly an image rose: the bloodied body of a man lying on the frozen Siberian earth.

The silence swelled up and became pure, white light.

Another person, separate from myself, exists. Someone, a being who until this moment did not exist in this room, now does. This sensation was unmistakable.

As if in defiance of this momentary but intense sensation, a feeble voice wailed.

"It's a boy, Mrs. Hata!" came the nurse's voice. Makiko opened her eyes. Glancing at the mirror, she saw the doctor's bald head gleaming and below it, something that was red all over. Then she looked to one side and saw a small thing wildly squirming and crying in a fragile but surprisingly lusty voice. The nurse picked it up and thrust it in front of Makiko's face. The nurse restrained the little object's movements with her large white hand and said, "Look, five fingers on each hand, five toes on each foot." Then she pointed at the part that was disproportionately large for that little body. "A perfect little boy."

The little living body, whose existence as a male human being had just been demonstrated, howled with all his strength, as if to say he would have none of it. All the blood vessels were distended, flushing the little body bright red as he wailed.

Makiko put herself in his place. So he didn't particularly like being born. Too bad. But I'm here. Makiko smiled weakly. I'm not much to count on, but I am here.

The nurse smiled and nodded at Makiko, then, still holding the baby, crossed over to the other side of the room. Makiko closed her eyes again, resigned to the realization that her body was still just something for the doctor to work on. It's over. This little being has left my body behind and has begun to live on its own. Makiko felt relieved, forgetting that she had never actually sensed a separate life living inside her. The pain swelled up, then the silence came; that was me dying for a moment. Then this person rose up.

"All right, we're done. Everything went fine, Mrs. Hata." The doctor came around to Makiko's head and smiled. She smiled back faintly and mumbled, "Thank you."

The black nurse came up pushing a wheeled mobile bed and lined it up next to Makiko's bed. She went around to the other side, then together with a blonde nurse counted, "One, two, three," and the two of them tugged on the sheet. Makiko, the conscious part and the paralyzed lower half, rolled over onto the mobile bed. She made another half-revolution, and found herself lying face down. Helga had told her in detail about this, too. Makiko recalled her warning: "Make sure you don't lift your head while you're on the anaesthetic. I saw Conrad waiting in the hall and I wanted to speak to him, so without thinking I lifted my head; afterwards it really hurt. Just stay lying face downwards."

When they went out into the hall, Motoo's pants came into view, striding up to her.

"Mr. Hata, could you wheel your wife to her room?"

Compared with the American husbands who showered their wives with tender words, the quiet, expressionless Japanese husbands must seem cold. From the time they had arrived at the hospital, the nurses kept assigning Motoo various tasks to keep him busy.

In the room, the two nurses again counted to three and pulled the sheet. Makiko made another half-turn and lay face up on the bed.

When they were left alone in the room, Motoo suddenly fell to

his knees beside the bed and pressed his face into Makiko's palm.
Makiko realized that he had probably felt just as tense as she had.
Poor thing. With that thought, the cold shadow of anxiety that
had been forgotten for these last few hours swept over her and
stroked her deep inside.

A tall man wearing a long white robe appeared soundlessly in
the thin darkness where Makiko lay with her eyes wide open.
When the Latin words of what seemed to be a prayer spilled from
the lips of the middleaged man, Makiko realized he was a priest.
Since it was a Catholic hospital there were a lot of nuns in white
habits; it wasn't that strange that a priest should suddenly appear
in her room. The priest stretched his white sleeve, his rosary
dangling, and inserted between Makiko's dry lips something even
drier. He made the sign of the cross and silently left. It's the com-
munion wafer, thought Makiko as her tongue dissolved the flat
wafer that stuck inside her dry mouth. It was Sunday. Maybe it's
some special holiday, she thought, but she wasn't a believer and
didn't know. Then the thought came to her that it might be
Easter.

When the anaesthesia wore off the pain returned. She knew
that it was the stretched uterus contracting itself back into shape,
but it was a rather strong pain. It came in waves, as if the womb
were trying to get back the being that it had lost.

Makiko thought about the tiny being whose life and safety
were being guarded in the nursery across the hall. Suddenly she
was seized by an inexpressible fear. Such a weak, helpless being
has entrusted his fate to me! The words "But I am here" that she
had mumbled in the delivery room merged with her fear and
swelled and changed before her eyes into something a hair's
breadth from terror. The moment of relief that had come when
the baby left Makiko's body behind and started life on his own
had disappeared completely, without leaving a trace.

The fear was especially intense in her weakened body. Makiko looked uneasily around in the semi-darkness. Suddenly she started: That magic spell, that almighty trump card, "I could die," could no longer help her. Without being aware of it, she had been searching in the semi-darkness for that valuable card that had disappeared from her hand, and now she realized it was gone for good.

She couldn't die now. No matter how frightened she was, she had to keep living. There was no way out. Terrified, she gazed after the retreating words, "I could die."

That midnight, with the words "But I am here" spoken in the intense white light of the delivery room, Makiko had made a promise to that little person wailing in his feeble voice. There he'd been, peacefully dozing inside the soft, dusky womb, when suddenly he was flung out—against his will—into a world where every imaginable danger waited for him. He was faced with the cruel task of growth. The thin little windpipe, which could have clogged up so easily, suddenly had to take in the rough outside air. The internal organs, no bigger than a fist, would start digesting food. The little living being waved his feeble arms and legs in protest. Poor thing: turning all red over demands that no one would grant. Makiko, imagining herself in the little being's place, mumbled the words, "It would be easier to die," that kept repeating themselves to her. It would have been easier not to have been born.

"You have to live."

The new, unfamiliar idea dazzled her. In order to protect the living thing that was even more helpless than herself, she had to go on living. How had she wound up shouldering this enormous, unimaginable burden? Now she absolutely must keep on living. She had destroyed the possibility of escaping through death. Why hadn't she thought it all over carefully before? Motoo had originally not shown any interest in having children. Though, in contrast to Makiko, he had had a happy childhood, he often said that he had no confidence in the way human society was headed. He especially didn't want a boy; "I can't even look at them, poor things," he had said. But neither of them had even thought of plucking and discarding the life that had sprouted in her womb. It was probably unrelated to the fact that abortion was strictly forbidden in France, where she had gotten pregnant; it was strange—the thought hadn't even crossed their minds. But, though the danger that Makiko personally knew was enough to fill the world all by itself, there was in addition all the suffering that only men could experience. If you looked at it this way, this little thing might well regret the very fact of his birth. And how could I possibly answer him if he did regret it, if he asked me why I had brought him into this world? Makiko's confused mind and exhausted body heaved with the strain.

The door to the neighboring room opened quietly. Makiko looked up and saw a young girl in a flowered robe and slippers. She approached Makiko's bed silently. Her golden curls were bound by a blue ribbon. The ribbon matched the bright color of her eyes. The girl's pretty lips parted, and she laughed.

"Shh! Don't raise your voice," she whispered to Makiko, who was speechless with surprise. "We're not supposed to visit our neighbors before breakfast. But I've been wide awake since the priest came, and there's nothing to do. Tell me, when was your baby born?"

"Late last night."

"Really? Is it a boy or a girl?"

"A boy."

"Mine too. He was born yesterday morning."

"And you're not worn out?" Makiko was amazed that the girl had such energy.

"Not really. But I'm only seventeen. They told me that you recover early when you're young; it's true. I'm almost back to normal. I'm supposed to go home the day after tomorrow, but I can't wait. I want to hurry up and get home, and start taking care of the baby myself. Don't you?" The girl whispered eagerly, her eyes gleaming. "The baby's so cute! I'm so happy . . . my baby, my very own baby!" The words tumbled from her lips, and she repeated them: "My baby, my own baby!"

A nurse pushing a breakfast cart appeared in the doorway to the hall.

"Dorothy! You know better. Hurry up and get back to your room."

The girl said quickly, "Bye! Show me your baby later, all right?" Then, apologizing gaily to the nurse, who was wagging her index finger at her, she retreated through the inner door.

The nurse's raven hair was tied up in a knot; she tilted her head back and, her chin jutting in the air, opened the curtains. As she raised the blinds, she spat out the words, "A baby herself, having a baby indeed!"

When the tray with the breakfast, which Makiko had barely touched, was removed, she was ordered to go take a shower. She had heard from Helga about this typical American method of speeding the mother's recovery, but it struck Makiko as cruel to make her walk down to the end of the long hall and splash water on herself so soon after giving birth. She just let a little of the water get on her for form's sake, fooling the nurse waiting on the other side of the shower curtain. On her way back down the hall she saw her energetic neighbor again. Dorothy was standing with her forehead pressed against the window of the nursery, staring intently inside. A gentle smile played on her cheeks, which still showed traces of her own childhood. The girl's red lips moved, subconsciously imitating the movements of her baby's mouth, and she didn't notice Makiko. Still hunched over, Makiko glanced around the inside of the nursery. It was easy to pick out the blackhaired one among the dozen or so bald babies. It lay there motionless; Makiko consecrated its image deep within her mind's eye and teetered back to her room. An official-looking woman was waiting there with some papers.

"Mrs. Hata. Your child's name?"

"Akihiko Hata." Makiko gave the name she and Motoo had already decided on, tracing the Chinese characters in her mind. They had heard that in America it was a good idea to think up the names in advance, and Motoo's father had sent one boy's name and one girl's name. Makiko had read the characters' literal meaning aloud, "child of the sun's rays," and Motoo liked the name too.

"Mrs. Hata. Your husband's name?"

"Motoo Hata."

"Mrs. Hata. The name of your child's father?" Makiko was puzzled; she had just said it. The lady, without batting an eye, repeated the question slowly. Then Makiko realized what she meant, and repeated, "Motoo Hata." Of course, sometimes the husband's name might be different from the father's. But she wondered if they would actually ask the question in a Japanese hospital.

The telephone by the bed rang.

"Makiko-san? I heard you had a boy. Congratulations!" It was Mrs. Ide's voice.

"I thought Papa and I could come for a visit; do they allow visitors?"

"They say no one but the husband . . ."

"What a stupid policy!" Mrs. Ide's voice sounded untypically petulant. It wasn't her fault, but without thinking Makiko apologized.

"Is the baby in your room?"

"No, in the nursery . . ."

"You'd better get him soon and start nursing him. If you don't, your milk won't come down."

"As you say. But the nurse . . ."

"Nurses don't know anything. You have to get the baby yourself. You have to make him start sucking. He's probably crying right now."

Makiko didn't know how to answer. It was the first time she had heard Mrs. Ide so worked up.

"It's a good thing you had a boy. A boy is always better."

"As you say."

"Japanese babies are cute, aren't they? A nice head of black hair; not like the red, bald heads of white babies. No matter what they say, Japanese babies are the cutest. Ken was too."

Makiko finally understood; she nodded to herself. The Ides' only son, now over thirty and living in Boston, had suddenly become a newborn baby again and was nestled within Mrs. Ide's stout breast. The news of the baby's birth had brought on a miracle in the nearly sixty-year-old woman. Makiko marvelled at the tenacity of motherhood. Suddenly she felt a sharp pain in her breasts. The pain throbbed and moaned like a living thing. Trying to suppress the pains in her breasts and uterus, Makiko put up with Mrs. Ide's admonitions for a few more minutes. Usually hospitals in California discharged new mothers after three days; Makiko stubbornly resisted when Mrs. Ide insisted that she come and stay with them at the house, where Mrs. Ide could look after her. "No, thank you, but I'm going back to the apartment. Motoo will help me. The university even gives fathers maternity leave. No, it's all right, really." Though Makiko's words were polite, she wouldn't give in, and Mrs. Ide finally relented. She set the condition that she should get to give the baby his first bath.

The phone call had exhausted her, but when she hung up it rang again. It was Motoo. He told her he had sent telegrams to their parents in Japan, and she blurted out, "Don't go and get killed in a car accident, all right?" Her voice broke and tears spilled down her cheeks. "What's the matter?" Motoo's voice sounded surprised; he must have been wondering why she was crying when everything had gone so well and she should be delighted.

"I'm afraid ... there's no way I can take care of the baby. I haven't been able to sleep at all. . . ." While on the surface she had spoken politely, inside she had fought desperately to shove aside the hand that Mrs. Ide had offered. As the built-up tension dissolved, she sobbed as though all her support were gone. She was dimly aware that, after all this time keeping her terror inside, not telling anyone of it since childhood, she had lost all control and was sobbing it out; the realization only added to the tension. Motoo was silent and seemed to be thinking, then all at once he spoke up, like a student who, taking a test, suddenly recalls a fact from his textbook.

"Oh, you've got that thing, the baby blues. After giving birth, you get a sudden change in hormone levels, and your nerves run wild on you."

Listening to him upset Makiko even more. It's not some physiological thing. It's deeper. I'm all torn up inside and helpless, and I'm asking my baby's father for support.

"That's not what it is. I really can't cope. I can't raise him. . . . Can you?"

Motoo did not try to soothe his sobbing wife. He spoke candidly:

"I've never done it before. It's like an experiment; you just have to try. I suppose everything will be all right, but of course you never know; why, there's even the possibility he might die suddenly. He's a living thing, after all."

It didn't occur to the young husband that his straightforward, scientific answer might seem cruel to the new mother with, as he put it, her nerves running wild.

"You know Mrs. Ide offered to look after you both—I can ask her again."

"That's enough!" Makiko shook her head wildly, still holding onto the receiver. No matter how desperate she got, she would never entrust that little living thing to a stranger. Even to her, it didn't make much sense, but the only possible thing for her to do was to hold him tight in her arms, even as she endured her own fear. If they went to stay in the Ides' huge house, the thing that lurked in the shadows of that luxurious furniture would steal the baby away from her.

Makiko clung to the receiver as if it were the baby being pulled away from her into the void.

"Mrs. Hata. It's time for the baby's first nursing."

The nurse stood at the door into the hall, holding something small, wrapped in a white blanket. The little person's face was red, his eyes closed, and he was making little sucking noises with his tiny lips.

Congratulatory letters and gifts came both from Motoo's parents in Tokyo and Makiko's foster parents in Hokuriku. Makiko's mother-in-law, who had raised four boys, gave a long list of assorted specific infant-care suggestions based on her own experience; her frustration at not being able to help bathe the baby and change his diapers spilled out onto the paper. Makiko's foster mother hadn't had a baby of her own; a dry, abstract odor rose from her letter and Makiko saw something of herself in it. Her foster father, a lawyer in the old provincial city, had built up an almost ideal bond of friendship with Makiko, whom he had taken in when she was six. Her foster mother had a matter-of-fact character, and Makiko had never suffered from being too clearly perceived by outsiders as a stepchild. Though her speech was uncolored by the local dialect and she created a private refuge for herself, excluding others, her self-contained attitude was interpreted as being typical of the only daughter of an established family, and she had no particular problems with her teachers or friends. In that district there was a tradition of taking in and giving out children for adoption; it was common for boys, beginning with the second son, to be adopted into their bride's family when they married, and being a niece rather than a daughter was not out of the ordinary.

In other words, I had a happy childhood, thought Makiko, repeating the thought to herself, trying to draw the conclusion. I was happy. Thinking this way will lead to Akihiko's own happiness; the idea took root in her mind like a superstition. On nights when she couldn't sleep, Makiko would peer into the baby's crib, going over in her mind her childhood in Hokuriku and picking out the proofs of happiness. The brand new child-sized skis her foster mother had bought her. The time the enthusiastic young clerk in her foster father's office had taught her how to ski. And English: She was the only one in her class who had private English conversation lessons. But no matter what she came up with, it was only words that came to her mind, words expressing only the idea of happiness: "I had a happy childhood." But what good was this idea of happiness, even when guaranteed by his mother, to Akihiko? The inexperienced young mother forgets the most basic thing, that a guarantee means nothing to a baby. At least I exist. I promise not to die. The last words that Makiko, exhausted, uttered before going to sleep were these new lines that she hadn't completely learned yet, and their dreadful meaning terrified her.

One night Makiko suddenly started up in bed, frightening Motoo.

"Are you sure you sent in the request for Akihiko's Japanese citizenship?"

"What are you talking about? You know I turned it in at the embassy in Los Angeles the day before you left the hospital. I even showed you a copy," he answered in a sleepy voice.

"Oh, that's right. Good. You know they have the draft in

America. We have to make sure he loses his American citizenship when he turns eighteen. They're sending more and more soldiers to Vietnam."

"Come on, that won't still be going on when he's eighteen. The French ran into all kinds of trouble there and got out."

Motoo fell asleep talking. Makiko had met several Vietnamese people in France. Their children were miniature versions of themselves, and the terror that the soldiers' guns had frozen in their eyes swept through Makiko, touching her deep inside. But Makiko refused to notice. Her subconscious mind made the decision for her; she would close her eyes to all the unhappiness of this world in a foolish attempt to gain the confidence to live on as a mother.

As if she had guessed Makiko's concern, Motoo's mother sent them a copy of the family register. To the right of the column where Akihiko Hata's birth record and request for citizenship were entered, Makiko saw the record of her own birth. She stared at the writing: Special City Shinkyo in Manchuria. A fabricated country, a country that should not have existed. But the setting sun that had dyed the wild fields of that country red, that sun had existed. Panicked, Makiko had tried to suppress the burning sunset that had spread across her brain and threatened to dye her whole body red. She was afraid that her baby, now a month old, would look into his mother's mind.

I want to forget. The thought came to her suddenly, forcefully.

"Look at the beautiful flame trees."

The guests, led out to the pool by Bob Ide, all drew in their breath simultaneously and looked up at the spreading branches of the tall flame trees. On the long, straight branches, the scarlet flowers were in full bloom. Lit by the twilight sun of the western sky, the blossoms, true to their name, blazed up like red flames.

Makiko realized that Papa Ide had planned everything to the

minute. To show flowers to people at the best possible time and overwhelm them with their beauty was more than just a hobby for the owner of a nursery—it was also his job. At the end of the academic year the Hatas would go back to France, and the Ides had decided to invite the Novozhilov group over in May, before the summer heat set in. Undoubtedly the beautiful flame trees had also entered into Bob Ide's plans when he set up the party for a May evening.

Julia, wearing a white dress remarkably becoming to her enormous figure, carried a silver tray around to the guests, serving champagne. When Julia saw Makiko's face, she smirked conspiratorially at her. Makiko was confused; she didn't have any secrets with Julia. The first time she had shown Akihiko to her, the huge Mexican woman chuckled, spreading wrinkles from both sides of her nose. "He's bigger than a mouse after all," she commented.

Vicky ambled around among the legs of the guests standing beside the pool with drinks in their hands.

"Is it a collie? She's a good dog, isn't she?" Professor Novozhilov followed Vicky with his faintly gleaming eyes.

"She *was* a good dog. Now she's gotten old and lost her spirit. She wouldn't be any help biting the Viet Cong," answered Bob Ide. Standing next to the tall Professor Novozhilov and Conrad, his short stature actually made him more conspicuous. With his silver hair combed neatly back, wearing a white shirt and tie, Bob Ide looked the part of the gracious, old-fashioned gentleman farmer welcoming his educated city guests to his house and pool. This diminutive, second-generation Japanese-American even gave the impression that he was bearing on his small, square shoulders the entire weight of an older, better America that was rapidly falling into ruin.

"Well, Mr. Johnson is younger than this dog," said Conrad loudly.

"But Vicky isn't stupid enough to go and get her beautiful coat dirty in some muddy swamp." As Motoo spoke, a dark-skinned hand brushed against Makiko's arm. Layers of gold bracelets on the wrist gently brushed together with a cool jingling sound. The swollen abdomen sagged under the bright blue sari with its arabesque pattern embroidered in gold thread.

"Vietnam, Vietnam, I'm fed up with it. I can't stand political discussions. Can you, Makiko?" Kamini's face frankly betrayed the bored, haughty expression typical of women who have spent their lives doing just as they wish. The Indian accent, with its crunching sounds, gave a strange, regal thrust to her English words.

"Your baby's next. Be brave!" Makiko changed the subject. Though the habit American girls had of covering their ears and pouting whenever men started talking about politics may have been just a mannerism left over from the days of *Gone With The Wind*, it nevertheless seemed to Makiko a mercenary kind of flirtation designed to show men how much they depended on their strong protection. Makiko wasn't sure enough of herself to openly criticize the resourcefulness of women who might change the course of political events through such flirtation. But in this case, she thought that Kamini's dislike of political conversation was just a case of arrogant ignorance. Even so, Makiko had no desire to get into an argument with the young Indian aristocrat. And who was she to judge? She, who even after all this time still didn't know what it was that had been destroyed inside her by that soldier's blue eyes.

"What did you do after you got out of the hospital? Did you get someone to come from Japan and help out?"

"No, somehow Motoo and I managed by ourselves."

"But . . . that's hard to believe. You left the hospital after five days, right?"

"Usually it's three days, you know. I stayed as long as I could and left after five."

"Where I come from, the mother stays in bed for two months without moving." Kamini looked earnestly at Makiko with her large eyes under the double lids. Gazing at the perfect beauty of her oval face with the rose-colored circle painted on the forehead and the jet-black hair bound into a knot, Makiko suppressed the urge to ask sarcastically, Is it a matter of caste?

"Could I ask you something?" Kamini bent her dark-skinned finger and touched Makiko's arm again.

"When you were admitted to the hospital, did you store your jewelry somewhere, like the bank?"

Makiko was taken aback, but with Kamini's eyes fixed so earnestly on her, she couldn't answer honestly that she didn't own any jewelry valuable enough to store away somewhere. She wondered if, when Kamini adorned her body, which was already so beautiful, with gorgeous saris and glittering jewels, it was her own way of showing her passion for living.

Makiko smelled the appetizing aroma of melted cheese. She turned around and saw Julia displaying a huge pizza as big as a washtub on the table that had been set out beside the pool. Mrs. Ide called out, "Try some of Julia's specialty, Mexican-style pizza!" Helga and Rose, each holding their babies, stared at it with shining eyes. Makiko noticed that Helga's hips had spread after she had given birth, and now she looked like a typical German matron. Makiko herself couldn't get into her old skirts.

In the baby carriage that had been set out in the shade, Akihiko started crying. Makiko bent over the carriage, but Mrs. Ide's fat arms stretched out to him, pushing her aside.

"Oh, why are you crying? Boys don't cry, boys don't cry."

Makiko reached out with both hands to the little being, who looked as though he were about to sink into Mrs. Ide's ample chest.

"I'll hold him."

"No, you go and entertain the guests." Mrs. Ide wasn't about to give him up.

"Aki-chan, come to Mama?"

The baby, not yet three months old, cooed and turned his face away from Makiko. Mrs. Ide laughed exultantly. "This baby doesn't like his Mama."

"You're right. He likes you better, naughty boy." Feigning jealousy, Makiko suddenly felt a pang in her chest. The baby's eyes were captivated by the flowers of the flame trees.

Scarlet flowers blazing up toward the heavens.

Of course, babies are always attracted to the color red. Makiko crossed around behind Mrs. Ide and looked at Akihiko's little face peering over her thick shoulders. His innocent, wide-open eyes flickered with the blazing scarlet flames reflected in them. Without thinking, Makiko started to raise her hand to protect the baby's eyes from the light of the flowers. But at that moment the scarlet color disappeared from his eyes. Makiko's hand stopped in mid-air, and she turned around. Behind her stood Mrs. Novozhilov, her tall shape blocking the red light of the flowers.

"So the baby's awake. He's so cute, may I hold him?" Lyudmilla Novozhilov gazed intently at Akihiko with her blue eyes. Makiko started and instinctively reached out toward him. But before she got to him, Mrs. Ide, addressing the baby, said, "How about it, baby? Get a hug from the Professor's wife." Then, turning to Mrs. Novozhilov, she said proudly, "He's a heavy baby," and handed him to her. Makiko stared at Akihiko, holding her breath. She was ready for him to suddenly burst out crying as though he'd been burned; when he did, she would immediately wrench him out of Mrs. Novozhilov's arms.

Too young to be afraid of strangers, the baby gave no sign of crying and instead cooed again contentedly.

"I suppose he will speak only Japanese with you. You're lucky."

Makiko opened her eyes wide in surprise. The words were so

unexpected from the lips of the woman who was always stressing how American she was and pushing the young foreigners to study English.

"It won't hurt him at all to speak Japanese, even in front of Americans. Our boys are all fluent in Russian, but they never use it around Americans. Even when we're walking down the road talking, if we pass someone, they stop talking immediately."

Makiko scrutinized Lyudmilla's pale eyes as she talked. Mrs. Ide nodded and chimed in her agreement, then under her breath added to herself in Japanese, "And for the same reason Ken never speaks Japanese anymore."

Akihiko tilted his head backwards as though searching for something.

"You want your Mama? Look, here she is, here's your Mama." Lyudmilla Novozhilov moved her arms so that Akihiko could see Makiko.

"No, he's not looking for me," she said, then, noticing, added, "He's looking for the red color. Look, it's those flowers."

"Oh, the flame trees." Lyudmilla Novozhilov looked up, convinced, and turned Akihiko's face in the direction of the flowers.

"Look at the bright red flowers. See how pretty they are. Babies always like bright colors, don't they?"

The brilliant scarlet rays of the setting sun shone through the flower petals straight into Akihiko's eyes. The baby squinted at the dazzling light. When Makiko looked up, she saw that the scarlet flames were blazing up in Lyudmilla Novozhilov's blue eyes as well. Makiko staggered back a step and looked at the tiny Japanese baby nestled in the arms of the large Russian woman. It may have been to avoid the blinding light, but Akihiko turned his eyes away from the flowers and looked up into Lyudmilla's face. As if sensing his gaze, Lyudmilla looked down at the baby in her arms. The two human beings, so different in age, in size, and in the color of their eyes, looked directly at each other. The innocent, guileless smile of a baby shone in Akihiko's tiny eyes. Lyud-milla returned the smile, saying, "Oh, good boy."

In Makiko's chest, her father's smile suddenly arose again. The baby's smile had superimposed itself on the smiling face the young father had left in Makiko's distant memory. The layers of time that had been stratified and separate now collapsed gently and joined together in a single eternity that glittered like light shining through a prism. From behind the window of the past that had frozen deep inside Makiko, a flickering sensation arose, dodging its way through the undercurrents of time. Without un-derstanding the sensation, Makiko raised her arms and groped for it in the empty air.

Surrounded by the blazing evening sunlight, Lyudmilla Novozhilov handed the baby back to Makiko.

MEI HUA LU

I

Outside Changchun the city street gave way to a rough, muddy country road, where deep ruts left by trucks and horse-drawn carriages alternated with scattered piles of debris.

The driver maneuvered the car over the craters and rises, nonchalantly turning the steering wheel in broad sweeps first to the right, then to the left. Riding the horn, he dispersed the clusters of bicycles and pedestrians in his way. Ueda felt like joking that Japan should send jeeps, rather than old-model passenger cars, for foreign aid, but of course he kept quiet. Especially since this car, a three- or four-year-old model, was probably paid for with Chinese government funds, and wasn't foreign aid at all.

Mr. Feng, sitting in the back seat behind the driver, said something to Ueda in Chinese. Yang Xiao-hong, seated next to Mr. Feng, leaned forward until her face nearly touched the back of Ueda's head, and interpreted into Japanese for him. Ueda had chosen to sit in the front seat so that he could have a good view of the scenery, but whenever Mr. Feng said something, he had to turn around. He wasn't just being polite; he really couldn't hear Mr. Feng's voice—not only was the engine racing because of the bad road, but the air conditioner made a loud noise and the horn was continually blaring. As if that weren't enough, he couldn't understand Chinese. Yang Xiao-hong's face nearly touched his ear; she probably wanted to save him from having to turn around each time.

"It's the same in every city; the roads are worst in the outskirts. Once you get out into the country, they get better. Neither the national government nor the city spends money on the places in between." The girl's breathing tickled his earlobe.

"It's the same in Japan."

Miss Yang interpreted the brief phrase, and Mr. Feng laughed aloud. Both Ueda and Mr. Feng seized the fleeting opportunity to laugh together whenever they could. Without a common language, this was their most effective way of communicating shared emotions.

Just as Mr. Feng had said, when they came out into the suburbs, the road turned into a splendid paved highway marked with white-lettered blue road signs just like those in Japan. There were only two lanes, but the road was wide, and separate bike lanes ran parallel to it. With the broad fields and gardens spread out on either side, it gave an impression of much greater safety than, say, Tokyo's main expressways. The modern highway itself, and the sight of its leisurely horse-drawn carriages mingled in among the cars and trucks, filled Ueda with a simple delight.

Forty-two years earlier, in midsummer, the neighborhood association had been thrown into a panic by the news of the Soviet entry into the war, and had evacuated en masse. Was this the route they had taken? Of course they hadn't gone in cars along a highway; they'd taken horse-drawn carriages, and the dirt road had sent up clouds of dust. Yes, it must have been that way, though Ueda couldn't recall it clearly; he'd been eight at the time.

"I get the feeling I must have been here before, a long time ago. At the time these were all sorghum fields, I think."

Yang Xiao-hong gave him Feng's reply, that he was probably right, but that now it was mostly cornfields.

"It may sound trite, but I feel like I'm dreaming."

Ueda repeated these words he had said countless times since his arrival in Changchun. He had visited Changchun before, four years ago. Though he had had business only in Beijing and Shanghai, he had also managed to include Changchun in his itinerary. He had stayed only two days. Using a map, he had located the place where he had lived as a child, but the house was no longer standing.

This being the second time, he hadn't experienced the same rush of emotion as before. Still this present-day Changchun, now a completely Chinese city, aroused in him a deep affection.

"Mr. Ueda, have you been to Jilin?"

"I think I have, but I don't know for sure. I was only eight. . . ." He caught himself and exclaimed, "Oh, that's right, isn't there a place near here called Domonrei?"

"Domonrei? How do you write it?"

"I'm not sure. If I could look at a map . . ."

Yang Xiao-hong spread out a map in the back seat and exclaimed, "I found it!" She gave Mr. Feng the Chinese reading for the name.

"I remember being taken there for a picnic."

It was a small hill. He had gathered some wildflowers there and taken them back to his sick mother as a present. She had stretched her emaciated hand out from under the covers to reach for them, and had broken into a coughing fit. Even now he vividly recalled her melancholy, brilliant eyes when, after the coughing abated, she smiled and said, "Aren't they pretty!" The next year, the winter of the last year of the war, she had died in Changchun.

"A picnic? Oh, that's right. Nowadays, all the Chinese go on picnics, too." Mr. Feng's tone of voice gave a sense of how much the lives of the Chinese had changed over the last few years.

They passed small food stalls with square red lamps, which had sprung up even out here along this rural highway. Ueda realized that, like the ones in central Changchun, they represented the new profit motive that had arisen among people who until yesterday had been putting on so-called People's Uniforms and going off to the factories or cultivating the fields. Four years ago virtually all the men had worn such uniforms, and the women had, at best, made do with plain colored blouses, but now the clothes seemed scarcely different from those in Japan. Today only the older women were wearing work trousers, and among the men hardly any could be seen in uniforms of the traditional style, with caps. Deng Xiao-ping had designed a three-part policy of actively opening the country to the outside world, broadening individual initiative in the internal economy, and forcibly advancing the industrialization that had fallen sharply behind during the ten years of the Cultural Revolution. Mr. Feng said the Chinese people were content with the results. For Ueda their satisfaction was clearly manifested in the clothes they wore.

They were going to see the world's largest meteorite, which had fallen outside Jilin, but Mr. Feng had gotten passes and set up a visit to an exhibition center on the way that featured products for which the province was famous. They weren't factory-made goods, but he wanted to show them to Ueda because of their special value as exports.

Ueda learned that there were three Treasures of the Northeast: ginseng, deer antlers, and the fur of the *suisho*. He had known, of course, that both ginseng and antlers were valued for their medicinal properties, but the word *suisho* carried no meaning for him. When they showed him the way it was written, he realized from the characters that it was a species of marten, a "water marten."

Though Ueda worked for a major household electronics company whose products were imported in large quantities into China, his own job had little direct connection with that side of the business. But he had spent his early childhood in Japanese-occupied Manchuria, and, feeling a certain meditative nostalgia for that time, he would help Chinese exchange students in Japan with part-time work or scholarship money. Though his efforts were modest, they represented a sacrifice of time on his part. That must have been why, when he had asked to go to Changchun during his trip to Beijing, the provincial administration had responded promptly by sending a guide and an interpreter.

The exhibition center stood at the edge of an immense, gently undulating field. The ginseng was planted in fields by the roadside, protected from the sun by reed awnings. Yang Xiao-hong kept up an ongoing, but detached, interpretation: that usually ginseng flowers are white, but there were some rare varieties with yellow blooms; that the ginseng growing wild in the mountains was highly valued for its medicinal properties, which far surpassed those of this cultivated kind. She had said that she had graduated from the foreign language school in Changchun. How old would that make her? She reminded Ueda a little of his daughter, Mari.

When Ueda got out his camera, Xiao-hong hastily retreated to one side. She must have thought he wanted to take a picture of the ginseng fields.

"No, stay where you are . . . ," said Ueda, then added, "together with Mr. Feng." But Mr. Feng didn't like being photographed; he waved his hand to one side and moved away.

Framed by the lens, Xiao-hong stood somewhat awkwardly, slim in her white dress. When he snapped the shutter, Ueda noticed that she looked more like his mother than Mari. His mother was Mari's grandmother, after all, and it made sense that if Xiao-hong reminded him of the one, she would also remind him of the other. Ueda had never thought of his mother, who had died in her early thirties, as Mari's grandmother, and he was struck with the awareness that it was through a complete stranger, a young Chinese woman, that he had been made conscious of the relationship.

Unlike the ginseng, which sprawled in broad fields, the animals were rather severely confined. Under the gate lay a box filled with white disinfectant. The three of them stepped through the powder, one after the other, into an open space that seemed disproportionately large in comparison with the row of metal cages in which the *suisho* were kept.

The animals were small, a little over two feet long. Twisting their long, slender bodies, they nimbly climbed up and down the iron railings of their cages. Ueda didn't particularly like their quick movements or their small, glittering eyes. His gaze fixed on their fur, and he noticed the wide variety of shades of color. Then he realized that the animals were minks. Of course he knew that mink was considered the height of fashion for women, and he remembered how his wife, Yasuko, had once made a point of showing him a coat with a mink collar. "This is mink," she had said. "Touch it, see how soft it is," and she had brushed it against his hand. But he hadn't made the association between the characters signifying "water marten" and mink coats.

Ueda thought they weren't very appealing animals, but he took a photograph. Yasuko had probably never seen a live mink either. He included Xiao-Hong's profile in the picture. Oblivious, she nodded her head up and down, wide-eyed, following the movements of the animals.

The third Treasure of the Northeast was confined in tall, clay-walled enclosures that reminded Ueda of Chinese farm huts. Here and there cross-shaped windows were cut into the walls. Seen through these windows, the deer stood or lay on the ground, their long, gracefully raised necks contrasting with their disheveled appearance. The hot summer sun beat against the brick floor.

"You see the white things on these deer?" Xiao-hong started interpreting Mr. Feng's words, but, apparently unable to recall the Japanese word for spots, she stabbed the air with her finger, "It's . . . like this, they have dots. . . ."

"Spots. Or you can say spotted. Usually they're called dappled," Ueda informed her.

"Since the spots look like plum blossoms, we call them plum-blossom deer—*mei hua lu*," she added in Chinese. The syllables slipped out gracefully, reminding him of the slim, graceful body of a young deer.

Mr. Feng, pointing out a deer with two bumps on its head, explained that the antlers were cut once a year, like mushrooms, then grew back. Seeing the soft, swollen scars, Ueda felt a rush of pity.

Someone came out the gate in the clay wall, leaving the doors open. When the three of them approached the doors, the twenty or so *mei hua lu* flicked their ears nervously and fled in a group toward the shed at the rear of the enclosure. It was a calm but cold gesture of negation, elemental as the tide rushing out. Their fleecy white tails waved above their slender legs. "The *mei hua lu*'s antlers have a special medicinal effect that other deers' don't, isn't that right?"

"Yes. But since the *mei hua lu*'s antlers are fairly small, they're doing cross-breeding experiments with ass-deer to produce bigger ones."

Without thinking, Ueda asked, "Asses?" Xiao-hong didn't seem to notice the double meaning of this word. "Yes, it's a kind of deer. You write it with the Chinese characters for horse and deer. It's pronounced *malu*." Then she understood, and laughed.* But she didn't seem to feel the humor as strongly as Ueda.

"So you breed the plum-blossom deer with an 'ass'?" Ueda smiled wryly. He wanted to add, "That's too bad."

The deer, still standing at a distance, looked back at them with frank curiosity. The fawns nestled close to their mothers' sides; though they must have been born just that spring, they already watched Ueda and the others with an attitude of adult wariness.

"This is the pen for the hybrids," said Mr. Feng, standing

*[The pun hinges on the Japanese word for "fool," *baka*, which is written with the characters for horse and deer, as is the Chinese deer's name. —Tr.]

in front and indicating the neighboring enclosure. The *malu* were
indeed bigger, and had larger antlers, but they didn't seem to
have any problem keeping their good sense despite their large
bodies. They observed the visitors with a gentle, peaceful expression that called to mind both the horses and the deer of their
name, and they made no attempt to flee.

"Your wife would like this one." Yang Xiao-hong looked at
Ueda, her eyes so wide open the upper lashes curled backwards; it
must have been an idiosyncrasy of hers. Ueda had no idea which
of the various shades of mink furs arrayed on the glass shelf would
please his wife. After their visit to the meteorite museum, Ueda
had been invited to go shopping and was taken to the special
store for foreigners. Apparently this was part of their agenda.
Ueda had intended to buy the usual souvenirs—carved jade or
Duizhu vases—the next day when he got to Dalian, before board-
ing the plane for home, but he said, "Well, as a remembrance of
today, maybe I'll have a look at the Three Treasures of the Northeast," and Mr. Feng nodded contentedly.

They told Ueda that both the dried ginseng and the antlers, cut
crosswise, should be soaked in strong alcohol to extract their
potency. He bought three boxes each for his co-workers at the
company; this alone would weigh down his luggage. He had
figured that if the *suisho*'s fur was too expensive he wouldn't buy
it, but, with the yen so strong, it wasn't too bad. The thing to do
was to get not just one fur but something larger, say, a shawl
made from several pelts; that would really make Yasuko happy.

That was Ueda's original intention, but he felt selfish, coming
right out and spending so much money on such a luxury in front
of Mr. Feng and Xiao-hong. Even one fur would probably
amount to two months of Xiao-hong's salary.

The one she had chosen was a glossy jet-black fur. Her clearly
defined taste showed in her unhesitating selection of this pure

black mink from among the rows of gray and brown ones. Ueda was touched by this gift of herself, revealed in her choice for a Japanese woman she had never met. He thought of getting her one too, but didn't have nerve enough to offer. He was afraid it might be considered rude. But then, conveniently, Mr. Feng suggested, "How about getting one for your daughter, too?" He had remembered their discussion in the car about Ueda's family.

Just to make sure, Ueda checked with Xiao-hong, "Is it all right to get something like this for a young girl?" At first she thought the question was directed at Mr. Feng, and interpreted it. Then, putting her own expression into Mr. Feng's answer, "All females like furs," she gave a childlike laugh.

"Well then, you decide."

This time, too, Xiao-hong chose quickly, without hesitation. It was a pure white fur. After the clerk took it out, she wrapped it around her own neck to show him how it looked and convince him of the wisdom of her choice. The clerk reached out and poked the mink under its small chin and its mouth popped open. He put the end of the tail into the mouth to make a ring. The soft, shimmering white fur cradled her youthful chin.

"Two of those, please." Without waiting for Xiao-hong's translation, the clerk saw Ueda's two raised fingers and started searching on the shelf for the right color. "Let there be one just like it!"—Ueda's thought was like a prayer, and he gazed fixedly at the movements of the clerk's hands. Even if they themselves were not aware of it, he wanted Mari and Xiao-hong to have matching furs. White minks must be rare; there weren't any more on that shelf. Another clerk went to look in the back room and luckily found one more. "It's the last one," he said.

"Do you have two daughters?" asked Xiao-hong, and Ueda nodded ambiguously.

II

"Ooh, mink!" Yasuko and Mari exclaimed in unison; then, as if they'd planned it beforehand, they simultaneously wrapped the minks around their necks. In their haste to try on the animals, complete with eyes and nose, without taking a good look at them, Ueda's wife and daughter revealed a side of their characters that was unfamiliar to him. And now that he thought of it, Xiao-hong, too, though she had just seen the living animals moving around, had immediately wrapped the mink around her neck without even commenting on its beauty.

"Do it this way," said Ueda, and reaching out, he put the *suisho's* tail in its mouth. They said, "Oh, that's right," and turned, satisfied, toward the mirror. But then Mari suddenly squealed and tore her *suisho* off her neck.

"What is it?" asked Yasuko, and Ueda, startled, chimed in, "What's the matter?" His first thought was that a needle, hidden somewhere in the soft fur, had stuck her in the soft flesh under her chin.

"Its eyes are all red, it's scary."

"Silly, they're glass eyes."

"But look how they're glaring!"

"What about yours?" Mari peered at Yasuko's *suisho.* "Oh, the brown eyes are pretty. That kind is better," she muttered, looking warily out of the corner of her eye at the white fur tossed on the floor.

Ueda decided to give her a scare. He took a bundle wrapped in plastic out of his travel bag and handed it to her. "Look, here's another souvenir; it's very valuable."

Mari took it casually, but taking a look at the packaging, which lacked the usual souvenir markings, she asked suspiciously, "What is this thing?"

"A deer heart."

The moment she heard her father's answer Mari shrieked, but, apparently lacking the nerve to toss the bundle on the floor as she had the mink, she thrust it hastily into her mother's hand.

"What did you say it was? A deer heart? A live one?" asked Yasuko stupidly, affected by her daughter's anxious expression.

"It's alive. See how it's twitching?"

Yasuko, though she realized that he was teasing her, kept her eyes uneasily on the package.

"What did you bring something like this for?" Mari looked at her father as though he himself had become some kind of alien creature.

"It was a gift. They use it as medicine. It's supposed to be really good for you."

"For what? First of all, how do you . . . ?"

"It's dried. Since it's dehydrated, you soak it in water, and when it's restored to its original shape, you boil it in the microwave oven and eat it."

That's what Xiao-hong had told him. She had spoken, raising her beautiful eyes, as if there were nothing out of the ordinary in what she was saying.

"Oh, come on! How can you talk about it that way?"

Mari was right: He shouldn't have spoken so plainly about cooking it in the microwave. . . .

Steam rises from the bloodstained, throbbing heart, lying on a plate. You stab it with a fork, cut it with a knife, and lift it to your mouth. . . . What kind of thoughts are these?

"What's the difference between this and the pig hearts they serve at the *yakitori* stands?" commented Yasuko.

She was the housewife. The word "microwave" seemed to have brought her back to her senses. She placed the package gently on the table.

"If it's dried, could you grind it into powder and drink it?"

"Who would grind it? Mama, could you do it yourself?"

"That's disgusting."

"If it's that bad what can we do? Since it's so valuable I guess we could hang it on the wall as a decoration," said Ueda, suggesting a compromise.

"Oh come on, Papa, that's enough!" Mari was even more disgusted.

Ueda went into the bedroom, which doubled as a study, and laid the package with the deer heart on the desk. He opened his briefcase and took out its contents. Among the papers was a pamphlet from the Jilin exhibition center. He pictured the expansive cornfields he had seen from the highway; then the sorghum fields from his childhood superimposed themselves over them. All the Japanese who lived in occupied Manchuria will mention its scarlet evening sun. Ueda, too, had countless times seen it sinking down beyond the boundless plain. It had been an omen of the destruction and death that would begin with the sudden Soviet entry into the war as well as a reflection of the Chinese blood that was even then being spilled there, as it had been in the past.

Nevertheless, though his memory of this land—as the point at which the sweet life of a child intersected with the smell of blood and death—continued to throb and expand within him, when he actually visited it he himself was nothing more than a common foreign tourist, foraging for souvenirs for his wife and child.

Ueda had been nothing more than a stranger. Muttering, he poked his finger into the briefcase and brushed against a lightweight, square, no-longer-new box. He now remembered this souvenir and took it out, but instead of going right back into the living room with it, he slipped his fingernail under the rusty metal clasp and opened the box. Inside was a row of small silver forks, blackened with oxidation: old-fashioned ebonite-handled dessert forks. The velvet covering the outside of the box, not to mention the wrinkled velvet lining, had faded completely. The gilt lettering inside the lid, "Ginza Hattori," was discolored, too.

Ueda pulled out another bundle, this one misshapen and wrapped in paper. It was a coaster made from glass inlaid into a silver frame. This silver, too, had blackened, and the glass was completely clouded over. He laid it next to the forks on the desk.

For a while Ueda gazed intently at these things that would arouse less pleasure than the mink stoles, and less disgust than the deer heart. What had made him buy them? Just a sentimental quirk.

As he had walked down a street in Dalian, an antique store had caught his eye. He went in and found the forks and coaster. Ueda had no memories of Dalian. He had simply gone there to catch the direct flight to Narita, but his emotions were stirred by the number of buildings that had remained from earlier times, both those built by the Russians, and those built by the Japanese who had come after them.

It was a large store with a number of sales clerks, but when he saw the Japanese customer without an interpreter, a fat old man, apparently the manager, came out to serve him. He spoke in fluent, though accented, Japanese, but his manner was blunt. Not only was it the normal course of affairs in a socialist country to lack the incentive to sell things, but the man himself proclaimed, "Whether I sell one item or ten thousand, my salary stays the same, so why should I try to sell something expensive?" As if that weren't enough, he added, "I can't stand it when Japanese buy expensive things from this shop."

Struck to the heart, Ueda sympathized, "I see what you mean. With the yen so strong, Japanese are walking off with all the Chinese antiques."

"No, that's not it. We don't sell things older than two hundred years. It's forbidden to take them out of the country. What we have here are just curios. Household things."

He was almost rude, but that was somehow gratifying to Ueda.

He laughed, and the clerk, more favorably disposed to him now, took out an embroidery in a wooden frame. "But this is a good one. It's just two hundred years old." It seemed awfully stiff, but Ueda didn't know how to evaluate embroidery. What would Xiao-hong have said if she had been there?

"It's really exactly two hundred years old?" he interrupted, and the clerk said, with a serious expression:

"I don't lie to Japanese. The Chinese and Japanese are in the same family. Sometimes I lie to Westerners."

"Why? You shouldn't lie, even to Westerners."

"No, to them you can. I do. But I never lie to Japanese."

Ueda grinned wryly. The old guy could be lying to him right now. He couldn't tell. He walked along the counter, looking over the glass shelves, and came across the silverware arranged in one corner. Though it was real silver, it wasn't anything special, just an assortment of small items, cups and spoons. But among them he found the coaster and forks. He called back to the clerk, "These are Japanese things from before the war."

The old man agreed, "That's right. They were left by the Japanese," and taking them out, he handed them to Ueda.

When Ueda saw the elegantly curved prongs of the forks and the delicate openwork of the silver setting of the coaster, suddenly the image of his mother, young again, rose before his eyes. His mother's illness must have begun during the war. She hardly ever went out, and she left the rough housework to a maid. She was always sitting in a chair knitting or reading. When even that wearied her, she would polish just this kind of silverware, her hands working delicately.

As a child Ueda would play outside in the mud after coming back from kindergarten or elementary school, but when he got thirsty or felt like having some sweets, he would dash into the house and, on his way, would ascertain out of the corner of his eye what his mother was doing. He was most reassured when she was knitting. Seeing her wearily turning over the pages of a book aroused his pity, and when he saw her, her brows knitted, polishing the delicate silverware, an indefinable anxiety would arise in his chest. With the movements of her thin hands, the silverwork seemed to emit small sparks. Perhaps it was the transitory nature of the light that aroused such apprehension in him.

One day when, as always, he glanced out of the corner of his eye to check his mother on his way back out, she called to him unexpectedly. When he came up to her, she beamed at him and, lifting her hands, stretched out her fingers for him to see. She had painted her nails; they sparkled bright red at the tips of her pale fingers.

What was his mother's reason for doing this? This particular scene etched itself into Ueda's memory, and even after he grew up, he would recall it vividly. At such times he would be overcome with an inexplicable emotion.

While polishing the silverware, she must have been taken with a sudden caprice to polish her own fingernails, then decided to see what they looked like painted red. The decorated silverware undoubtedly had been part of her dowry; it may have triggered a desire to return to her girlhood amusements. Then, after she'd finished painting her nails, there was no one to show them off to, and when her small son chanced by she called out to him. . . . Even this innocent coquetry of a young girl had disappeared somewhere, pointlessly, into the vast continent.

It was impossible that the final days of the war, beginning with the evacuation, would pass without affecting her fragile health. By the time the Soviet soldiers invaded the house in their muddy boots, she couldn't even get up out of bed, much less polish the silverware. Her lungs continued to hemorrhage, and, within six months of the end of the war, one bitter winter morning the child was brought to view his mother's dead face. Another six months after that, the family abandoned all their possessions and joined the evacuation. The boy carried, in addition to his knapsack, his mother's ashes. "The Soviets took most of the Japanese possessions of any value, but the things that were left behind are concentrated in Dalian," said the old man to Ueda, who was looking down at a fork, toying with its prongs.

"Maybe things from Changchun, too." He figured it couldn't be something that had belonged to his mother, but he wanted to ask.

"Yes. And from Xinjing, and from Haerbing, and Fengtian." The old man, without hesitation, pronounced the old place names from the "Wei Man" era, the occupation period.

As he paid for the silver, Ueda said, "They come and go, don't they? Who knows, maybe this coaster will return to China sometime."

"That's right. It's history." The old man nodded, then added, "Perhaps in the meantime the governments will negotiate and things like the paintings by Taikan that are precious to Japan will be returned there."

"But once you start talking that way, Japan, too, and other countries as well, have a lot of things that should be returned to China. There's nothing wrong with China having Taikan's paintings."

Having unilaterally decided this issue, Ueda thanked the clerk and said goodbye in Chinese, "Xie xie zai jian," and offered him his right hand. Though he had been raised in China until the age of eight, these were the only words he knew—which itself suggested to him the extent of the Japanese oppression of the Chinese.

The old man shook his hand and said stiffly, insincerely, "Excuse me for not being more hospitable." His fat body jiggling, he accompanied Ueda out to the front of the store.

It could have been the child of long ago having a conversation with a familiar old neighbor. If he had come out and said, "Uncle, this might have belonged to my mother," the old man might very well have given him his guarantee that it was so. . . . Ueda blew onto the coaster and wiped it with his handkerchief. Though its former brilliance would not return to the oxidized silver, the aged glass gave off its own gentle glow. The pattern of ice crystals engraved in its center shone faintly. When he recalled the ice crystals that had gleamed in the window on the morning of his mother's death, Xiao-hong's youthful chin wrapped in the shimmering white fur appeared before his eyes.

Ueda had found a moment when Xiao-hong was away to entrust the *suisho* fur to Mr. Feng. He took a piece of paper and wrote, "For Yang Xiao-hong." Mr. Feng's expression showed his surprise at such an extravagant gift, but he accepted it for her. Ueda gave Mr. Feng a quartz watch and a solar-powered calculator he had brought from Japan—pretty banal souvenirs when compared with the Three Treasures of the Northeast.

The next morning, when Ueda set off for Dalian, Mr. Feng and Xiao-hong came together to see him off. It was then that Xiao-hong had given him the deer's heart. "Don't worry; it's from the *mei hua lu*, not the hybrid. You won't make a fool of yourself." When she smiled at her play on words, she reminded Ueda even more of the mother in his memory.

Hearing footsteps in the hall, Ueda instinctively hid the forks and the coaster in the desk drawer. He didn't actually intend to conceal them from Yasuko and Mari, but, at least for now, he didn't want to expose these things to the eyes of people who didn't know the land of Manchuria.

Yasuko came in and started to close the curtain in front of the desk, but gave a little startled cry.

"What is it?"

"The heart; I don't like it. It's twitching, as though it really were alive."

"Silly. It's just the way the light is hitting it." He reached out, but suddenly hesitated. What if it really were beating?

Xiao-hong herself had told him it was dried, and it had been as hard as a rock when he touched it through the plastic bag, so he hadn't even thought to open it and see. But if it hadn't been completely dried, it could really be a mess. He opened the bundle.

Inside lay a brownish thing that really did have the shape of a heart.

"Oh, disgusting; the blood vessels . . ."

From behind Ueda Yasuko nervously pointed at it with her finger. The two tubelike main arteries had been cut off, and their mouths gaped open. He gazed fixedly into one dark cavity, and from afar he heard the lively pulsation and the plaintive call of the *mei hua lu*, and its soft back, scattering white spots, slipped past and vanished.

THE PHOENIX TREE

I

Her apron crumpled into a ball in her hand, Mitsue returned to the house. She stopped in the kitchen for a drink of water, then sat down on the living room sofa. The house was hushed; her brother and his family were still asleep.

She folded her arms and pressed her stomach tightly just under her chest. That didn't calm her, though, so she drew both legs up onto the sofa and embraced her knees. She had often curled up this way as a child. . . . Rather than just sitting here idly, she knew she should start breakfast for her brother's family as usual, but this morning she couldn't bring herself to do it.

Mitsue had risen at the first light of dawn, gone over to the "wing," and slid open the rain shutters. This small cottage was all that remained of the main house, and stood solitary in one corner of the overgrown lawn that marked the original walls. She had intended to wait in the wing for her aunt and her cousin Shiro, due to arrive that morning from Tokyo, but had somehow felt uncomfortable there and had started back; the chilly caress of the early morning breeze coming across the yard had kindled a tiny flame deep in her breast and she had been overcome by a sudden fear.

The clock on the wall struck once, quietly: 5:30. The Hokuriku overnight train would arrive at T– Station in thirty minutes. Her face already washed, Obasan would be looking out at the Japan Sea through the dull gray morning. . . . Shiro was probably still asleep on the top bunk. When Mitsue pictured his sleeping face, something knocked in the pit of her stomach. Rounding her back, she pressed her chest to her knees and tucked in her chin. She always looked forward to the return of her aunt and cousin, but this time Shiro's phone call three days ago had sparked a burning impatience in her.

It was only a ten-minute taxi ride from T– Station to the house. Once out of the city, they would pick up speed on the prefectural highway that cut through the rice paddies. . . . It really would have been better to wait in the wing.

Although this was the Sogi family's ancestral home, it had not sheltered a permanent resident for several years. Obasan had lived here alone before that, but by then the big house itself had already been sold and dismantled. It sounded strange to keep on calling what remained the "wing," but, even after all this time, it still seemed to Mitsue that the run-down cottage had been only temporarily vacated and was just waiting for its mistress to return from her son's house in Tokyo. Mitsue and her older brother Kohei, who were orphaned when she was a baby, had been raised here by their aunt. She had been very close to her cousin Shiro; he had treated her with special tenderness when she was a child, but since his graduation from a university in Tokyo, he returned only for the annual Bon festival in the summer. It didn't seem right to consider him the master of the house. Then there was Shiro's wife Rika, who with her brisk Tokyo way of talking didn't seem part of the family at all. Mitsue was apparently not alone in feeling this way; old Genji, who had lived out his whole life in the village, continued to address the almost forty-year-old Shiro as he would a child, never granting him the status of master.

Kohei was up; there came the sound of his heavy tread as he went down the hall to the bathroom. If he was planning to do some work in the fields before leaving for the Agricultural Cooperative, he would need some breakfast. Mitsue raised her head slightly, but the footsteps thumped back the way they had come.

Again she rested her forehead on her knees. When she was very young, before she could even remember, her face had been burned, and she had been left with a scar. For this reason, and also because of an innate shyness, she had always felt awkward among strangers. During the fourteen or fifteen years since high school, she had just stayed here at home, doing almost nothing. She had not married nor found a job, and was supported by her brother. Though she took care of most of the housework while her sister-in-law, Kazumi, worked in the neighborhood supermarket, she found no satisfaction in this responsibility. In the past she had occasionally taken correspondence courses in dressmaking or handicrafts, but lately she had lost interest. Now, though often vaguely frustrated and restless, she idled away the daylight hours when she was alone in the house. For the past several years, particularly during the late spring when the trees were beginning to bud, she would fall into an almost feverish melancholy that would continue until the end of the rainy season in June. She desperately wanted to rid herself of this depression and irritability but at the same time felt slightly intoxicated by the need to maintain a stoic endurance. She also found some bleak consolation in the realization that without some such stimulation she might as well not be living at all.

And now this sudden phone call from Tokyo—not, as usual, from her aunt, but from Shiro—had come to jolt her out of her lethargy. Whether or not Shiro was aware of it, when he told her that the two of them would be coming from Tokyo, she had heard a note of portent in his voice. And there were still two months left before the Bon holidays, the time of their usual annual visit. Mitsue was on her guard; something was not right. Shiro had begun by telling her that Obasan was ill, but then he hastily added that she did not want visitors, and asked that Mitsue not tell anyone.

"Anyone—not even Kohei and Kazumi?" asked Mitsue, flustered.

"Well . . . I don't suppose you can keep it from them, but that's the way she wants it. If possible, only you . . ." The words came haltingly, and Shiro spoke as if to himself. Quietly he repeated,

"Only you, Mit-chan," then, returning to his normal tone, he gave her the day and time of their arrival and hung up.

Since he had been speaking in the Tokyo dialect and other voices could be heard in the background, Mitsue guessed that he had called from work. At the other end of the line stood Shiro in a business suit, the buildings of Tokyo's financial district in a panorama behind him. What had he meant by calling his cousin from his busy office? Had it been so that his wife would not overhear? At this thought, suddenly his low, halting words, "only you," burned like a secret deep within her breast, their fragrance welled up in her, and her heart raced.

Her aunt rarely gave advance notice of her visits. Twice a month or so Mitsue would open the shutters in the wing to let the air in, occasionally going through with a broom to sweep down the worst of the cobwebs, but she never actually gave the place a proper cleaning. This time, though, she and her brother knew that Obasan was coming. Beginning early in the morning, Kohei had mowed the grass around the wing, and Mitsue had spent the whole day thoroughly scrubbing the house, from the tatami floors inside to the pillars on the veranda.

When Mitsue was a little girl the wing had seemed cramped and small compared to the main house, but now she found that cleaning it was a major task. Though called the wing, it was really a house in its own right. There were three tatami rooms, and a long passage led to a kitchen and a bath that had been added on to the old tea house. Two of the three rooms, the ten-mat room and the eight-mat room next to it, opened out onto a long open corridor facing south; this part of the house had always been known as the "new rooms." The third, a snug little six-mat room, was affectionately called the "dressing room." It was bordered on the north and west by an open veranda.

A rainfall two days earlier had brought out rich new vegetation all around the wing, but when she stood on this veranda, Mitsue was struck by an especially deep, vivid jade color.

Directly facing the veranda stood a phoenix tree, with its spread of fresh new leaves. Back when the main house was still standing, Obasan had found the seedling in a corner of the front garden and moved it to this spot. She called it her *wakagiri*, her sapling, and treated it with special care as it grew. Mitsue knew this, and when she looked at it she felt with deep clarity that it was waiting for her aunt's return.

When Kohei was five and Mitsue not yet one , they had lost their father to tuberculosis. He was a native of Tokyo, and the children had both been born in the city. After he died, there were no close relatives there who would help the widow with her small children, so she brought them back to Hokuriku, where she had grown up. Her younger brother was now the head of the family, but he, too, was suffering from tuberculosis and was bedridden. Nevertheless, the mother and her children were welcomed in this small town, whose people were used to the way of life of the extended family, and, as representatives of the old manorial clan, they were made to feel at home.

Before long, it turned out that the young widow had also been carrying the disease. Hers was an especially acute illness—a "galloping" case—and she soon followed her husband in death. The sick uncle arranged for the orphans to be officially adopted by a childless, distantly related elderly aunt, but they continued to be cared for at the main house together with their cousins Shiro and Haruko.

Shortly afterward the uncle also died. Although she had been too young to remember, Mitsue would later recall the story as she had heard it from others; it continually amazed her that the three of them should have died in such quick succession—even granted the contagious nature of the disease. And others had suffered worse. In the provinces facing the Japan Sea with their deep snows, and in this area in particular, it was not unusual to

hear of entire families that had been wiped out by tuberculosis in
the postwar years. All four children, their ages spaced neatly two
years apart, with Shiro the oldest, then Kohei, Haruko, and Mitsue, escaped the disease. For this they were undoubtedly in-
debted to Obasan, the only remaining adult, who had progressive
views on sanitation and nutrition.

But her aunt was not one of those people who reeks of disinfectant and antiseptic, Mitsue mumbled absently to herself. Her
hand stopped its scrubbing and she gazed out at the deserted
yard, spread out beneath the soft sunlight that shone through a
momentary break in the overcast, monsoon sky. It was hard to
believe that this land had once been occupied by the old mansion, with its rows of dark, deserted rooms.

The roofed front gate, called the "storage gate" because of the
sheds that made up its two sides, was still standing. Three other
sheds also remained, but all the rest—the main entrance with its
broad wooden platform and the earthen flooring that spread out
beside it, the four tatami rooms arranged in a square with sliding
doors that could be removed to create one spacious hall, the Buddhist altar room with the intimidating gloom of its altar made of
black lacquer and gold, the miso storage room with its rows of
earthen pots, and all the rooms stretching out beyond—all this
had utterly vanished.

The death of Mitsue's uncle had left his wife with the responsibility of singlehandedly caring for not only their own children
but also his niece and nephew. Obasan's training in Tokyo at an
Ueno music school was a rare asset in this remote region, and she
soon found work teaching at the local high school. Though the
cleaning alone, even if kept to a minimum, took up an enormous
amount of time, she managed to maintain the main house until
Shiro graduated from the university in Tokyo, perhaps because
she had thought he might want to settle here someday.

Soon after Kohei graduated from the agricultural high school and started working at the local Agricultural Cooperative, Obasan arranged his marriage to a local girl who was distantly related to her. She set them up in a house of their own, and Mitsue went to live with them. Then, when Shiro got a job in Tokyo and his sister, Haruko, entered a college there, Obasan waited no longer; the house, after being sold to a temple in the area, was dismantled and rebuilt on the temple grounds. Mitsue didn't know to what extent Shiro, the heir, had been consulted, but she felt a secret despair when she heard her serene cousin Haruko's simple assent to the sale: "Whatever you do, Mother, is fine with me." The temple had wanted to buy the tea house as well, but Obasan would not part with it. Instead, she remodeled it, adding a back entrance, and had a new bathhouse built.

"It doesn't have to be anything special; after all . . . ," said Obasan, but the carpenter, an old man who had been doing work for the family for generations, took it on himself to use the finest quality cypress, so that the fresh fragrance of the wood, mixing with the steam, would soak deep into the skin.

This was to be the carpenter's last project. Mitsue had heard her aunt encouraging the old man: "Your skills are wasted on a mere bathhouse; I should have you add on an entrance hall as well. . . ." But the carpenter had not answered. Obasan left it at that, and a front hall never was built for the wing. The only ways to get in were through the back door or directly over the veranda.

For the next ten years or so Obasan had lived alone in the wing, but then she retired from the high school and began spending most of her time in Tokyo with Shiro or Haruko and their families. She now returned only once or twice a year. Even the specially built bathhouse gradually fell into decay as the months of disuse turned into years. The leaves of the persimmon trees outside were reflected in the frosted glass of the high windows; thin, careless rays of the sun became specks of green shining on the cedar walls. Mitsue, scrub brush in hand, stood still in the weak light and lingered there, feeling the gloom again after all these years. Black mold appeared in random spots on the surface of the cypress, and trails left by slugs gleamed eerily. The wood had long ago lost its fragrance. It wasn't Mitsue's fault, but somehow she was overcome by an irrevocable sense of failure.

She returned to the ten-mat room and, on a sudden impulse, pulled the tassel of the altar door. When the main house was torn down, the altar had been salvaged and moved here. In this well-lit room, it seemed to have lost its former majesty. Mitsue intended to set out some matches so that Obasan could light incense for her husband's mortuary tablet, but was startled to find the altar nearly empty: There were only a few vases and a censer giving off a somber glow. The tablets that had been crowded inside were gone. Mitsue was puzzled, then remembered that they had been entrusted to the temple. It was as though the family spirits, imprisoned in the wing, had fled its bright cheerfulness, longing for the quiet gloom of the old altar room.

When death at last quit the house, after taking first Mitsue's grandparents and then her mother and uncle in such rapid succession, the number of visitors moving through its halls also noticeably declined. Wherever the child Mitsue went in the house, she would open the sliding doors between the rooms only to be greeted by the same damp caress of confined air on her small face. On occasion, though, when she would turn her back on the open doorway of a dark room, two hands would suddenly descend from behind to cover her eyes. What happiness! It was always Shiro, of course, home for a school holiday. When school was in session he stayed with relatives in his mother's home town in the neighboring prefecture, attending the middle and high schools that were affiliated with the university there. Mitsue, though generally unsociable, would nevertheless respond to his attention, and he spent more time with her than with the sullen Kohei or the indifferent Haruko. She would twist her small body and free

herself; flustered and bashful with delight, she would circle behind him and jump up onto his broad back. At such times she
completely forgot about her scar. . . .

The phone rang. Mitsue started up from the sofa. She ran to
the telephone in the corner of the kitchen. She swallowed once,
then answered curtly; her voice always sounded sullen when she
was nervous.

"Mit-chan?" It was Shiro.

Something snapped open in her chest. It was as though some
giant hand had plucked the tension and irritability that had built
up from all the waiting and covered them—covered them, leaving
behind a sense of relief and openness. Hearing the broad sounds
of the local dialect, Mitsue got the strange impression that she
was the one who had dialed, and that Shiro had answered.

"We've just gotten home." It was his unmistakable calm,
deliberate way of speaking.

"Obasan?"

"Grandma's with me, of course."

He called her "Grandma," not "Mother," so Mitsue wondered
if he had brought along his wife or children. She waited an instant, then asked, "Did Rika come too?"

"No, she couldn't come. The children are still in school."

"Oh, that's right." Mitsue felt the tension leave her voice.

When she began to ask about her aunt's condition, Shiro interrupted and thanked her for opening the shutters. She had to suppress the urge to remind him that she had also cleaned the house.

"Well, then, if it's no trouble, could you come over now?"
Though there was no urgency in his words, his voice seemed to
betray a note of impatience.

"Of course, I was intending to." She was about to tell him that
she had cooled some beers and barley tea for them and had
started breakfast but remembered that she was going to see him
in a few minutes.

"Mitsue?" His voice became suddenly quiet. Pressing her ear to the receiver, she strained to catch all the contours of his voice. "I'll be at the zelkova tree behind the house—could you come around the back way?" He spoke almost in a whisper. There was nothing unusual in this request; she always came to the wing the back way, but nevertheless her heart suddenly throbbed intensely.

"How are Kohei and Kazumi?" His voice returned to its normal level, and he asked about the whole family, one by one.

"It will be a lot of trouble, especially for you, Mit-chan. . . . It's a real shame."

She did not answer. His voice had lowered again at the words "it's a real shame," and they echoed deep in her ears. His tone was different now from when he had told her to come by the back way. This time he did not seem to be concealing something from his mother as much as lowering his voice to address something in himself.

She hung up and, picking up the crumpled apron again, put on her sandals and left the house.

Until about ten years ago there had been only a narrow, one-lane dirt road running through the fields from the bus stop on the prefectural highway to the front gate of the estate, but recently the road had been widened and paved. Small houses had cropped up along either side and the traffic had increased. Even if Shiro had not asked, Mitsue would not have wanted to come by the front way.

Mitsue looked over the golden waves of winter wheat ready for harvest and saw Shiro, leaning against the zelkova tree. Lost in thought, his head bowed, he was not looking in Mitsue's direction. Shiro was of average height and build and wore an ordinary beige open-collared shirt and dark brown pants—an absolutely typical middleaged company man. But it suddenly seemed to Mitsue that the Shiro she had been seeing every year at the Bon festival for some fifteen years now was a counterfeit, that the real Shiro had been hidden all this time and had just now slid open the door of one of the dark rooms and emerged from inside the old house.

What could he be thinking about so deeply?

She reached out to a clump of bamboo grass at her side and passed her hand through it tentatively. It gave off a gentle, dry rustling sound.

Shiro lifted his eyes slowly and smiled, recognizing his cousin. It was a gentle smile, but it passed over his face like a puff of wind over an empty sky, without feeling.

The pain in the pit of her stomach returned, this time raw, as though an actual wound had opened there. She felt a sudden urge to cover her face and turn her back, to retreat and run away somewhere under the gray, overcast sky. Closed up in the house, secluded from the outside world, she had recently come to accept her scar with indifference and with the kind of awakened understanding that comes after the age of thirty. But now this serenity had crumbled instantly.

It was not really such a disfigurement: A glossy mark extended from the forehead to the cheek on the left side of her face. She could conceal it under her hair, or, if she cared to, she could camouflage it with a thick layer of makeup. But the burn had also left her eyelid with a twitch, which Mitsue felt was a mortal wound to her appearance. Responding to changes in her facial expression, the lower eyelid would turn down, showing a thin line of red, as if it had been flipped outward. The deformation was very slight, but it was especially stark because there were no eyelashes, and as a result the white of the eye was abnormally highlighted. It had an unsettling effect on people. When Mitsue was in elementary school, some of the children had nicknamed her "Red Eye" and teased her cruelly.

This time the defect had served to her advantage; it had

prevented her sudden agitation from showing in her expression. Shiro drew nearer, as if nothing was wrong. She forced herself to stand her ground. He came so close that the front of his shirt became a wall in front of her, then he cleared his throat and averted his eyes slightly.

Even villagers who had known Mitsue her whole life would usually look aside after first greeting her. Mitsue herself made a point of not meeting other people's eyes; she felt much less awkward that way, but her aunt, Shiro, and Haruko always faced her directly when they talked to her. When Shiro looked away now, it seemed to Mitsue that, oddly enough, it was from a kind of reluctance to face himself, rather than any avoidance of the scar.

Shiro's expression was strained. "Mitsue," he began, skipping the usual greetings, then hesitated. "You remember I told you about the illness." Shiro seemed to be in good health, but he spoke so strangely that Mitsue had to ask to make sure it was Obasan he was referring to, and not himself. He nodded, then cast a quick glance over the field.

"We might be seen if we talk here," he said, then beckoned to her and moved away from the back of the house toward the part of the yard that was hidden behind the earthen wall.

The backyard had been exposed to much more sunlight since the dismantling of the main house, and it had gone a long time without the care of a gardener. The trees had changed completely, and the entire garden was now so overgrown it seemed more like a small grove. Shiro led Mitsue to a place under the trees that reminded her of the musty shade of the years when the house had blocked the sun. Evergreen yatsude shrubs spread out their thick, hard leaves.

Shiro's behavior was unprecedented, and Mitsue was overcome by a strange, trapped feeling, an uneasiness, as if she were pinned down, body and soul. She stared directly at him, emboldened by the semidarkness under the trees.

"What we've been saying is that she's sick," he began, looking down at the dark ground. Then, raising his eyes, he met Mitsue's gaze. Speaking with sudden force, he added, "But the truth is, it's cancer."

Mitsue drew in her breath soundlessly. In an instant, something between despair and resignation flooded her chest. What could she have been expecting from him for the past four days? His hesitant "only you," his whisper this morning asking her to meet him behind the house, and finally, now, his strained expression and urgency, almost seizing her hand to draw her into the shade where no one could see . . . All of it had been only to tell her this. It was that one word that had trapped him and had been striving to snag Mitsue, too—only that.

The blossoming that had begun in her chest faded away, and the void it left was slowly filled with the meaning of the word "cancer." She lifted her eyes slowly.

"What kind of cancer?"

Shiro told her it was in the breast. "She's had it for the past ten years," he added.

Obasan had quit teaching eight or nine years ago. Though it was early for retirement, she told everyone that she wanted to help Shiro and Haruko with the care of their young children. This would mean that she had had breast cancer even before she had retired. Under ordinary circumstances she would have had an operation years ago, but Mitsue had never heard anything about her aunt having a mastectomy or even going to the hospital. She now recalled that Obasan had not come back for Bon last year; instead she had gone to America to stay with Haruko, whose husband had been transferred there three or four years ago, and who was expecting her third child. She couldn't have been very ill then.

"She told me straight out herself, that she's had it for ten years." Shiro lowered his eyes and added, "She also told me to tell absolutely no one, so even Rika doesn't know."

"What do the doctors say? I understand that doctors often don't give a clear diagnosis to the patient. . . ."

Shiro raised his head and looked directly at her. "She has not been to see a doctor at all." He clipped the words, pronouncing each one separately.

"What?" Mitsue was puzzled. She stared at him, unblinking.

"She says she doesn't want to get involved with doctors, and I understand and respect her feelings."

He turned slightly and added, "I hope you will understand too. Rika would not, nor would anyone else. But you . . ." He looked straight at her and stopped talking.

The shade of the trees in the back garden began throbbing like a living organism. She had never before faced Shiro as an equal and looked into his eyes this way. Her body ached with the tension, and from inside her rose the words, "I understand."

Not to consult a doctor or undergo treatment; to face death directly and go forward to meet it—if she herself were ill, this is what she would want to do. Still the commonsense question, contradicting this feeling, came to her lips: "But why?"

"It's not something I can explain." The expression on his face told her nothing.

"You knew about it before?" She asked with a serious expression; she wanted to be sure. Then she wondered why she had so emphasized such a trivial question.

"She told me herself. Her side got cramped and she got so she couldn't play the piano. She said she had breast cancer on the right side."

"But they say that if you discover it early breast cancer is the easiest to cure."

Then Mitsue caught herself. Could it be? Was it possible that a woman past middle age, already a grandmother, could still feel such reluctance to lose a breast that she would exchange her life for it?

Shiro was sensitive to her thought and caught the question, though she hadn't said it aloud. He spoke emphatically.

"It's not being disfigured that disturbs her. It's completely different." His eyes probed the yatsude leaves, searching for words. "She wants to leave it up to nature, not to go against the natural way. If I had to put it into words, that would be the general idea."

Although Mitsue felt that she understood and that there was no need to "put it into words," she cut in.

"It must be that she doesn't want to go through an operation, cobalt treatments, and all the side effects of the drugs."

"It's not that she's not thinking about those things, too. And I can't say for sure whether there's more to it than that; I can't speak for her." He became pensive again. "Anyway, as far as I'm concerned, it's a simple matter of respecting her wishes. I'm convinced that she's not just childishly stuck on something she doesn't understand. . . . I don't know what to say. I think it's just that she doesn't want to get lost in making decisions about dying."

The deep insight of Shiro's words soon calmed the throbbing of the shadows. Or rather, as he spoke, a deep silence rose out of the damp earth and stretched through the air to the branches above.

Carefully, so as not to disturb the calm, Mitsue asked, "What is her condition now?"

"Not good." Shiro's thick eyebrows drew together sharply. "It's impossible to say, since she hasn't been to a doctor, but it may have begun as a benign tumor that remained unchanged for ten years, then suddenly became malignant two or three months ago. It really was unwise to bring her all the way out here, but she was very anxious to come."

Anxious to come. It's true, Obasan, and I've been waiting here like this since I was a child.

The unexpected words rose to Mitsue's lips, startling her, but, unspoken, they disappeared noiselessly into the shadow of the yatsude bushes.

When Mitsue was very small, and even after she entered school, she would always wait impatiently for her aunt's return from work. Until she reached the third or fourth grade, she used to come directly home as soon as school was over, and without even starting her homework, she would begin waiting. Though she did not realize it at the time, that's exactly what she was doing—waiting.

Inside the storage gate and the earthen wall stretched a spacious garden, with a wooden inner fence cutting across it lengthwise. Mitsue had taken as her landmark a small knothole in the darkened wood. She had a special spot that she located by counting precisely ten steps from the knothole. Crouching down on her heels there, she would curl up into a tight ball. Bending her head down sharply until it seemed her neck would break, she would press her cheek against her kneecaps and gaze intently at the movement of the sun's rays along the ground.

Had the child Mitsue been aware that her special spot changed with the lengthening of her stride over the years, or that the sun's rays themselves moved in different patterns with the changing of the seasons? Mitsue tried to identify the season and year of the particular day whose sun's rays now appeared in her memory. There was no snow, so at least it was clearly not winter.

Toward evening the rays began slanting and the shadow of the roofed gate lengthened and stretched over the garden. Though the gate itself was one solid, squarish bulk, the sun shining on it diagonally created a shadow that was strangely elongated, like a spire. This shadow advanced slowly, inch by inch, toward Mitsue's feet as she crouched, watching. The ground in front of her gradually turned to shadow, and her little curled-up body stiffened in anticipation as the space in front of her toes narrowed and was invaded. When she was completely covered in the shade, she changed her angle and watched intently as the gate's shadow crawled onward toward the inner fence.

On the other side of the fence at that time had stood a cedar tree that was hundreds of years old. Later the tree was cut down and its wood sold, and old Genji had accused Obasan of killing a holy tree. There was no shrine there to make the tree holy, and Obasan had dismissed the accusation with a laugh.

When the shadow reached the trunk of the old tree, Mitsue pictured in her mind her own small shadow, enfolded in the gate's large one, reaching higher and higher up to the very top of the tree's branches.

There was a bamboo grove beyond the inner fence at the opposite side of the garden, and a rice storehouse stood at one edge of it. The shadow of this storehouse, like that of the gate, took on a strange shape, and Mitsue watched as it, too, reached out toward the house. She imagined that the two shadows were in a race to see which would reach the goal first.

Eventually Mitsue heard the creaking of a bicycle, and her cousin Haruko arrived home from school. She greeted Mitsue but continued pedalling on past up to the house. It was some twenty minutes by bike to the T– town elementary school. When winter came with its deep snows, Haruko couldn't take her bike, and would go by bus instead, her bus pass in its little red folder hanging from a corner of her school bag. When she got back from school she would do her homework, then spend some time practicing the piano—Obasan gave her daughter a lesson every Sunday. Haruko had spent her first years in the same neighborhood elementary school as Mitsue but transferred to the city school when she reached the fifth grade. Mitsue had assumed she would also have to transfer after the fourth grade; she had dreaded the thought of having to face unfamiliar teachers and students and endure their stares at her scar. But it turned out that she didn't have to transfer after all. Then there were the piano lessons, when her aunt's usually kindly face became stern and she would rap Haruko's knuckles sharply. Mitsue dreaded the prospect of piano lessons, but here again she was spared.

Her brother's situation was similar. Shiro had gone from middle school to the prefectural university high school, but when Kohei finished middle school he went on to the agricultural high school. He disliked academic subjects like English and math but showed great enthusiasm for learning about crops and cultivation techniques. In his eagerness he was different from his sister, who was utterly passive.

The shadow of the gate, engulfing Mitsue's own small one, joined with the shadows of the inner fence and the cedar tree, and together they all melted into the evening haze. Mitsue, choosing the right moment, thought "NOW" and drew in a deep breath, as if to drink in the whole dusk and enclose it in her breast. Why she did this, and how she chose that particular moment, she couldn't tell.

At the moment when a thin sliver of light still floated above the bamboo grove but the roots of the cedar where she crouched were already in darkness, Mitsue would strain her ears, and from beyond the faded sky and the evening mist would come the clicking of high heels, and her aunt was home.

She was beautiful.

Every time she saw her aunt coming through the wooden side door of the storage gate, Mitsue was lost in admiration. Before Obasan noticed the small, crouching black figure, Mitsue drew back quickly and leaned over, pretending to be drawing something in the dirt. When the footsteps drew near, she looked up and gazed at the white ankles moving briskly under the nylon stockings. Sometimes her aunt wore a flared skirt, its hem swinging against her slender calves, and sometimes she wore a tight school-teacher skirt that cut a straight line across the back of her knees.

"Mitsue, I'm back," she said, her voice, vibrant and tempered from singing, descending from above Mitsue's head. "Is Haruko home?" Even as the words came, the white ankles continued on past. Mitsue raised her head and mumbled, "She's home," but of course her voice didn't reach her aunt, whose back was receding toward the house.

Even with her back turned, Obasan gave an impression of simple elegance. Seamless stockings had not yet come into fashion, but the seam, as always, stretched reassuringly in a neat straight line down the back of her legs. In those days it was unusual to see a woman over thirty in this remote region with a shoulder bag, but Obasan had a small bag hanging from her left shoulder on a short strap, while in her right hand she carried a thin music portfolio, or sometimes a violin case.

Photographs of Mitsue's mother showed a plump, kimono-clad woman who reflected none of the brilliance you would expect to find in the daughter of an old landowning family, and Mitsue felt no affinity to her. She often imagined how radiantly proud she would have been to be Obasan's real daughter, and it never occurred to her to feel guilty toward the mother who had given her life.

From her vantage point Mitsue could see into the house as, just when the clicking of the high heels stopped in the entrance, the hall light went on and Haruko came out to greet her mother. Haruko was a rather independent child, and from the time she was very small Mitsue could hardly remember ever seeing Obasan embrace or caress her daughter. For her part, Obasan showed no special partiality toward Haruko, while at the same time avoiding any forced favoritism toward Mitsue or any discrimination in her affections toward the children. Thus Mitsue would feel an excessive anger when the old ladies of the village, who considered Obasan a little too "chic" for the widow of a distinguished family, comforted her behind her aunt's back for being a poor orphan.

When she got home from work, Obasan would prepare supper. Looking back, Mitsue realized how much work it must have been for her, but Obasan had never made Mitsue or Haruko help.

A light shone through the kitchen window, and there came the sound of running water. Obasan often sang while she was cooking—songs like "In the South Country" and "Caro mio ben'" that she must have been teaching in the high school. When Mitsue heard her aunt singing, she would get up lazily and start for the house, without waiting for her brother to trudge home, carrying his scythe or plow back to the storehouse. Kohei enjoyed farming and had a feeling for it, and he had worked in the fields from the time he was in middle school.

On Obasan's days off she would sit at the piano and patiently do voice drills, then practice the Japanese folk songs that were printed with piano accompaniment in the school textbooks. Her voice was a clear soprano well-suited to Italian arias, and it had seemed funny to Mitsue to hear her singing traditional Japanese songs like "Aizu Bandai Mountain" in the operatic style, interrupting herself in the middle to exclaim "No good!" when something sounded wrong.

A kind of frenzy seized Mitsue, and she broke the silence. "There's no point in that kind of worrying now. I'd just like to see her face." Really, the only important thing now was that Obasan was facing her death.

Suddenly she felt afraid. If, as Shiro said, she did have terminal cancer, then might she not have already become a painridden, clay-colored apparition? I don't want to see her like that, Mitsue thought, and an acute, instinctive urge to run away flowed through her.

They went in the back door, and Mitsue asked with her eyes only, Where is she? Shiro whispered that she was in the dressing room. Muffling the sound of her footsteps, Mitsue went down the hall to the sliding door and knelt to open it. She looked up once at Shiro, but, without returning her glance, he said in his deep voice, "Mit-chan is here."

She slid open the door without waiting for an answer. Obasan was sitting right on the tatami floor, without even a cushion under her, facing the door. She had changed, had become terribly thin, and her eyes seemed much larger now, but the smile that she gave when she saw Mitsue was the same as when she had come back two summers ago. Her face was pale but certainly not "clay-colored." The tension left Mitsue's shoulders.

On the contrary, Obasan looked lovely in her silk gauze yukata, with its pattern of tiny lavender flowers spreading their long stamens over the deep purple of the cloth. Like a dim memory, words from something she must have read, "crystal pure she was," rose in Mitsue's mind. Obasan's collar was slack and her obi was fastened low, as is common with invalids, but she did not give an impression of sloppiness or carelessness. Although she had long preferred western-style clothing, she had always looked beautiful in traditional Japanese dress as well. Even now she still looked younger than her age—not at all like the grandmother she was.

"Mit-chan, thank you for cleaning up. The cobwebs must have been awful." Her voice was clear, but its tone had weakened noticeably.

"You must be worn out from the trip." Mitsue bowed her head formally, then, looking at Shiro, she added, "The night train takes more time than the daytime ones, doesn't it?"

"On the night train you meet fewer people," said Shiro, then added jokingly, "so we made a point of coming like thieves in the night, but when we got to T– Station—the only place we could have been recognized anyway—it was already broad daylight."

"Even inside the taxi I sat sideways just to be sure no one would recognize me through the window."

"If someone like Genji saw us we'd be in trouble."

"He'd say the reason I'm ill is that I cut down the Guardian Cedar and sold it—that it's a curse."

Like a young girl, she poked the tip of her tongue out between her teeth, then looked back out over the veranda. "But the phoenix tree is healthy—look how thick the foliage has grown."

It was at the same time she had had the cedar cut down that Obasan had found the sapling and transplanted it here, outside the dressing room veranda. Now she herself had grown so thin you could almost see through to the bones, and she gave the impression of some kind of ethereal tree nymph rather than a human being; she could have just now materialized from inside the phoenix tree. Of course Mitsue said nothing of her thoughts.

"How are Ko-chan and Kazumi and the children?"

"They're fine. They'll be over to see you later. . . ." Mitsue hesitated, confused. Kohei had been raised by Obasan since he was five, but now that he was a grown-up with a household of his own, maybe he too was one of the "villagers" his aunt wanted to avoid.

Shiro rescued her: "I've told Mitsue that you don't want to see anyone."

Obasan gave a simple nod in assent, adding, "That's right."

A slight wind rose and rustled the leaves of the tree, and the sky darkened. With the puff of wind came a strong odor. Mitsue had noticed the bad smell earlier, riding faintly on the morning breeze, and now with a shock she realized what it was. The breast of Obasan's kimono bulged out unnaturally on the right side, as if it had been packed with some padding material. The thought floated up in Mitsue's mind that the tumor must have broken open and the resulting wound covered with gauze or some kind of bandage. The bad smell must be a mixture of pus and blood seeping out. . . . She imagined it as some foul sort of broth. At the same time, for someone whose condition had deteriorated that far, Obasan did not seem to be in terrible pain.

"Mother," began Shiro, with renewed energy, "You've worked hard for many years. Mit-chan also understands that you need a good rest. So while you're here I want you to relax completely and let her take care of you; if you need anything at all, just ask her."

As he spoke, Mitsue felt something opening again inside her. Of course; there was no one better suited for this role. It didn't matter whether the disease really was cancer or whether she could actually be of any use; she would stand by this woman who had decided to die. If she couldn't do this much, could there have been any meaning in the little girl who had drawn in the twilight and enclosed it deep within her breast?

Obasan looked at Mitsue with a serious expression in her eyes, but her thoughts were elsewhere, and she did not seem particularly affected by Shiro's emotional words. She answered absently, in Tokyo dialect, "I'm so lucky to have Mitsue to take care of me."

Mitsue was just about to ask about breakfast when Obasan suddenly winced and, relaxing her posture, drew in a strained breath. "I'm worn out."

"Bring a futon," said Shiro hurriedly, then, "I'll get it." He stood up but hesitated, confused; he didn't know where to look. Mitsue hastily started toward the closet of the dressing room, and he followed her.

It was just a lightweight summer futon, but Shiro tried to help her. Still standing, he took the sheet by one end and shook it vigorously, trying to get it to spread out flat. Mitsue couldn't repress a giggle, though she felt guilty laughing in the sickroom. She couldn't have said why, but she felt a kind of pure happiness. She tried to suppress the flush in her cheeks and, kneeling down, she took the other end of the white twill sheet, folded it back, and spread it over the futon.

Obasan's breath was labored. She watched vacantly as her son and niece worked. "You'll need to get some kind of plastic cloth to put under my back; even a bag from the cleaner's would do," she said. Without thinking Mitsue glanced at Shiro's face, but his expression hardened slightly.

"There must be some vinyl cloth," she mumbled, then stood up. "I'll go to the house and get some."

Obasan interrupted her. "There ought to be something in the tool shed; there was two years ago."

Mitsue stopped Shiro, who had already begun to go out, and left the room herself, half running. Why should she need a plastic cloth under her shoulder? She must have blood or something oozing from her breast that could soak through the sheets and soil the futon. Mitsue's face stiffened at this ominous thought.

It was the first time she'd gone into the tool shed since childhood. The outer door hung open, its latch broken, but the bolt on the inside door was rusted, and it resisted when she tried to open it. As she rattled and tugged at the door, Mitsue remembered a time long ago when she had been locked inside. She had gotten into some mischief, and suddenly old Genji, grimacing horribly, had come chasing after her. (Why Genji had been called "old" even then, Mitsue, looking back, couldn't tell.) She and Haruko had been running from him together, but, as bad luck would have it, only Mitsue was caught. Old Genji had picked her up and pinned her under his arm, carried her to the shed, and locked her in.

Inside the dark building old folding screens cast their huge black shadows, and short-legged trays stood in tall piles where someone had stacked them up without putting them away in boxes. Then there were paulownia wood boxes of all sizes, labelled with ink in illegible handwriting, their contents a mystery, bound with braid and leaning one against the other for support.

Mitsue had felt it her duty to flee, sobbing, until she was caught. For one thing, that was what Haruko had done; also, Mitsue had thought that it would somehow be inappropriate for a child not to cry for help, that someone, or maybe even all of the adults, would scold her if she didn't. But now, trapped irrevocably within these walls, she no longer felt the need to struggle or call out; obviously it would do no good anyway. With a calm, almost adult, resignation, she stopped crying and crawled into one of the spaces between the paulownia boxes.

She wondered what it would be like to just stay there for days on end, years, decades—for eternity. Though she didn't know that word, her small body was overcome with the consciousness of it; she had the urge to crouch without moving, hidden inside forever and ever, and wait for something to come to an end.

The awkwardness in the behavior and language of small children gives the impression that they are unable to understand any but the most simple emotions, but when Mitsue looked back at her own childhood she realized that this was not true. Although at the age of three or four she couldn't have put it into words, she had understood the true nature of life and death then at least as deeply as she did now.

Mitsue finally managed to push the thick, heavy inner door open just enough for her to be able to squeeze through. When she looked around the inside of the shed in the dim daylight that came through the glass of the high windows, she felt a sharp pang in her chest. There was practically nothing left of the assorted boxes that had been piled up high enough to bury the child Mitsue, and the household items that had been left here without boxes were gone as well. It was natural that the rice storehouse should be empty, but Mitsue had not imagined that the toolshed could have become this huge, gloomy, empty cavern.

She didn't have to look for what she needed; her eyes fell on a pile of large plastic sheets that had probably been used to wrap up the things that had not had boxes. She gathered them up in her arms and ran back to the house. She had taken a long time.

She was out of breath when she reached the veranda of the new rooms. Muffling the sound of her footsteps, she proceeded to the dressing room and peered in. Shiro had his back to her. He was sitting crosslegged with his arms folded. His head was bowed. The sheets had been left half-spread and there was no sign of Obasan. The pure whiteness of the sheet, folded sideways, reflected like an ill omen in her eyes.

His broad back, a shadow between her and the light, looked terribly sad, and Mitsue couldn't move. From the way he was facing the phoenix tree with his head bowed, it looked as though he were praying.

Shiro twisted his thick neck and partially turned toward her, but his eyes avoided hers. "Did you find it?"

She nodded and stepped into the room, then suddenly blushed. She remembered how happy, even playful, she had felt when she and Shiro had spread the starched sheet for Obasan; it spoiled the feeling to cover the mattress with the old, stiffened vinyl. To make matters worse, the plastic was a depressing dark purple color. She decided to buy a soft, transparent one later, and hurriedly covered the vinyl with the sheet. This time Shiro didn't help.

With an effort to make her voice sound indifferent, she asked, "Where's Obasan?"

"In the bath."

"But there's no hot water ready," she said, flustered, and started for the hall. Without turning, Shiro stopped her with his voice alone. "She has something she does in the bath twice a day, in the morning and evening, and she doesn't let anyone in. So it's best to leave her alone."

What had it been like for Obasan to live in Shiro's suburban house with his high-strung wife Rika and citified children? Mitsue glanced again at his back and knelt in the hall. She pictured Obasan's emaciated body in the bath, the exposed breast with its strange swelling. . . . Did Shiro have any idea of what she did in there? The flesh was split open like a pomegranate, the meat exposed. . . .

"I imagine you find it hard to understand why she won't see a doctor even in her condition."

"But what about Rika? What does she say?"

"The children are still young. She was so busy with them that she didn't notice anything for a long time, but then recently she commented that Mother was acting strange. You know that Rika, being from Tokyo, likes to have everything just so; if she knew the truth, she'd get her to a doctor, even if she had to trick her into it." Shiro hesitated a moment, then added, "All that aside, I imagine Mother would rather be at her own place in the country than at her son's house."

He turned and sat facing Mitsue. "She said that she would spend just a couple of weeks here and then go back to Tokyo, but in reality she wants to stay here. And I agree that at least while it's so hot, this is a better place for her. I told her that as long as she was not going to see a doctor, she should go somewhere cool, like a mountain resort, but she insisted on coming here—and I understand that. But if that's the way it's going to be, I mean, even if it's not her intent, she's going to need your help . . . and she's getting it already."

"Well, of course. She's the one who raised me."

Suddenly Shiro placed both palms before him on the tatami and bowed his head low to the floor. "I'm sorry, Mitsue; I beg you. Even out here in the country, if she went to a doctor, he'd put her in a hospital immediately. And once she was in a hospital, they'd try to keep her going forever, like some kind of machine."

Then he lifted his face, and in a low voice, almost to himself, said, "In my heart this is how I want her to die, in a natural way." He looked deeply into her eyes with an expression she had never seen before on his face: desperate, intense, and gentle. Mitsue was overcome by a wave of suffering and pleasure; her body stiffened, and she could only nod in reply.

Obasan, her diseased body worn out from the overnight trip, came back from the bath in a terrycloth nightgown. She drank a cup of barley tea, then, without a word, as if even speaking was too much of an effort, she lay down on the futon.

Her weakened condition was especially noticeable as she lay there on her back. Her closed eyelids had lost their resilience, and the eye sockets were caved in and exposed in circles that you could trace with a fingertip. In contrast to the sunken cheeks, her mouth was more prominent now, and Mitsue noticed again the facial structure that she had always thought so beautiful. In reality, her aunt's face was anything but beautiful: Her eyes were small, her mouth too big, and her nose set too low in the face. Nevertheless, just this morning that face had seemed so lovely, even radiant; how could that be? Mitsue, forgetting even Shiro's presence in the room, gazed intently at her aunt's face.

Shiro leaned over toward his mother and asked in a low voice, "Aren't you hot?"

"Oh . . . I'll go turn on the fan. . . ." Mitsue started up, but Obasan, with her eyes still closed, said, "I don't want an electric fan; later you can leave a paper fan for me." Then she raised one hand and moved it as if to dismiss them. "That's all. . . ."

Mitsue raised her eyes. Shiro, his expression unchanged, nodded and got up. He withdrew toward the smaller "new room" but stopped in the open corridor and stood there with his hand on his hip, shaking his head from side to side. Mitsue took a beer out of the refrigerator, put it on a tray with a glass, and brought it to him.

"Would you like some breakfast? You should at least have some toast and coffee. . . ."

"No, this is fine, just what I need."

As he poured his beer, Shiro gestured with his chin toward the overnight bag that he had put in one corner. "There are some things in the bag that she'll need while she's staying here." Then his brow relaxed, and he continued, "Mit-chan, even though the trip may have been difficult for her, I'm glad I could bring her back here. It looks as though she's really at peace. We should have come earlier." He tilted his head back and finished the beer.

"Why don't you stay awhile too?" She took a floor cushion from the closet, folded it over and slapped it, then pushed it up next to him. "Shall I heat up the bath for you?"

"No, I'll wait. I'm sorry, Mit-chan. Forgive me." Even as he said it, Shiro took his socks off and pushed them out of the way, then stretched out on the tatami floor. "We're really busy at the office these days. The day before yesterday we had a meeting from five to ten in the evening. The whole economy is changing so fast; no matter how much we discuss things, we can't get anything settled. And it's even worse at the division and section levels—just ridiculous." He spoke with his eyes closed. This had nothing to do with Mitsue. Then he laid his arm, bare below the short sleeve, across his forehead. Mitsue hadn't realized how muscular his arm was. His complexion was paler than Kohei's, but it seemed strange that he should be as sturdy as her brother.

Mitsue felt that it was wrong to sit here and watch him like this, but she could not bring herself to leave. It was awkward and unnatural to remain silent, but she didn't want to interrupt the feeling of liberation and peace that enveloped Shiro; she couldn't find the proper words. Unexpectedly she thought of her cousin Haruko, two years her senior. How would Haruko act toward her brother at a time like this?

As she stared half-consciously at Shiro's arm, she suddenly stirred; it felt almost as though Shiro was looking back at her from under the shadow of his arm. Her hand rose automatically to cover her left eye, but at the same time she noticed deep, regular breaths seeping out of the darkness beneath his arm. His lips were slightly parted, and he snored slightly with each breath.

Watching him intently, she noticed that the area on both sides of the brown belt that bound his waist was rising and falling in a steady rhythm with the inhaling and exhaling of his snores.

This is what's ridiculous, thought Mitsue with wry bitterness, and she stood up. Was Shiro the kind of person who could fall asleep, just like that, with someone watching? Did he think so little of Mitsue as a human being that it didn't matter that she was there? Or should she be glad that he felt at ease with her, just as he did with Rika or with Haruko? She'd like to ask him directly.

But then, when she had moved into the kitchen, she had a sudden doubt. Maybe Shiro had noticed her staring at him and had just pretended to be asleep . . . there was no way to know without asking him. Mitsue felt a darkness, as though a giant hand had descended and gently covered her eyes.

In an effort to seal inside the questions that kept welling up in her, Mitsue turned her thoughts to lunch. Meals at her brother's house, too, were her responsibility, but since she was alone there during the day, for lunch she usually just had leftovers. Now she had to figure out something to fix for her aunt and Shiro.

Until the year before last, Mitsue hadn't done any housework in the wing, even when Obasan was back from Tokyo. Obasan had lived there alone during the years after Haruko left for college, and even after she herself had moved to Tokyo, she was still considered the mistress of the house. So Mitsue had never thought of her as a guest who needed to be cared for. Now Mitsue was faced with this new, unexpected burden, but strangely enough, she began to see not this, but her usual work of preparing meals for her brother's family, as an unfair demand on her. Shouldn't her sister-in-law help with supper or with preparations for the next day's meals when she came home, the way people did in most cooperative households? From now on she would cook here and eat with Obasan and Shiro. When she made this decision, she suddenly felt estranged from her brother's family, though she had been living with them for some twenty years. Now she had rediscovered her home in the main household, her aunt's home, where she had been raised until she reached high school.

When Kohei married Kazumi, he and his sister received, as the inheritance of the branch family, some fields and a ramshackle house in a state of near collapse. The three of them were young, and felt no hardship in living in the old shack and sharing it with an army of field mice. But when the first baby was born, Obasan sold one of the fields, which had begun to appreciate in value, and had a new house built for them. Since then Kohei had put on some new additions, and now his house was much larger than Obasan's wing.

It was wrong to call it "Kohei's house"; naturally it was Mitsue's home, too. It wasn't that she didn't belong there, but she had always felt that if she could have returned to the main house she would have; that somehow the Mitsue who had wandered, searching for someone, through the dark rooms of the old house—the house that was no longer there—only that self was the true Mitsue.

Thinking over the menu for lunch and supper, she picked up an old shopping basket and went out the back way through the kitchen door. The thin morning light had clouded over, and the murky monsoon sky spread out over the field. As she came through the wooden side door of the storage gate onto the road that passed between the two rows of small houses, Mitsue noticed an old man coming toward her on unsteady legs. There could be no mistake—that small, bent, and feeble body could belong to none other than old Genji.

Oh, no, thought Mitsue and stopped short, thinking she could turn off the road, but it was too late. And of course she couldn't very well just run away the way she had as a child. There was also the possibility that he hadn't seen her coming out from the gate of the main house, and she could simply pretend that she had come along the fence from her brother's house. If so, she could get by with a simple greeting and go on as if everything were normal. In the meantime the shrivelled-up little face, dry as a raisin with its coarse wrinkles, advanced into her line of vision.

"What's the young master doing here? It's not time for the Bon festival yet." Genji skipped the usual greetings and got right to the point.

She would have bluffed and told him that Shiro wasn't here at all—that he must be seeing things—but realized that he'd probably gotten the information from someone who had seen Shiro and Obasan.

"You're as perceptive as ever; when did you see him?" Trying her best to answer him courteously, she strained to think of a way out. Genji's curiosity was aroused even more by Mitsue's unusual cordiality, and his beady eyes gleamed. He muttered an explanation.

"I was talking on the phone with my daughter, the one that got married and moved into town, and she mentioned that she had seen him this morning in a taxi."

Mitsue remembered her aunt laughing as she told of how she had sat sideways in the back seat of the taxi so as to avoid being seen. She decided to keep Obasan's presence a secret, at least for the time being, even at the risk of being found out.

She couldn't count the times when, looking out over the veranda as someone from the village came through the storage gate and headed for the front entrance, Obasan had said with a light sigh of resignation, "Here they come again." Even as a child Mitsue had felt sorry for her aunt, having to make tea and serve it all afternoon while the visitor went on and on about some endless petty property dispute.

"Shiro's here, but he came on the night train and is tired. He's sleeping now and doesn't want to be wakened." She assumed a condescending tone and clipped the words.

"I don't have any intention of waking him up," answered Genji. Mitsue thought that he was about to take offense at her haughty manner, but he adopted an uncharacteristically conciliatory attitude: "But what's he doing here this time of year?"

"It's a . . . some kind of business. I think he's going to try to sell something again."

Though it was obvious that Mitsue had simply said the first thing that had popped into her head, Genji's eyes gleamed even more, and he pressed on: "What's he selling?" Even if it were Obasan doing the selling, Genji surely knew that except for this house and land there was nothing left to sell; in fact, it was probably with a scheme to buy it himself that he had come in the first place. The instant Mitsue thought of this possibility, she recalled the hollow emptiness of the storehouse this morning.

"I don't know what he's selling. At any rate, an old family gone to ruin has got to get rid of everything, and actually it's a great relief to be free of property. But there are people claiming influence with the family who are a little too eager to act as middlemen and skim off all the gravy in the process." She had hoped that this lie about Shiro's intent would make Genji angry and drive him away, but then she hit on a still more promising scheme: "Shiro has a friend in the tax office who told him that they are going to have to investigate windfall investment profits in this area." This last part was true. But the man who mentioned it had also said that, though an investigation was needed, at the same time it was practically impossible to carry out. Furthermore, Mitsue had heard it not from Shiro but from Kazumi, who had gotten word of it somewhere else.

Nevertheless it worked perfectly. Genji's stingy, wrinkled lips clamped down at the corners and he lapsed into a disgruntled silence. At heart he was an honest man. When he was young, he had loyally served Mitsue's grandfather, the old "master." But the agricultural reforms had come during his middle age, right when he was beginning to lose confidence in his own physical well-being. Rural land values near the city rose rapidly, and Genji lost all sense of proportion. In the course of four or five years he divided up his fields into lots and sold them at a considerable profit, then built himself an ostentatious and luxurious mansion. As a result he had come to understand the awesome power of the tax bureau on the one hand, while on the other his desire for cold cash continued to increase.

It was not just Genji. Even after the main family had dwindled down to the widow and children, the people of the village had continued to besiege the house whenever they had a wedding or funeral, expecting money, as if nothing had changed.

Obasan was much too generous, giving out her "little tokens" for these occasions freely, whether they were solicited directly or hinted at in more subtle ways. But she gave without ceremony. Some of the people of the village interpreted her offhand manner as showing a lack of sincerity, a concern that was only paper-thin, and felt insulted by it.

The villagers lived on land soaked with the labor of their ancestors, who had worked for generations as tenant farmers, and it was natural that an unprecedented worship of the value of money should arise in them when they began selling that land. Of course, even in the politics of the village that controlled the land, it was money, in the guise of "election campaigns," that spoke loudest.

From the point of view of the villagers, Obasan's cool generosity, thin and transparent as a length of gauze, seemed to rebuke this new but already entrenched set of values. They couldn't very well criticize her for her casual manner alone, but eyebrows were raised when she sold off not only the furniture and garden stones that were the inheritance of the Sogi family, but finally even the house itself. It was as if this woman and the one who gave out the money were two entirely different people.

Even the labor and offerings, such as the seasonal pickled scallions and plums, the rice cakes for the new year or the first gleanings from the fall harvest, and gifts in memory of Mitsue's grandparents, offered on the anniversary of their deaths—even these lasted only until about the time Mitsue finished elementary school. If Obasan hadn't gone and become the high school music teacher but instead had worked ineffectively at cultivating her land, it was very unlikely that the villagers would have sympathized with her and helped support the five of them—including Mitsue and Kohei—for the ten or twenty years that she had.

But Obasan continued to live in her own way, with an attitude toward this thoroughly contradictory treatment by the villagers that could only be called total unconcern. Mitsue felt a piercing ache in her chest when she realized that the journey of her aunt's life was coming to an end in the dim light that floated in the air of the cavernous storehouse and the gray dust that had settled there like a layer of fine silk.

"So I think that Shiro came to see his friend in the tax office," added Mitsue, just to make sure Genji got the message, and, her head lowered, she started to walk away. But Genji caught up with her and asked, "How long will the young master be here?"

"How long?" Mitsue stopped short, as if the question had physically tripped her. How stupid of her—of course Shiro was a working man now and couldn't stay long. The way he had bowed formally to her and said, "I'm sorry, I beg you," must mean he was going back very soon—maybe even tomorrow. The houses by the road, the trees, and Genji himself began to fade into gray and disappear into the distance. She lowered her eyes and saw the toes of her sandals chafing against the asphalt, and her chest contracted with the realization that at least Obasan would remain after he was gone.

Shiro left even sooner than Mitsue had expected; he took the night train back to Tokyo that same evening. They got up after noon and had clear soup and tempura for lunch. Obasan hardly ate anything, taking a bite or two for the sake of appearances, but Shiro ate a surprising amount, and after lunch both of them went back to sleep. Mitsue was amazed; it was as if they hadn't slept for days. She imagined what their thoughts must have been as they lay awake in the train all night listening to the sound of the wheels.

Obasan woke up in the evening completely refreshed by her nap and in good spirits. She was dressed neatly in a clean yukata. Rain had been threatening off and on all afternoon, but toward evening the sky cleared again, and the leaves of the phoenix tree, bathed in the western sun, were fresh and bright.

"Shiro has also been having a good rest," said Obasan, looking into the eight-mat room where he was sleeping. She raised her voice: "You'd better get up or you'll miss your train." Mitsue had assumed that Shiro would be staying here at least overnight, and she was more angry than surprised.

After a bath Shiro sat and ate his dinner ravenously while Mitsue waited on him and his mother watched. When he finished, he stood up and said, "Now Mother, you rest and let Mitsue take care of you."

Obasan laughed her assent. Certainly those few hours of rest couldn't have caused any great change in her weakened body, but her condition seemed improved and she even looked less thin than before.

Shiro's spirits were high, as if Obasan's refreshed complexion had affected him. Mitsue accompanied him as far as the storage gate. He restrained his stride to keep pace with Mitsue, who was walking slowly on purpose.

"It's good to be out in the country," he said, in a tone that reflected the relaxation in his face. "There are people out here who can get on your nerves, but somehow my heart is at peace when I'm here. . . . I don't know what it is exactly."

He was half asking himself.

Mitsue, in contrast to Shiro's and Obasan's good mood, was beginning to fear that she had gotten into something way over her head. To judge from her appearance, Obasan seemed to be in good condition now, but if she should suddenly take a turn for the worse, there wasn't much Mitsue could do besides call a doctor. She opened her mouth, but Shiro spoke first.

"Mit-chan, it may seem strange for me to say this, but there is a possibility that it's not cancer. Usually with cancer there's terrible pain. She's fatigued and has difficulty breathing, but she's never said anything about pain."

This time Mitsue didn't even mention that one visit to a doctor could tell them what the problem was. The question rose to her lips but she sealed it inside.

They reached the gate. Shiro stopped and looked back at the wing. Suddenly he muttered, "It's no good in the city."

"If it's that bad, you could always come back here—but you never do," said Mitsue peevishly. She knew it was unthinkable that his mother's illness could bring Shiro back here to live, but she said it anyway. Futile as it was to bring it up, this was probably her last opportunity. Once Obasan was gone there would be nothing left to bind him to this land.

You know, our people are buried here. . . . She herself did not expect these words to come to her lips, so she closed them inside . . . bad luck to speak of such things.

"That's right . . . why don't I just come back?" Shiro, his arms crossed, looked off into the distance, and again it seemed as if he were looking into himself.

"If the problem is your job, there's bound to be something here . . . if it doesn't matter what you do." Mitsue feigned indifference and pressed him further, though it was unlikely he was serious.

"That's right, if it doesn't matter."

"It's Rika, isn't it?" That's why Genji and the others had gossiped behind his back that he should have married a local girl.

"Is it Rika? She was born and raised in Tokyo. The place you were raised shouldn't have any effect on whether you can live here. . . . But she goes on and on about the children's schools." It was as if he were talking with Rika now.

Last year Obasan had gone to America instead of coming back here, but Shiro had stopped in with his family on their vacation. They had observed the Bon ceremony at the temple. Mitsue, who hadn't seen Shiro's children in quite a while, thought they seemed clever in their own way, but there was something artificial about them; they lacked the charm of childhood. In contrast, Kohei's children were not as sharp, but they seemed completely natural. They were endowed with an innocent nobility like that found in wild animal cubs. Mitsue sensed that Kohei's children would grow up free of corruption and live naturally and spontaneously, whereas Shiro's children would never be fulfilled, would always be missing something important. She said simply, "The best way to raise children is to just let them grow up naturally in the country."

"I agree. I understand that, but I still don't bring them back here. I wonder if it's that I can't come back. . . ."

Shiro again fell into such a deep meditation that Mitsue felt uncomfortable.

"I guess it's that, living as we do in the city among thousands of other people, it seems we'll be left behind unless we do as everyone else does."

Mitsue kept silent, swallowing the words, If people like me worried about being left behind, we couldn't live at all.

"Anyway, if I came back to the country, as you said just now, I would feel secure inside, and maybe her illness wouldn't seem like cancer anymore."

A monologue. Finally, in what seemed like a conclusion without actually being one, he said to himself, "It doesn't make sense." Then, at last, he looked at Mitsue.

"Well, I'll really think about it during the trip back to Tokyo."

Mitsue gave a bitter laugh and answered, "You do that, if you like." But she thought, Instead of that, try thinking about what is going on in this old maid's head beneath her scar.

How would he react to her sarcasm? He smiled and said, "I'll be back again soon—so you won't scold me." She was surprised by the effect his simple smile had on her.

When have I ever presumed to scold you? She was suddenly overcome by a confused feeling, leaving her both sad and angry, that in this case it would be more convenient for Shiro if she did assume a dominant role. She could neither reveal nor dispel this feeling, and so she remained silent and motionless.

Shiro continued: "If it's too much for you by yourself, you can always get some kind of help, say, hire a woman to come in. Or I could send Rika. . . ."

He hesitated, as if thinking of his children, and Mitsue interrupted him in an unusually emphatic tone:

"But if Rika came, she'd insist on consulting a doctor."

"I'll talk her out of it."

"There's no need for that; it would just cause problems. Let's see if I can simply take care of her myself," said Mitsue firmly, already forgetting the fear that had gripped her just moments before. She wanted to be the only one to bear the burden of Shiro's and Obasan's secret; she didn't want to share it with Rika.

Then, remembering, "What about Haruko?"

"We can't avoid contacting her. She's in America with the new baby, and Mother doesn't want to tell her, but I think we'll have to."

"There's nothing to say yet—not until it gets serious."

Shiro smiled again, gently. "All of a sudden you've become so responsible."

She was at a loss for words. Why did seeing his smile make her feel so angry and bitter? Finally she said in a severe tone, "At any rate, it's better if Rika doesn't come."

Mitsue rationalized to herself: It's more trouble than it's worth to have someone come to the country who's not used to life here, but her voice stuck in her throat. Shiro suddenly suppressed his smile, and his eyes, serious now, looked intently at Mitsue. He said nothing, though, and, lowering his head, he bowed to her, turned his back, and walked out through the side gate.

She braced herself against her anger and watched the back of his shirt until it was gone. Then she noticed that, instead of blood oozing from the wound deep in her breast, cold drops of water were sliding down her cheeks. She was faintly surprised.

The expression left on Shiro's face after his smile disappeared seemed to show that he had come to a deep comprehension of something. He had understood, but then he had left her there without saying anything. It was unfair. You could only call it unfair, thought Mitsue, and at the same time she suddenly wanted to take that face and press it directly on the wound deep within her, then sink down to the earth as twilight descended.

There came the sound of a motorcycle passing on the highway

beyond the wall. Mitsue couldn't bear for the rumor to get out that Mit-chan had seen the young master off with tears running down her scarred face. The discernment appropriate to her age returned to her, and she hurried back to the wing.

Her aunt was sitting in the dressing room with her back to the door. The lights had not been turned on yet and dusk pressed in onto the edge of the veranda; only the area around the phoenix tree was a thin green, as if it had escaped the darkness. She didn't turn around, even though she must have heard Mitsue's foot-steps. Mitsue called to her. She couldn't possibly have died, just sitting there that way, but her pose gave such an impression of tranquility that for a moment Mitsue wondered if she had.

Obasan turned, and a smile appeared on her thin face. She did look like Shiro. "I'm sorry to ask, Mit-chan, but there's some mos-quito incense in the lower cupboard in the kitchen."

"There's also some bug spray."

"I'd rather have the incense."

Mitsue lit the dark green coil and put it down at the edge of the veranda.

"Somehow I've already come to count on you completely, Mit-chan . . . though I hadn't intended to." She wasn't exactly making excuses, but then she continued as if in spite of herself. "I guess the train trip affected me—now that I've come home I'm truly ex-hausted. When I was at Shiro's I could still help a little with the washing and housework. I didn't feel this drained. . . . I wonder why." She had slipped into the Tokyo dialect. Perhaps Shiro's departure had saddened her; her cheerful expression of a short time ago seemed false now, and wrinkles had appeared on her brow.

She began to have difficulty breathing again, and her shoulders labored with each inhalation and exhalation. Mitsue, uneasy, called to her.

"If you're tired . . . ," she began, but all too soon the words "we could get the doctor to come" rose to her lips, and she broke off. Not to see a doctor, to hide the disease from outsiders, this was what it was all about. No matter what was going on in Obasan's heart, the person alongside her was forced into this awful state of anxiety. Could Shiro have realized this and still have left Mitsue this way, entrusting her with Obasan's care? Obasan herself, as if she saw through her perplexity, spoke to her.

"Shiro must have said something to you. What did he say?"

After a pause, Mitsue answered: "That your condition is bad . . . but that you don't want to see a doctor." Then, keeping her voice low, she concentrated her strength and asked, "Is it true that you don't want to see a doctor?"

Her brow still tense, Obasan peered deliberately into the thick twilight and looked up at the phoenix tree.

"Indeed it is. I'm sorry for Shiro, having to keep this secret from people, but don't you think that a person also has the right to take care of her own illness by herself without seeing a doctor?"

Rather than simply "nursing oneself," "to take care of her own illness" sounded like "to accept her own disease and cherish it."

". . . It's a matter of a person's whole body, that person's entire life."

As she finished talking, her voice, punctuated by her labored exhalations, became hoarse, but Mitsue did not have to strain to understand. Suddenly she saw clearly. This morning, when she had heard the news from Shiro, she had pictured a kind of tragic intoxication in facing death and advancing toward it boldly, and she had answered, "I understand." But maybe when her aunt spoke of "that person's entire life," she had meant simply to cherish that life along with the illness it included, or the death itself that was a part of it. Mitsue couldn't very well ask, though, and so she remained silent.

"But it won't do to trouble you; all I want is to stay here quietly the way I am. You can go on home now."

Go on home. Of course, Obasan must not think of her as belonging here. With some resentment, she addressed her aunt formally: "So I'm troubling you by being here?"

Obasan looked back at Mitsue's face in the darkness and smiled. "You know how happy I'd be if you'd stay with me. It's just that by not seeing a doctor I'm being very selfish. You have your own life. Shiro and I can't very well force our self-indulgence on you."

"There's not that much in my life. If I weren't taking care of you I'd only be helping out Kohei with his family." Mitsue casually spoke the words. It was the truth.

"That's what you say, but Mit-chan, isn't that what living is— taking care of someone, helping out . . . is it really possible to live for your own sake alone?" Towards the end she was mumbling absently, as if to herself.

"It should be," answered Mitsue decisively. "Isn't it the same thing—you say that you have the freedom not to see a doctor because it's entirely a matter of your own life, and you can nurse yourself alone; I want to help you here instead of working in Kohei's house—aren't we both acting in our own interests?"

It was only the darkness of the room, half submerged in twilight, that gave Mitsue the courage to say it. Obasan, as if Mitsue's unprecedented boldness were nothing unusual, answered in a voice that reflected her deep contemplation.

"Are we? You can't say definitely that it's only for yourself; but then when you ask for whose sake . . ." Her thin shoulders stirred and her gaunt face looked again through the darkness up at the phoenix tree. In the twilight that had gradually thickened in the garden, even this tree, standing directly in front of her, was almost invisible.

"Maybe for the sake of someone you haven't even met." Facing the tree that she couldn't see, only her smile, showing dimly white, floated up and away.

Hearing her aunt's unexpected words, Mitsue felt a sudden emptiness. *Someone I haven't even met. Who is she talking about?*

They both were silent, and there was an almost frightening stillness all around them. In the evening at Kohei's house the television was always on and the children were always making noise. Even Mitsue had forgotten the calm of an evening in the country. Obasan had lived for some time alone with Haruko in that huge main house; then even after Haruko had gone she continued to live by herself for years in the wing that was left standing, isolated, in the overgrown yard. Someone like Mitsue couldn't begin to imagine the depth of thought that Obasan must have cultivated as she spent those evenings in the terrifying silence and darkness.

"Ah . . ." Obasan made a soft sound. Mitsue panicked, wondering if she was in pain. But her aunt continued: "I can hear the frogs—it's been so long." She listened intently, almost as if she were exchanging greetings with the frogs in the distant rice paddies. Even in the deep darkness, frogs were innocently singing out their short lives.

Mitsue made up her mind: no more hesitating. Even if it meant she would be here alone to witness her aunt's last moments, she would stay here without fear. Let the villagers blame her for not calling a doctor. She pictured herself standing here alone with Shiro, the two of them facing the censure of the townspeople together, and felt a defiant exultation.

II

Mitsue had made her commitment, but by the middle of the second week, when summer had marked the end of the rainy season and the cicadas began their evening wailing, she had already found herself wavering in her resolve on more than one occasion. Actually, as she had concluded after moving in with her aunt, there didn't seem to be any danger that Obasan would suddenly be stricken in the middle of the night while Mitsue was asleep; in that sense her illness was very different from something like heart disease. Of course, Mitsue had no idea whether this sense of security was justified. In fact, Obasan was visibly losing strength daily, as if she were gradually descending a hill, and Mitsue almost thought she could determine the day Obasan would reach the bottom. Nevertheless, she sought the reason for her aunt's weakness in the heat that increased with each day. Even a healthy person is easily fatigued in midsummer; maybe her strength would return to her in the fall. . . .

Unsure of which of these two equally plausible theories to believe, Mitsue began to want to consult a doctor and find out the truth. Even if her supposition was wrong and the doctor told her that it could happen suddenly, she still wanted to ask. She rationalized to herself that even if nothing came of it at least she could feel prepared—then she realized the irrationality of her thinking: Anyone can die suddenly in something like a traffic accident or a natural disaster, even Mitsue herself—and yet was it a mark of health that she did not consider the possibility? If so, mightn't her aunt's way of thinking, ill as she was, be closer to the reality of the human condition? Perhaps Mitsue's desire to find out something about her aunt that her aunt herself didn't want to know was itself a kind of arrogance.

Shiro must have gone straight to his office when he got back to Tokyo that first day; in the evening Rika called. She seemed surprised when Mitsue answered the phone, and Mitsue did not know how much Shiro had told his wife; she quickly turned the phone over to her aunt.

"Yes, yes, I'm feeling just fine; it must be the fresh air out here." Obasan addressed Rika cheerfully, then she assumed her "young grandma" voice and spoke in the Tokyo dialect to the children, who came one after the other to the phone.

The next day Shiro called. Conscious of her aunt lying nearby, Mitsue couldn't tell him of the occasional difficulty Obasan was having with her breathing, but he soon guessed her meaning.

"I'm sorry. I'll come back as soon as I can," he apologized again. Then Obasan came to the phone and talked cheerfully in the same tone she had assumed the night before, almost singing the words: "You know you don't have to keep calling me every day; I'm very happy to be back in the country."

Shiro had only left the day before yesterday, and Mitsue already wanted to call a doctor—for the wrong reasons. It would have been all right if, unable to bear the anxiety of watching her aunt suffering, she had wanted to turn to a doctor and ask for treatment. But instead she simply wanted to find out—and tell Shiro—whether or not it really was cancer. It sounded like such a simple thing, but there was a lot going on in her mind that even she herself didn't understand. It didn't seem to matter to her aunt whether it was cancer or some other disease—she seemed already to have prepared for death long ago. Since Shiro had accepted his mother's way of thinking, he didn't need to know the exact nature of her illness, either. To Mitsue, her own desire to know was not simply an idle whim; she saw it as a dangerous temptation.

Her brother Kohei was not the sort to interfere, and he wouldn't even think of protesting at anything Shiro and his aunt did. He simply cooperated with Mitsue and followed her suggestions, as when he built a privacy fence just in case someone from the village should get onto the property and come up to the wing. In these long midsummer evenings they didn't turn on the lights until late, and no one had noticed that Mitsue was taking care of the mistress out in the ramshackle wing of the old house.

Kohei's wife Kazumi showed some curiosity, but she respected

Obasan as the person who had raised her husband and Mitsue. Without prying into the situation, she kept Mitsue supplied with what she needed.

In the old days, a dilapidated estate like this would have become an exploring ground for neighborhood children, but the children living in the new houses down the road were busy with clubs, extra classes, and television, and the ruins, forgotten, stood there like a gaping hole. Now, after all this time, Mitsue noticed that there was actually more privacy with the crowded neighborhood nearby than there had been before, when nothing but fields stretched as far as the eye could see.

Perhaps he had seen Shiro leave for Tokyo, or possibly he felt apprehensive at what Mitsue had said; for whatever reason, even Genji kept his distance. Without making any special efforts to conceal her aunt's presence, Mitsue had prepared herself mentally to repulse any attack by villagers who might discover that Obasan was here, but it was certainly easier to live this way, without interference.

Obasan kept getting thinner, but though at times she was unsteady on her feet, she could still bathe herself; she would even go to the kitchen and prepare simple dishes and sauces. When the children were young she would fry things for them, but she herself had always avoided heavy foods. When Mitsue followed her aunt's wishes, she found herself preparing cold noodles for both lunch and dinner during the hot summer days. As she served herself meat or fish regardless of what Obasan was eating, she caught herself worrying that her aunt's body couldn't hold out for long nourished this way, then realized that if Obasan didn't particularly want her body to "hold out," Mitsue didn't have the right to force her to eat nutritious food. If she did, it was possible that that in itself could cause the cancer cells to multiply, and her aunt could actually suffer more.

Sometimes on her good days Obasan would take it on herself to make *shiraa-e*, a cool tofu salad. Mitsue took a self-deceptive consolation in her aunt's activity. Though she herself didn't like to go to the trouble of making the sauce, Obasan had figured out some clever shortcuts, and effortlessly produced *shiraa-e* with a rich flavor and texture. She has such a sense of elegance, thought Mitsue with renewed admiration.

Obasan would not make any effort to get up in the evening after she had finished her early supper. It was hot, so they would leave the lights off and watch the indigo-colored twilight through the screens of the veranda. Mitsue would light the mosquito incense and, sitting by her aunt's side, move the fan lazily back and forth. In the evening the cicadas could be heard, and after dark the frogs joined in their chirping, their voices meshing like a green mosquito net surrounding the space Mitsue shared with her aunt.

Mitsue would try to imagine Shiro beside them but realized that if he were actually there she wouldn't feel this serenity. She longed for him when he wasn't there and realized that ultimately it was the absent Shiro who attracted her most. And now, staying here alone with her dying aunt, she felt Shiro's absence even more intimately.

"It must smell bad...." Lying on her back, Obasan gave a strained smile and groped with her left hand for the cologne bottle. The hand, trained by long experience, picked it up and sprayed a little cologne onto her breast. The smell of the old-fashioned mosquito incense and the sweet odor of the cologne could not mask the rotten smell of blood that rose and mixed with them.

Mitsue had not seen her aunt's right breast and could not tell what its condition was, but it was already clear that there was a ruptured ulcer that was continually bleeding; Obasan was using up enormous quantities of gauze and absorbent cotton. Mitsue thought it strange that she had never once seemed to be in pain. It seemed that all of the pain spent itself in the weariness of her exhausted body and in her labored breathing.

At times Mitsue vaguely felt that she would like to ask her aunt something, but she couldn't come up with any concrete questions. Perhaps something about her own parents, who had died so young . . . but Mitsue was actually more curious about Obasan's husband—the man who was Shiro's father.

Mitsue's aunt had had a privileged childhood as the daughter of a doctor, and her education at a fashionable music school in Ueno set her apart from her peers, but Mitsue had heard that after her new husband had fallen ill she had spent the rest of her marriage—until she became a widow—acting as his nurse. But she had been more than a nurse: She had given birth to the two children Shiro and Haruko. It was romantic to think of the hopeless love of the young couple fighting together against his tuberculosis, which was a fatal disease in those days. Obasan had an open, outgoing character, and Mitsue could also understand her acting naturally and not resisting her sexual instincts. Mitsue herself had lived for over thirty years without knowing anything about sex, but her aunt had arranged a marriage for her brother before he reached the age of twenty. Mitsue guessed that Obasan's reasons for this were related to her own earlier experience. The fact that her aunt had not sought a marriage partner for Mitsue against her will must be partly related to the scar. But at the same time Obasan, in spite of her own past, might have felt that if Mitsue did not experience any relationships with men she would not miss them in her life, that as a woman she was capable of living in this kind of innocence.

One day as Mitsue sat fanning the smoke from the mosquito incense, she blurted out a question. "What kind of person was my uncle? Was he like Shiro?"

Her aunt was lying down as usual, and she kept her eyes almost completely closed while she spoke. "He was more like Haruko."

Mitsue realized this must be true. Although Shiro looked the part of the generous landowner, he actually had a sensitive character. It was Haruko, with her unconcerned manner and broad outlook, who seemed to have inherited the personality of a landowning patriarch in the tradition of this district. "Shiro is more like you, isn't he?" The words "especially when he smiles" stopped in her mouth. It was such happiness to be able to talk quietly about Shiro with her aunt, steeped here in the thin blue twilight. Opposite the veranda, the young phoenix tree seemed pregnant with a faint light.

He was her treasured only son; she too must want to talk about him. But, contrary to Mitsue's expectations, her aunt simply answered, "He is," then changed the subject to her late husband: "Your uncle was ill for so long, but he never lost his good humor and was always making me laugh."

Mitsue was lost in thought. "He didn't go to the hospital?" she asked cautiously.

"In the old days people stayed at home when they were sick. We were limited to whatever nursing was possible at home. We did try a change of air, though, and were here in this house at the end."

Mitsue wondered if Obasan had chosen to die this way to follow her husband's example.

"Your uncle loved natural things, you know." Obasan opened her eyes and looked at the dark ceiling. "Not natural in the sense of mountains and rivers and growing things—of course he liked all that too—but he used to say that it was wrong to rely too much on science and technology, on artificial things. And now look—recently people have begun to talk this way. A long, long time ago, for example, when they came out with artificial flavoring, he was already saying that it was a mistake for people to develop a taste for it."

Mitsue was silent; she didn't feel like providing the usual easy responses, that he had had a lot of foresight, was ahead of his time. She moved the fan back and forth.

"He even thought the flush toilet was a mistake."

Now Mitsue understood. The toilet here in the wing was the old style, the kind you had to bail out. Ten years ago they had changed the toilet in Kohei's house to the flush style. At the time, Genji had made a point of coming to poke around and had made snide comments about a farmer getting a lavatory. But no doubt when Genji himself had built his own mansion, he had had a flush toilet put in.

"What's wrong with flush toilets?" Mitsue thought it was a peculiar philosophy.

"He thought that the way people clean up everything dirty, hiding it from view, was the cause of human unhappiness. It's funny for me to talk this way when I myself am facing death, but recently somehow sickness and death too have become something that must be tidied up. It's an abnormality that shouldn't happen, so it seems that if it does, it's got to be cleaned up in a hurry. It might sound strange to say that sickness and death are acceptable, but they do actually exist, and shouldn't they be a part of everyday life that people can become accustomed to?"

Obasan had talked for an unusually long time. She smiled weakly. "But nature's wisdom has animals like the elephant or the cat hide themselves when they are about to die. I thought that I could learn from their example and die alone in this old shack, even by starving myself. But a human being is incapable of it. I can't tell you how happy I am to have you here with me."

She took a deep breath and, without changing her position, flexed her back painfully.

"Does it hurt somewhere?" Without thinking, Mitsue reached out and put her hand under Obasan's back. The backbone fit

right into her palm. Her aunt moaned slightly and made an effort
to push against Mitsue's hand; her back was so thin it didn't seem
capable of supporting her body. "It doesn't hurt, but it's stiff,"
she murmured.

"Shall I massage it?"

"If you could just keep your hand there . . . I used to do that for
Father; a person's palm feels good."

Mitsue felt an innocent happiness in hearing her aunt say
"Father," not "your uncle." Even if it had just been a slip of the
tongue, she felt as though she had become Shiro's sister.

She hadn't intended to put so much force into her hand, but
the abnormally frail back lifted slightly and at the same moment a
strong stench rose from Obasan's breast. Mitsue felt nauseated,
and without thinking she covered her nose and mouth with her
other hand.

About three weeks later Shiro came again. It was the height of
summer, and Obasan had been spending more and more of her
time during the day just lying listlessly in her room. Shiro came in
complaining of the heat, and Mitsue gave him a cold towel. He
wiped his face and neck roughly, then questioned her with his
eyes. Mitsue pointed mutely with her chin toward the dressing
room. During the days she had spent alone here with her aunt,
Shiro had seemed even more real to her because she was so deeply aware of his absence. Now, actually seeing his face, she felt a
mixture of tenderness and irrational anger and could not speak.
At the same time she became disagreeably conscious of the tic in
her eyelid, which she had completely forgotten about until now.

Judging by the energetic way he had wiped his face, Mitsue expected him to put on an offhand manner and tromp into his
mother's room saying, "How're you doing, Grandma?" But this
was the same old Shiro, and he entered her room quietly with a
simple "I'm home."

Mitsue wished she could see the expression in their eyes when they met. She took some barley tea and a beer from the refrigerator. Her aunt was constantly thirsty, probably because of the liquids she lost through blood and sweat. When Mitsue realized that the plastic cloth she had spread out on the first day was a precaution against a sudden loss of blood, she removed it and replaced it with an old thick cotton cloth folded into several layers. If Obasan should suddenly lose that much blood, it would probably mean the end; if so, one or two sleeping mats were a trivial matter. Then, in spite of herself, she found herself wondering if even in such an extreme case a blood transfusion was unthinkable.

As she approached the room, she heard Shiro's voice: "She says that if we don't force them to learn swimming their physical education grades will fall and they won't make 'fives' and 'fours.' " Obasan answered, "It's better not to make them do it against their will, but I guess Rika is like all those other pushy 'education mamas.' " Mitsue could hear the same smile in both their voices and felt the affection between mother and son in their comments at Rika's and the children's expense, and she had an urge— something between envy and loneliness—to put down her tray right there and disappear somewhere once and for all.

Obasan took the cup of tea from Mitsue's hand and turned to Shiro, her eyes serious: "You can see how well Mitsue has been taking care of me." Shiro nodded. It seemed to Mitsue that they had exchanged some kind of silent signal.

She answered, "It's only natural that I do," straightening the back seam in her aunt's yukata. She wanted Shiro to see how accustomed her aunt was to her care. Before Shiro arrived, Obasan had closed herself in the bathroom and spent a long time dressing her wound; she had done a good job, for there was no bad odor from her breast.

"What should we do for Bon?" Shiro seemed to be consulting

Mitsue rather than his mother.

"Shall we say I went back to America?" She said it mischievously, like a young girl.

"Me too, then?" Shiro became serious.

"We could say Haruko is having her fourth child." Obasan kept her bantering tone.

"Not only her fourth, but twins to boot, so we all had to go?" Shiro joined in.

Their joking irritated Mitsue and she took the proposal seriously. Suppose they used this lie; then to be consistent they'd have to say that these imaginary twins had died soon after birth. As if Mitsue had spoken the word "death," Obasan said casually, to no one in particular:

"Ultimately I suppose the graves should be turned over to Kochan to maintain."

Shiro, a little surprised, looked at his mother's face.

"It's the perfect occasion. I haven't told you in any detail yet, but the cemetery plot is about the only property we have left. This property was mortgaged to the bank a long time ago." Obasan continued in a lighthearted tone, as if she were talking about the weather.

Shiro, his expression unchanged, was silent. He did not move his gaze from his mother's face.

"Genji has had an eye on this place for years and years, but . . . at any rate when I die I'll be leaving those debts as part of my inheritance; what's left of the land will go mainly toward paying back the bank and taxes. If there's anything left after that, I'd like it to go to Kohei. You and Haruko have houses in Tokyo, and that's all you need; if Kohei will take care of the cemetery plot, you can stay in Tokyo without worrying about what people here might be thinking; you won't have to come back here at all."

The old resilience of her singing days had returned to her voice, though at times her words were interrupted by labored breathing. Without thinking, Mitsue wanted to shout at her aunt, "Isn't that a little too much?" Without taking the time to ask herself why she felt this way, she blurted out: "When Shiro represents the thirtieth generation of the Sogi family?"

Obasan looked up at Mitsue and smiled. "It's funny to hear you talking like Genji. Everyone dies, and when they do, they become transparent, nameless spirits and board a boat that takes them beyond the seas. From beyond the seas they mount the wind and vanish somewhere. While we're alive we rid ourselves of our possessions and try to lose our attachments; at the end when there's nothing left we leave the body as well.

"Well, we don't want to upset Genji; at least the cemetery plot should stay in the family. After that it will be more than enough if Kohei gets a piece of the old Sogi family land to keep under cultivation. Don't you think so, Shiro?" She turned and looked gently at her son. Her eyes had grown bigger in contrast to her face, which was emaciated from illness, and they overflowed with an expression of serene affection. It was unbearable. Shiro nodded, his eyes lowered, and answered "uh-huh," like a boy.

In the end she's taken only Shiro's happiness into account, thought Mitsue. She felt a burning deep in her chest. I have to keep living here on this land that she and Shiro are abandoning.

"I'm glad I've been able to talk about this." Obasan, her eyes distant, looked relieved. "Now that's settled," she muttered.

It rained briefly in the afternoon and Mitsue returned to Kohei's house for the first time in several days. Her ironing had been piling up, and the iron at the wing was terribly old-fashioned. She had gotten used to Kazumi's steam iron and missed it, and now that Shiro was here she didn't want to wear blouses that were wrinkled from the wash. No one was in the living room. She turned on the air conditioner, sat down on the sofa, and took a deep breath. The wing was well-ventilated, but when she had to stand up and work there were times when she missed air conditioning. And now that Shiro was there she couldn't have a decent nap. A feeling of drowsiness came over her as she lay there, then unexpectedly she heard the sound of Kohei coming home early.

"I'm home." Mitsue stood up and greeted her brother. He gave her a strange look—why had she said "I'm home," not "Welcome back," when she was the one who had been there first?

Feeling half foolish, half amused, Mitsue reflected that Kohei looked like a bear. "This house is pretty civilized compared to the wing—living there is like living a hundred years ago. There's not even an electric fan, much less air conditioning."

"It's because the wing is well ventilated," answered Kohei, and he got some barley tea from the refrigerator. As he poured himself a glass he asked, "How's Obasan doing?"

"Not very well. She just now started talking about her last requests."

"Is that right. . . . I see."

Kohei's face darkened and he looked down. Mitsue wondered if maybe he, too, under that coarse exterior, had idolized their beautiful aunt all these years. Kohei thought deeply, his face serious. But unexpectedly he changed the subject. "I've just been talking with Shiro," he began.

"Where did you see him?"

"He called me at work and we met at the station hotel lobby."

This was unprecedented. By the way Shiro had reacted to Obasan's talk about the graves and the land, Mitsue had assumed that he was hearing it for the first time. That couldn't have been an act. But what had he talked about with Kohei, then?

"You probably came over here to ask me about this."

Things were getting stranger and stranger. "About what?"

Kohei uncharacteristically stumbled on his words. "Well . . . I had meant for Kazumi to bring it up with you," he began, "but Shiro is concerned about your scar. He says if it's all right with you he can get a letter of introduction to a well-known plastic surgeon in Tokyo. The main house can cover all the expenses. So why don't you think about it?"

Kohei spoke haltingly, measuring his words carefully.

This was totally unexpected, and Mitsue couldn't speak. She realized with chagrin that her face had turned scarlet right in front of her brother.

This wasn't the first time the subject of plastic surgery had come up. When Mitsue was still a child, her aunt had thought about it seriously, and once had even gone to Tokyo to find out about doctors. Mitsue had cried and said she didn't want to have it done. The reason she gave was that she didn't want to go through the pain, but in her heart she felt that an operation somehow posed a deep threat to her self-esteem. There was no point in forcing something on her that she didn't want. In fact, there was no guarantee that the operation would be a success, and indeed it might even result in greater disfigurement. And then, if the doctors made a mistake with the anesthetic, Mitsue could be far worse off than she was now. Obasan reflected on the possibilities and gave up the idea.

Why had the subject suddenly come up again now? Mitsue even suspected that her aunt had sensed her yearning for Shiro and had devised this as part of a strategy to marry her off.

Kohei began again. "There are some new techniques for transplanting skin over scar tissue, and even if the operation itself should leave a scar, it would probably be smaller than the original one. Then, when it comes to tics on the lower eyelid . . ." Mitsue heard Shiro's way of speaking behind her brother's words, and she shuddered.

Mitsue had gotten the scar about the time she was learning to walk. She had heard that an old housekeeper who had worked for them had accidently upset a pot of hot oil on her when she got underfoot in the kitchen. Now, regardless of its cause, the tic was part of her face. Everyone has some defect—a flat nose or dark skin. Some people aren't particularly smart or athletic; some are irritable and a little eccentric—nevertheless these failings all go into making a "self." And in Mitsue's case, her present character was a product of the thirty-odd years she had lived with that face. Suppose now, after all this time, her face suddenly became beautiful; Mitsue felt that somehow it wouldn't make sense—that she would be rejecting her self as a whole. Now she thought she had come to an understanding of the resentment she had felt, but not understood, as a girl.

Whether or not Kohei had noticed her blushing, he continued in a subdued tone: "Shall we try the operation? Nowadays even men are changing their faces, even if there's nothing wrong with them. People are lengthening their noses or giving their eyelids an extra wrinkle."

"In that case, if someone offered to take your puffy eyes and give you elegant Western-style eyelids, you'd just go along with it?"

Mitsue was cross-examining him. Kohei gave her a strange look. "It's two different things. You're just getting back your original face, the one you were born with."

Her eyes unexpectedly blurred with tears. "You say 'my original face,' but this is the only one I know. What about the one I had when I was ten? Even if you go back to when I was three or four, I had the scar then, and the face I have now was forged through its bond with it all this time. My character and the circumstances of my life are the same thing; I am only the combination of all these different things. It's just an illusion to think that I could have or can have a different face."

"You're just rationalizing," Kohei muttered in astonishment. It had been years since he had seen Mitsue cry, and he hesitated, not knowing what to say.

Mitsue dried her tears. She was amazed at the way she had changed. Earlier this year she couldn't even have imagined that she could talk to her brother this way, or that she could have silenced Genji with that expedient lie on the day Obasan had first come.

Kohei was utterly defeated. "If you're satisfied with the way things are, then it's all right with me."

He seemed on the point of saying "That's enough!" and turning his back on her, but then he suddenly sank into thought.

Satisfied? Mitsue's heart mumbled the question over and over. Of course she could only answer herself that she was not. But perhaps it was more truthful to say that she was satisfied with her unsatisfied self, the defective self that endured the dissatisfaction. It was this defective part of her that had created her present self, and that was the true Mitsue. And if she couldn't be satisfied with this self as a whole, she might as well commit suicide.

Countless times, beginning when she was very small, she had imagined how wonderful it would be to live without the scar. But if that had been the case, she would have been more extroverted and wouldn't have been so attracted to her cousin, who only came home for school vacations. She would have promptly fallen in love with one of the local boys and by now would be a housewife and mother like Kazumi, without a care in the world. Of course she might have been happier that way, but she nevertheless preferred the self that clung to this hopeless yearning for Shiro, and that was now nursing this dying woman. Maybe this was what was meant by "human nature." If a person, in spite of enjoying the most fortunate circumstances in life, was fundamentally dissatisfied with her very existence, how could she live with herself? Mitsue had experienced transitory despair at times, and had wished that she could strip off her face and throw it away somewhere, but she had never thought of suicide; she was too important to herself.

Reconciling herself to the fact that she couldn't explain these complex thoughts to her brother in a way he could understand, she was suddenly overcome by the desire to simply come out and tell him that she loved Shiro, and that she loved the self that loved him.

Kohei took a couple of steps back and forth like a bear worn out from the effort of thinking, then shrugged his shoulders sluggishly and lifted his tanned face: "Obasan doesn't have much time left, does she?" he muttered.

"I'm not a doctor; I can't tell. What did Shiro say?"

"Nothing, really. . . . But he did say he'd like Obasan to see your face without the scar before she dies."

"You know, I'm not pretty anyway . . . ," Mitsue said spitefully, then added, "I didn't know she cared that much about it."

At Mitsue's harsh words Kohei shook his head gravely. "No, she really does."

"But she has nothing to do with it." She continued to herself: Unless she thinks she has to marry me off and get me away from Shiro.

Kohei looked surprised. "You mean you really think that?" he asked.

"Think what?"

"That she has nothing to do with it."

Mitsue was struck with something like foreboding, and she stared at her brother. Kohei, perhaps oppressed by her gaze, hesitated a moment, then said, "But she was the one who burned you to begin with."

"Obasan?" It couldn't be. Mitsue rephrased the question. "You mean it wasn't some housekeeper?"

"The fact that it was Obasan who burned you—that in itself was a tragic accident," he said as a preliminary, then explained how it had happened.

They called it a tempura pan, but it was actually a large round-bottomed Chinese wok, as Kohei recalled it. He himself had been very small, and Mitsue could barely walk at the time, but he had made a point of investigating the circumstances of her injury. Obasan had only recently had the propane gas stove put in; up to then, she had done her cooking on the big old kitchen stove. Looking back, Kohei figured that she hadn't yet gotten used to cooking on the little gas range. Haruko and Mitsue were running around the earthen floor of the dark room. Suddenly they got tangled up with each other and ran into Obasan, and she lost control of her hand. If the pot had been completely upset, not only Mitsue but also Haruko, Obasan, and the old housekeeper—who had indeed been there—would all have been burned. Instead, it had only tipped sideways and most of the oil had not spilled. It was just Mitsue's bad luck that the oil that did spill hit her on the side of the forehead. Kohei had been standing in the shadow of the old kitchen stove. He didn't have the slightest recollection of how his little sister had howled or how his aunt had panicked and rushed to give her first aid, but for some reason he retained one image clearly, as though it were on an old, worn-out film, gray and streaked like rain, running in slow motion. At the moment the pot tipped, Obasan knocked Haruko out of the way of the hot oil with her hand.

Mitsue listened, holding her breath.

"She really pushed Haruko out of the way? Just Haruko?" She said it in a low voice, slowly, emphasizing the words.

"It must have been a mother's instinct," answered Kohei simply. "I think it was raining that day," he said absently, his eyes distant, then added, "as if that had anything to do with it."

For the first time Mitsue felt a rush of love, not for Obasan or Shiro but for her own brother, who had kept the image of her accident in his memory for so long.

"Does she know you saw it?"

"I wonder," he said dully. "Probably not."

Something screwed tight in the pit of her stomach. "She's a liar under that pretty face. She figured no one knew." The caustic words tumbled out.

"It's not fair to her to say that." Unexpectedly, Kohei's deep voice chastised her. "If she hadn't taken care of us, no one would have. And she didn't have to do it: We call it our own family, but you know our mother left the Sogi house when she married into the family in Tokyo. By rights it was our father's relatives in Tokyo that should have taken us in, but they palmed us off on the Sogis."

Kohei was unusually eloquent. He continued, "The fact that we were adopted by a branch family means that there was nothing left here but the Sogi name. There may have been a lot of land, but in those days land wasn't worth a lot of money like it is now. Just the opposite—and beginning with the death of our adoptive mother, we all just burdened Obasan down even more."

Mitsue watched her brother intently as he spoke. Had this coarse, bearlike older brother, who had always come up short when she compared him to Shiro—had he really kept these details straight all this time, secretly hidden in his thick farmer's chest?

"There were a lot of things. . . . Remember all that she's done for you. She must have thought that if you started holding this against her, that kind of resentment would affect your character, and so she just kept quiet about the burn."

"And that's why you kept quiet too?"

"I guess so. . . ." Kohei's dull expression stood in contrast to his words. He nodded sullenly, then continued: "But if this is something that has been weighing on her heart, they'd at least like to raise the possibility with you before she dies, even if nothing comes of it. And then I thought that maybe you might even have had a vague memory of it."

"You know there's no chance I'd have remembered it. I had

just barely learned to walk."

He nodded.

"Does Shiro know ... that Obasan was the one?" She asked the question in a bitter tone. She could understand if Obasan wanted to fix the scar to show her appreciation for Mitsue's care during her illness, but was she supposed to undergo the operation just to put Obasan's conscience at ease? And had Obasan given her little speech about the graves this morning just to ease Shiro's conscience about abandoning his family home?

"I don't know whether he does or not. Does it really matter?" Kohei brought the subject to a close, irritably: "Why do you have the air conditioner on 'high' again? If you're going to have it on, can't you try to keep it on 'medium' or 'low'? If you keep on running it that way, you're going to wind up a rheumatic old lady like Mrs. Tanaka." He turned the switch angrily.

The cold air had penetrated to every corner of the room, and Mitsue noticed that she had been trembling without being aware of it.

Mitsue stuffed the clothes she had intended to iron back into the grocery bag and left the house. The shadows were already lengthening, but the sullen heat and humidity hovered over the fields, shimmering dizzily above the tops of the wheat stubble. Coming directly out of the cool house, Mitsue was especially affected by the heat and humidity; no wonder Kohei didn't like air conditioning. On the other hand, Kazumi spent her whole day in the cold air of the supermarket, and when she came home and found the air conditioner off she would say, "It's uncivilized ... ," and switch it on.

Parting the bamboo grass, she entered by the back door. She opened the refrigerator to get a soothing drink of barley tea, and suddenly, as if called by the sound, Shiro appeared. He was dressed casually in a running shirt and bermuda shorts.

Shiro's face turned hard, as if it were reflecting Mitsue's own stiff expression. Suddenly Mitsue stretched out her right hand. Shiro, perhaps assuming she was handing him something, instinctively extended his own right hand. She grabbed it without a word and pulled him toward the back door and into the backyard. Shiro, stumbling, caught a pair of women's sandals on his toes and followed her out.

When they got to a place where the yatsude bushes cast dense shadows, Mitsue stopped short and turned to face Shiro head-on. She herself couldn't say why she had lured him all the way out here.

Mitsue remembered the morning when Shiro had brought his sick mother back; for the first time she had faced him as an equal, and it had seemed that Shiro had been about to say something . . . could it have been only that, that he had only had words for her? But wait: It could be that she had been led by some impulse from Shiro himself to subconsciously expect more from him.

The cicadas wailed, filling the void created by Mitsue's sudden silence. She felt an urgent need to say something before their voices overpowered her completely.

"Kohei told me, you know," she said suddenly. Her tic started, and her red eyelid was exposed, but ignoring it, she stared straight at him.

"Already?" He mumbled the word, a little taken aback. His expression, strained from the experience of being dragged out here without warning, slackened at her unexpected words. The tank top exposed the shoulders that were usually covered, and they seemed surprisingly muscular.

Mitsue blurted out the words. "I know that only an operation would make this face look normal. But it's mine, so just leave it alone."

Shiro's face looked as if she had slapped it.

She was conscious that something uglier than her red eye was now exposed in her face, and that a thought was coming to her which once present could not be forgotten. In a panic, she searched the vacuum field of her mind . . . if she stripped off her face and cast it away, what could she put in the hole that would remain? In the vacuum field there was nothing, not even the hint of movement. Oppressed by this sense of desolation, she continued:

"Tell me whether or not it was really Obasan who burned me."

Shiro looked shocked; the question was utterly unexpected. Mitsue sensed something irreplaceable in his defenseless expression of surprise, but she destroyed it. She couldn't help herself.

"She was really cruel. She made me take Haruko's place. She upset the oil, but Haruko was the one she pushed out of the way."

Shiro, his face drained of expression, stood mute. Mitsue's whole body ached in pity for him, but she went on.

"Kohei saw the whole thing and knows all the details. I even remember a little myself," she added in spite of herself. She hadn't intended to tell a lie. Rather, in the short time it took to listen to Kohei's story, the scene of that one moment in the dark kitchen on that rainy evening had branded itself onto her brain. No matter how far back she went—tens, hundreds, or even thousands of years, it seemed that that scene had always existed inside her and was only awaiting her summons to make its appearance.

The rich voices of the cicadas closed in on the space around her, and Mitsue stood in the void which had opened at its center, listening to the sound of the rain and looking down at the earthen floor.

It's not anyone's fault; I'm not blaming Obasan. So why did I say it? This is going to distance Shiro from me once and for all. As the regrets welled up, she felt a chill in her fingers and toes, and a cold sweat seemed to gather at the pit of her stomach. The colors around her faded to white and shade, and, suddenly nauseated, she fell against the trunk of a yatsude bush.

She heard Shiro's frightened voice calling her name faintly and was dimly aware of his arms embracing her. Deep in her sickness, she was lifted and carried, then laid down.

Obasan's voice descended from above.

"A fainting spell . . . a cushion, that one is all right. Fold it in half, that's right . . . under her feet. Keep her head down."

Mitsue tried to shake her head, but she couldn't move any part of her body. She was aware only of her sickness. Everything else was dissolving into a muddy gray haze.

The cold sweat was wiped gently from her forehead. At last she opened her eyes and looked up into her aunt's emaciated face.

"Ah, you've come to." A tender smile appeared on Obasan's sunken cheeks. "It's too hot and humid, and you're worn out from taking care of me, poor thing. . . ." As she mumbled the words, she again stretched out her hand and wiped Mitsue's brow. The stench that came out of the open underarm of her yukata hit Mitsue head-on. Mitsue made no effort to suppress her reaction, and with a violent grimace she turned away.

"I'm sorry." Obasan immediately noticed and, apologizing simply, she withdrew.

"Please rest, Mother. I can see to her now." Mitsue lay with some ice wrapped in a towel on her forehead, and her nausea soon vanished.

"Are we doing the right thing by cooling her down? Shouldn't people with fainting spells be kept warm?" Obasan's voice rang out clearly.

"I wonder." Shiro wasn't sure. Mitsue was just about to say that she was all right now and didn't need them any more, when tears blurred her eyes and she closed them, hard.

Breathing heavily, Obasan returned to the dressing room. Shiro bent his knees stiffly and sat down at Mitsue's bedside. She whispered, "Go away." She didn't want him to see her lying this way with her eyes closed.

His voice was cool. "Should I get Kohei or Kazumi to come over?"

"No, it's all right. I'll get up in a few minutes. Just go away," she repeated and, with her eyes still closed, averted her face.

Shiro left the room hastily, trying to muffle his footsteps. Taking the sound as a signal, Mitsue furtively opened her eyes. Shafts of light, yellowed like the rich rays of the evening sun, bathed the room, and through them Mitsue caught a glimpse of his legs with their dark hair.

She closed her eyes again. If she could only stay here lying this way forever, without feeling . . . tears formed at the outside corner of one eye and slid in a single line down her cheek, then fell, and she saw a thin white corpse floating in the air beyond the yellow dusk.

III

It is not a cramped, tight feeling to be snowed in during the winter in Hokuriku. Instead, under the big thatched roofs of the spacious country houses, there is rather a comforting sense of being gently enclosed by thick bamboo and earthen walls. During the day vast glittering white dunes stretch as far as the eye can see; at night you sit hunched over the *kotatsu* in the heart of the boundless white darkness. It's too cold to move and you crouch motionless, resting your chilled hands against the frame of the foot-warmer.

As a child Mitsue had come to like the feeling of being snowed in like this. Now the summer's hot sunlight, the chirping of the cicadas, the grassy lawn, even the mosquito incense that was lit in the evening, all this seemed to isolate her from the outside world in the same way.

After Shiro returned to Tokyo, Mitsue was left alone again with Obasan, who continued to lose strength and hardly spoke at all. As Mitsue gazed out at the lawn from the veranda, her body soaked up the voices of the cicadas, and she found her own happiness in the desolate solitude.

The sudden attack of anemia had come unexpectedly to save her from the consequences of what she had blurted out. Though it had been brought on by her intense remorse, the attack was like a divine blessing that had gently swept everything away at the right moment. She had been terribly sick at the time, but if it hadn't happened, she thought solemnly, she would have been left to live in a continual state of vague semi-awareness.

Within the boundaries of her clouded consciousness, the child Mitsue, who had been running around that dark earthen floor that rainy evening, and the adult Mitsue, unconscious and inanimate, were joined together in the horizontal light of dusk, and it seemed to her that the interval between them, which should have been buried by the passing of time, had only been snowed in and, engulfed in the snow, had dissolved into nothing.

This came to Mitsue's mind as she sat vacantly one hot afternoon on the veranda outside the dressing room, mumbling to herself like a dying person. Soon Obasan would breathe her last in that room of death with its stagnant rays of yellowish light. They would move her body gently out and leave it in the grass; soon it would stiffen and start to decay. Enclosed by the voices of the cicadas, the earth and the roots of the bushes and trees would drink in all the organic matter from the decomposed body. Mitsue would sit crouched out there on the lawn like a dead person until there was nothing left but white bones . . . the consciousnesses of the dead woman and the one who had nursed her and now was mourning her would merge together and dissolve into the interval between life and death. Isn't that how they used to mourn the dead in the old days? Obasan had wanted to hide her body like a dying wild animal, and when she had said how inexpressibly happy she was to have Mitsue by her side, this must have been what she meant. Even at the very beginning of Mitsue's life Obasan had branded her on the forehead with her own hand as the person who would mourn her.

If so, the wing and the yard too, closed in by the cicadas' voices and the hot summer sun, might already have left the world of the living. Mitsue gazed out over the expanse of sunlit yard, and it seemed to her that she was sitting at the entrance to a gloomy yellow floating cavern, the Kingdom of the Dead. The words "aerial sepulcher" floated up in her mind like a distant memory.

Suddenly she thought, It's all over. That figure in the elegant white dress making its way across the lawn from the storage gate could only be Rika. A little messenger from the real world, she teetered along in her high heels, lugging a large suitcase up toward Mitsue.

Once he learned the circumstances of Mitsue's accident, it was reasonable for Shiro to consider it improper to entrust her with his mother's care, and of course he must have thought her fainting spell was related to exhaustion from nursing Obasan. He was probably even vaguely aware of her attraction to him and naturally would want to avoid taking advantage of it on the occasion of his mother's illness. No matter how hard it must have been for him to send Rika, he must have decided on this course as the only one he could take.

Mitsue, suddenly dragged back to this world from the shores of Hell, started up abruptly and went out the back door. She walked to the well and waited there until Rika was close enough to hear her voice. Shiro's wife hadn't seen her, and when Mitsue called out to her she stopped still in surprise, her thin body trembling. Under the eyelids with their conspicuous double fold and the eyeshadow that made her eyes seem particularly large, she stared at Mitsue a moment, then drawing a breath, said, "Oh, it's you."

It was Mitsue's turn to be surprised; had she really frightened Rika? Maybe Rika, looking at her, was reminded of the tale of O-Iwasama, the vengeful woman with the terribly disfigured face. "You didn't have to come," Mitsue said bluntly. Without even being aware of it, she was figuring out how to make Rika understand that even after traveling all the way out here she could be of no use, that someone not used to life in the country would only get in the way, and that she ought to turn right around and go back the way she had come.

"Not at all. I'm sorry I didn't come earlier to help you." Rika bowed her head politely as she paid her compliments. "I've been so anxious about the way we've been imposing on you."

Rika was two or three years older than Mitsue, but she looked much younger. Unlike Obasan, she was a classic beauty.

"But you've got the children; what did you do about them?"

"It's almost summer vacation, so they can stay at my mother's. . . . But this is no time to worry about them. And Mother—" She shrugged her thin shoulders and surveyed the empty foundation of the old main house, then asked, "It seems to be cancer, doesn't it?"

Mitsue, suppressing the urge to come right out and scowl at Rika, covered her irritation with an expression of dull placidity. The only person who had actually said it was cancer was Obasan herself, and there hadn't been a biopsy, so even Obasan must be aware that they couldn't be one hundred percent sure. And with everyone maintaining the ambiguity and supporting her, even with her difficulty breathing Obasan was able to live in balance with her illness and maintain a delicate clarity of mind. If it were positively diagnosed as cancer, it was possible that Obasan's suffering would increase. After all, at least in the opinion of outsiders, cancer was a wicked, detestable enemy that made a nest inside the body and fed on it like a parasite. To fight the cancer was to perceive the tumor and the self as separate entities, but even cancer cells are part of the body. The cancer reminded Mitsue of the tic in her own eyelid, and she thought that she understood her aunt better because of it.

Rika's pointed little chin tightened in response to Mitsue's dumb silence and she began speaking: "You must think I'm a terrible daughter-in-law for not taking care of Mother. It's all right; I won't make any excuses. But my husband . . ." She bit her lower lip and stopped a moment, then continued quickly, her eyes lowered: "I myself don't understand Shiro's way of thinking. If she doesn't want to see a doctor, it should be our duty to take her, even if we have to force her. . . . What's more, nowadays diseases like breast cancer . . . well, even if it's discovered late like this, there are ways of taking care of it. I've talked about it to one of my relatives who's a doctor. Of course I didn't say who I was talking about."

"I don't think there's any need to find out whether it's cancer or not," Mitsue interrupted in a quiet voice.

Rika opened her large eyes wide. "Well, that's not the important thing. What we have to do is take her to a doctor immediately," she said, urgency in her voice.

"You know, I think it's too late for that," Mitsue said sullenly, even though the words conflicted with what she had just said.

"Is it really that bad? Shiro also said that in the short time since she came back here she's gotten much worse." A tone of fear rose into Rika's nervous eyes. Mitsue understood—Rika was afraid of death.

"She's in that room over there," Mitsue said.

Even though Mitsue had pointed out the dressing room, the hesitant expression lingered on Rika's face. But suddenly, as if she had come to a decision, she shifted the suitcase to her other hand and went in through the back door.

Obasan, like Mitsue, had had no time to prepare for Rika's sudden visit. Though the heat and the illness had considerably

weakened her, she was still generally presentable, but Mitsue—
for reasons she herself didn't understand—worried that she
would seem terribly sick to Rika.

Ever since she had found out that it was Obasan who had given
her the scar, her aunt had become a kind of new scar inside her.
Though she ought to hate her, Mitsue had already come to love
her as part of her own fate—in spite of herself.

She arranged cold towels and cups on a tray, then poured some
cold barley tea. She could hear Rika's voice in the dressing room,
talking a blue streak, but when she started out the kitchen door
with her tray she nearly collided with Rika herself, who was coming back down the hall. Mitsue dodged her nimbly, and at the
same time Rika stepped aside and, pressing her back against a
pillar, burst into tears.

The cups of tea clattered. Mitsue steadied them and, taking a
kitchen towel from the tray, dabbed at the spill. Rika was holding
a handkerchief to her face and seemed about to start sobbing, and
without thinking Mitsue took her by the shoulder and pushed her
out the back door into the yard.

Rika meekly let herself be pushed out, then slowly lifted her
head and said, "I can't believe it."

"What can't you believe?"

"How could you have let it go this far? Can't you see? She's so
utterly . . . emaciated, she can't breathe without heaving her
shoulders, and her face is all gray." Mitsue hushed her, bringing a
finger up to her lips—Rika's voice had a disagreeable piercing
ring.

"She's only been here a month and a half . . . how could she
already have gotten to this state?"

For someone who saw her every day, it did not seem like such
a sudden change, but Rika's words made Mitsue realize that
Obasan had indeed wasted away at an alarming rate in the short
time she had been staying here. When she first arrived, though

unsteady on her feet, she still had been able to stand up and move around the house, but now, except for her trips to the toilet or the bath, all she did was lie in bed. She bathed herself once in the morning and once in the evening, and afterwards her face showed the effort it had cost her. Mitsue didn't make any attempt to fool herself by blaming Obasan's weakness on the heat.

"Does she eat?" Rika continued, cross-examining Mitsue.

"Some . . . just a little, really."

"Only liquids?"

"Cold noodles, some tofu, watermelon. . . . It's so hot now."

Rika sighed deeply. "I'm sorry for making you take care of her all this time, Mitsue."

Rika didn't say it maliciously, but Mitsue took it as criticism of her care of her aunt. She wished Rika could see how cool and refreshed Obasan looked when, her transparent blue-veined hands lifting the noodles, she half-closed her eyes and said, "This tastes so good in this hot weather."

"I'm going to call a doctor," declared Rika.

Mitsue stared straight at her. What right did this woman have to say that?

"Even Shiro won't oppose it." Under Mitsue's intimidating glare, Rika's voice weakened and she choked back her tears. Then she continued, "We have a responsibility to Haruko. Any daughter would want her mother to live longer, if only for one minute, or even a second. Shiro's a man and he doesn't understand. It's a frightening disease, so he just keeps procrastinating; he's just scared. My little brother's the same way. If the baby so much as spits up, he gets all worried."

"So he insists on calling the doctor?"

Rika nodded.

"But in this case Shiro doesn't want to call a doctor. . . ." Mitsue stopped; she was on the verge of advocating Shiro's position, and it was strange to be trying to explain to his own wife Shiro's desire to respect his mother's wishes.

"That's because she's his mother. He's completely different when it comes to his own children. Men don't care about their parents." Rika's big eyes clouded over for an instant; did she think the same way about her own son?

So that was her point. He's acting this way because it's his mother; if it were his child his attitude would be totally different. Maybe there was some sense in what Rika said, but she went too far when she made that remark about men in general. Mitsue was convinced that Shiro's attitude had nothing to do with some theory about men being indifferent toward their parents, but she didn't put her thought into words.

"I agree that it's cruel to make her go into a hospital and keep her alive like some vegetable, but we won't know whether that's going to happen if we don't try to help her. At least we can do all we can to the bitter end, and only then can we say that it was God's will. But not even to try, to avoid doctors and hospitals . . ."

Mitsue half-expected Rika to continue, "You're just a typical farmer, can't come to a decision," but not even Rika would say that. Instead she assumed a businesslike tone, as if to say, This is no time to bicker, and asked, "Where's the closest university hospital?"

Mitsue couldn't withstand the pressure, and she whispered her answer, "I guess the Agricultural Cooperative Hospital. . . ."

Rika's expression showed her disapproval. Mitsue figured that she was reacting this way because she didn't know about the brand-new modern building and facilities of the Agricultural Cooperative Hospital. She continued, "But anyone with a serious illness goes to the K– University Hospital."

"Oh, that's right; K– University has a medical school, doesn't it? We'll have to find someone with connections and get a letter of introduction to one of the doctors there." Then, as if she had just made a quick, clever round through her mind and struck on something, she clapped her thin hands together. "There's that uncle we see every year at the memorial services: Mother's younger brother, the one who opened his office in K– . . . how *could* she? . . . her own brother a doctor . . ."

Now Mitsue remembered. "But he's an ear-nose-throat doctor," she answered.

"It doesn't matter what his specialty is; he can introduce us to colleagues. And you know, he goes to K– University Hospital once a week; that's right, he told me last year during Bon."

Mitsue was impressed. Rika really did have a quick mind and a sharp ear. Mitsue herself knew that Obasan came from a doctor's family and that one of her brothers was a doctor, but, whatever the circumstances, Obasan didn't stay in touch with her relatives. Naturally you wouldn't expect any intimacy between this uncle and Mitsue and her brother, but he wasn't close to Shiro or Haruko, either. Nevertheless Rika had managed to get this information from him about his work.

"We can't hide this any longer. Don't you agree? I mean, this doctor is her own blood brother. If we don't tell him, Shiro will be blamed; it will bring disgrace on us both."

Mitsue didn't answer; wasn't it irrelevant whether someone was blamed or disgraced? She wanted to tell Rika that no one had the right to interfere with Obasan's freedom to stay in control of her own life, but now, unlike the times she had faced Genji and Kohei, her tongue wouldn't move. Rika was a tough opponent.

"What about Haruko? I wonder if she could be totally unaware of Obasan's illness?"

Mitsue pulled herself together with difficulty. She didn't know whether or not Shiro had given in to his wife, but she desperately wanted to know what the serene, even-tempered Haruko would say if she were here. She wondered if they had talked about it last summer when Obasan had visited Haruko in America.

"She must suspect something. I started noticing years ago that something was wrong. She got so she didn't want to carry heavy things, and she tired easily . . . and then . . ."

Mitsue didn't know what Rika had been about to say, but she knew there were things that couldn't be hidden from people you live with, day in and day out, in the same house. Now Mitsue, who alone had lived all these years without suspecting anything, felt like an outcast. Shiro had said that he had kept it secret even from Rika, but . . . Something trembled inside Mitsue. So that was it. Could Shiro have been protecting his wife? Considering Rika's character and point of view, Shiro must have known she wouldn't just stand by and let things be. But her children were still very young, and Rika actually needed her mother-in-law's help. There was no way she could have taken on the burden of her care if they diagnosed Obasan's cancer and put her in a hospital. So Obasan and Shiro must have kept it from Rika to protect her and the children. It dawned on Mitsue that she had been taken for a fool, and she felt a sudden anger.

"You do whatever you want. It's beyond me," she declared, and took off her apron. "Now that you're here, I can just go on home."

"What?" Rika's eyes were confused.

Mitsue faced Rika, and her expression spoke for her: Isn't that the way it should be? After all, you're the daughter-in-law. It was all she could do to keep from adding, As for me, I'm fed up with volunteer work. Without a word she went out the back door.

She entered the living room and again turned the air conditioner to "high," sat down right on the floor, and, drawing up her legs in her arms, rested her face on her knees.

Though recently Rika had been coming here with Shiro every year for Bon, in the old days Shiro had come by himself, saying that the children were too young for the trip. Rika, who had no connection with this land, had stayed in Tokyo at her parents' place. Mitsue imagined how Rika must feel, abandoned in this strange place with a terminally ill patient and utterly at her wits' end; part of her felt it served Rika right, but at the same time she felt guilty. She did feel sorry for her aunt, but then Obasan had brought it on herself. Mitsue didn't know what to do about these mixed emotions; she found herself thinking that if Rika called for help she would go on over, but the phone was silent.

There was some rice soaking in a pot for Obasan's evening meal, and Mitsue had put some frozen flounder on the bottom shelf of the refrigerator. She realized that Rika, with her instincts as a housewife, would know what to do with these things and wouldn't have any need for her help; in fact, now Mitsue herself felt left out.

Kohei or Kazumi had kept Mitsue supplied with food, bringing it to the back door so no one would notice. Without showing any desire to see Obasan or giving any particular explanation, they often made a point of including some light foods that the invalid was likely to enjoy.

When she thought of him, Mitsue realized she was truly grateful to her brother; unlike Shiro, he treated her like his own flesh and blood. And the two wives had a completely different attitude, too, thought Mitsue in spite of herself.

Cold air is heavy. Pretty soon it got too cold to sit on the floor, and Mitsue lazily pulled herself up to turn the switch down to "low."

It was getting dark outside, but Rika made no sign of calling for help. In spite of her sophisticated no-nonsense attitude, she normally didn't seem to have much inner strength; nevertheless she was showing an unexpected stubborn streak now. Mitsue's tense mood wouldn't let her body relax, and she paced restlessly in the kitchen. During the month and a half that she had spent in the main house, this kitchen had changed subtly. The soy sauce was still in the same place and the kitchen cloths were folded the same way, but here and there Kazumi had left her mark on the

room. Undoubtedly Kazumi had something in mind for tonight's
dinner, so there was nothing for Mitsue to do here either.

Still restless, she returned to the living room and, sitting with
her legs crossed on the sofa, sank into thought. There came a
sound from the back door, and Mitsue lifted her head, expecting
to see her neice or nephew. But again it was Kohei who appeared.
Kazumi must have been right when she confided to Mitsue that
Kohei was too preoccupied with Obasan's illness to work in the
fields as he usually did. As soon as his work was done at the
Cooperative he would come home, apparently just to be there in
case something happened with Obasan and they needed his help.

He stared at his sister's face, startled, but didn't ask what she
was doing there. Mitsue felt a sudden desire to beat her pent-up
frustration against her brother's thick, solid chest, but she
couldn't find any words to express this. She just said bluntly, "I'm
back here for good."

"Why?"

"I'm not going to just keep on being the maid over there, that's
why."

"What're you saying?" Kohei asked, as if he hadn't quite
grasped her meaning.

"Rika's come from Tokyo. I can't stand listening to her brisk
'young mistress' talk." It was a rash thing to say, but she was being honest.

Kohei was silent for a moment, but, looking closely at her puffy
face, he seemed to understand. "Don't be stupid," he said abruptly. "Cut out your petty complaining and get on over there. Rika
doesn't know how to take care of things; think of Obasan's position." He wasn't going to take no for an answer. Her normally
taciturn and impassive brother had turned against her, and Mitsue flared up angrily.

"You're the stupid one. Compared to Shiro . . ." She couldn't think of how to finish what she'd started, and added, "you're just a loser."

"I'm not a loser," Kohei answered sullenly.

Well, he was right. Whereas Shiro had made it into the university in Tokyo, and Kohei only got as far as the local farm school, Mitsue had to admit that both had gotten exactly what they wanted. Rika was more beautiful than the woman Obasan had chosen for her nephew to marry, but Kazumi was good-natured and Kohei lived in harmony with her. Of course this was not a question of winners and losers.

"Get going." Kohei pointed his tanned chin toward the main house.

"I don't want to," Mitsue stubbornly refused.

"You really are an idiot." Kohei's little eyes opened wide in disbelief and he scrutinized his sister's face.

"Obasan's just getting what she asked for. She's in the terrible shape she's in now because she hid her disease and refused to see a doctor. I'm not the one who got her this way. At first she wanted to just die of hunger out here, and I prevented it."

Kohei gave an uncharacteristically deep sigh. She was hopeless. "If you don't watch out, it's all over with you. Once you've given in to the dark side of your soul, that's the end."

Startled, Mitsue looked up at him. Was it some accident that had made him say "the dark side of your soul"? Or had he really meant to allude to something inside her?

"What do you mean, 'dark side of my soul'? I never thought I'd hear you talking like some priest." Mitsue feigned indifference, fearing all the while he would hit on the truth.

"There's also what I told you about your burn . . . and there's more . . . like the sin of lust." Kohei spoke quietly, evenly. "Sin of lust": The only response would be to laugh it off as just more religious nonsense, but Mitsue was shocked. Could Kohei, without saying anything, have been aware of everything, including Mitsue's desire for Shiro?

"Who's 'getting what she asked for'? Instead . . ." Kohei gathered his strength and continued slowly: "What I mean is, who's the one who's suffering most right now? Think about what it must be like to have your body break down, decaying little by little until death finally comes."

Kohei stood motionless and impenetrable like a guardian god, his body telling his sister, herself standing in stony silence, that he wouldn't move an inch until she went back to the wing. Then, after three or four minutes, there came the sound of a bike stopping at the back door and Kazumi rushed in, out of breath. She was back much earlier than usual.

"Oh, you're here." Kazumi seemed to be talking to Mitsue rather than Kohei. Panting for breath, she pressed her hands against her enormous bosom. It seemed to Mitsue that Kazumi was some kind of divine being who had come to rescue her just in time.

"What's all this fuss about?" Now even Kohei seemed agitated, and his criticism of his wife was unusual.

"Well, I'm surprised, that's what it's about. Shiro's wife, what's her name . . ."

"Rika?" Without being aware of it, Mitsue leaned forward.

"Yes, that's the one; even her name is elegant. She came up all of a sudden in a taxi."

"Where?"

"To the Marufuji." This was the name of Kazumi's super-market. "Well, she's a stranger around here, and a real beauty as well, so of course she stands out, and she just keeps piling up all this stuff to buy, so she asks me to help her." The Marufuji sold both food and household goods, and Kazumi worked back in the appliance section.

Her round eyes wide open, Kazumi continued, "She gave this

elegant bow," and she twisted her round little waist in imitation of Rika's bow. "And then she says . . ." Kazumi drew a breath and imitated Rika's style of speech. " 'I wonder if Madam would be so good as to let me use her employee discount for this?' I was wondering who 'Madam' could be and then realized it was me." Kazumi added this explanation without so much as a smile. "Well, I was completely floored, and I just said, 'Yes, ma'am,' and rang her up. But then, when I saw that taxi leave, I started wondering if something had happened, and took off work right then and there, and here I am."

"There's nothing to be that surprised at," Kohei reproved his wife, then turning to Mitsue he ordered her again: "Get on over there, you."

Now Mitsue realized that they could no longer hide Obasan's illness. Although the people who shopped at the Marufuji were for the most part residents of the newly developed neighborhoods, many of the clerks who worked there had longstanding connections with the original villagers. The opening of the new supermarket had had an enormous effect on life in this small town; it had been the focus of a major political struggle with the village potentates, who had been shopowners for decades. Kazumi complained that even the clerks were drawn into it. Mitsue herself had been amazed at how quickly information and rumors spread, and the usually talkative Kazumi had been especially careful to keep Obasan's illness a secret from her co-workers.

Old Genji had been right when he complained that Shiro should have married a local girl. Pretty soon the old villagers would descend upon the house in throngs, and there would be only Rika to greet them, come specially all the way from Tokyo. In the eyes of the old people, Tokyo was another world, as remote as it had been in the old days. Righteous indignation would be raised against Mitsue, who, though she lived right next door, wasn't there to help.

As she walked over toward the wing, Mitsue realized again that since Rika's arrival she had been absorbed with her own feelings and had put Obasan's needs in the background. Her aunt's desire to hide herself and die alone out here was not unreasonable. Kohei's words, "Who's the one suffering most right now?" and Obasan's voice saying, "You know how happy I'd be if you'd stay with me," came back to her, and the "memory" of that rainy evening and the dark earthen floor was superimposed on the words like a double exposure. That eternal vigil of mourning out in the field, wrapped in the slanting rays of dusk—had it been nothing but an illusion? Mitsue peered through the back door into the kitchen; the floor was lined with Rika's purchases. The first thing she noticed was a large electric fan. Among the groceries—yogurt, cans of soup—there was nothing that Obasan would be able to eat, she thought; then she heard Rika's voice coming from the veranda of the new room.

"I'm much obliged to you for coming to call." She spoke in an earnest, loud voice, the kind used at elementary school literary programs, as if her listener were some old lady with a hearing problem. "But she's terribly tired and can't see you."

Mitsue nearly burst out laughing. Contrary to her expectations, Rika was proving to be very useful. Though Rika herself wasn't aware of it, her manner of speaking was probably the best possible weapon against the onslaught of the old townspeople. And sure enough, after some indistinct mumbling a voice said, "Oh, I see, I see. I'll come back later," and then Mitsue heard the sound of footsteps retreating.

When Mitsue entered the dressing room, Obasan's eyebrows were knit in pain, but at the same time she was grinning mischievously. Mitsue had worried that her aunt might have heard her quarrelling with Rika earlier, but Obasan's face gave no clue.

Rika came back, making little mincing steps. She showed no

surprise at Mitsue's presence and reported earnestly, "I turned them away."

"You did? Thank you." Obasan bowed her head slightly, then looked out over the veranda at the phoenix tree. Her expression was so peaceful that Rika and Mitsue joined her deep silence and, aligning their gaze with hers, looked out at the tree. Of course leaves change with the season, but it didn't seem likely that the trunk itself could change color in this short time. Yet as Obasan lay facing the tree all day long, her eyes directed at it during every waking hour, the tree seemed to take in her gaze, and its green color gradually assumed a deep clarity; now Mitsue had an eerie feeling that the trunk itself had become transparent. Mitsue caught herself wondering if Rika had already, by some quick maneuvering, gotten hold of a doctor, but then realized that Obasan's bedside was no place to be competing with Rika. Instead, she directed her gaze at the twigs of the green tree, whose tips still shone with the light of the western sun.

That evening marked a turning point in Obasan's illness, and her weakness increased considerably. She hardly spoke at all, and sometimes she would seem to be asleep, but suddenly an expression of intense suffering would appear on her face. Rika was perceptive in her own way, and perhaps she had discerned something in Obasan's expression, or maybe she was vaguely afraid of the dark thing that lurked inside Mitsue. At any rate, she didn't bring up the subject of doctors again. She just planted herself at Obasan's bedside, a somber expression on her face. Obasan by now had no strength left even to show how Rika's attentions oppressed her. In the evenings Rika would call her parents' house to talk to her children, then, calling her mother to the phone, gave detailed instructions for the children's homework or lessons for the next day. The children had apparently been told to expect her calls at a particular time each day.

Within a very few days Rika, burdened with her various cares, had lost so much weight that even Mitsue felt sorry for her. She wanted to persuade her to return to Tokyo, but, watching the increasing, prolonged agony in her aunt's face, she lost the courage to weather it out alone. If Rika were again to bring up the subject of calling a doctor, Mitsue herself would agree to it without hesitation. Apparently Rika kept in touch with Shiro, using a public telephone so that Obasan wouldn't hear their conversations; now and then, lowering her voice, she would give Mitsue brief reports: He should be able to get here by such-and-such a day; he's called Haruko in America; as soon as Haruko can get a ticket, she'll come.

When Haruko at last arrived from America and walked in with Shiro through the back door, Mitsue greeted her with some surprise. She hadn't seen her for years, and Haruko had lived abroad and given birth to three children in the meantime. Mitsue had figured that she wouldn't even be able to recognize her, but Haruko hadn't changed a bit. She had always seemed somewhat homely in comparison with her beautiful mother, but when you looked closely, you could see she had the same nose and eyes. With the passage of time her skin had slackened and she had gained weight around the waist, but she still had exactly the same matter-of-fact nature that had marked her from childhood. Perhaps because of this, Mitsue was struck with an illusion that Haruko had been living here with her all these years.

"Mit-chan, thank you for all you've done." Haruko's smooth, low voice was veiled as if by some delicate gauze, and her gentle accent had survived, dodging the onslaughts of circumstance and time.

As the three of them started down the hall they heard Rika's thin voice exclaiming, "Oh, Mother, that must be Haruko!" It was such a contrast that Mitsue, without thinking, looked sideways at Haruko, but Haruko's expression didn't change and she continued on calmly into her mother's room.

From behind the threshold of the room Mitsue peered in nervously over Shiro's shoulder. Just one year ago Obasan had gone to America to help Haruko with her baby. How would Haruko react when she saw how her mother had deteriorated since then? . . . If she broke down, it could mean that Rika had been right, that Shiro and Mitsue's way of dealing with Obasan's illness had been a mistake.

With incredible nonchalance Haruko knelt beside her mother's futon and fixed her sensible eyes on her face. Her eyebrows knit slightly. "You've just wasted away, haven't you, Mother." Haruko's own pain blurred into her voice, which neither reproached nor consoled.

Mitsue couldn't see her aunt's face, turned sideways from the door, but Obasan nodded, and it seemed she was smiling in her usual way. She began asking Haruko about her family, beginning with her husband and bringing up each of the children by name. "So is the baby standing up yet? Children nowadays develop faster than they used to." Except for her difficulty breathing, Obasan's voice betrayed no emotion, and neither of them showed any signs of repressed feeling. Mitsue felt somewhat let down now that Haruko, after all her anticipation, was actually here, but at the same time she envied her. The daughter and mother were united body and soul, bound by a sense of trust deeper even than the one that existed between Obasan and her son. Haruko looked at her mother's illness with a calm recognition, as if she saw something of herself in it. For several minutes she said nothing but simply explored her mother slowly with her thoughtful eyes. Finally she reached out her hand and gently laid it on her mother's chest. Her expression, which up until then had conveyed a calm wisdom, broke into a smile of such complete childlike innocence that, of all the people in the world, it seemed only Haruko could convey it. Mitsue suspected that even Shiro would be jealous, seeing this child's smile, so completely full of trust, resurrected on the face of a woman about to enter middle age.

Obasan's lips moved slightly in response, and then, as if relieved of an enormous burden, her eyes closed.

In front of Mitsue, Shiro's back suddenly stirred and, grazing Mitsue on the way, he left the room. Instinctively she looked up, and their eyes met. His eyes were filled, and she winced. He smiled self-consciously, then, holding back his tears, he whispered, "No one can hold a candle to Haruko."

Mitsue took the presents Haruko had brought and went into the kitchen. Rika, her little chin set firmly, was intently grinding some vegetables in a mortar. She had heard that fresh vegetable juice—ground by hand—was effective against cancer, so she had taken to mashing greens in the mortar, then straining them through gauze. She must have thought that since Obasan didn't want to see doctors, she would prefer folk remedies. Mitsue watched with scorn: There was no point in going to all that trouble, because Obasan wouldn't force herself to drink the juice if she didn't like it. Still, she suddenly felt a rush of sympathy for Rika.

No matter how they tried, neither Rika nor Mitsue could give Obasan anything that could top Haruko's smile. Even Shiro couldn't achieve that sense of complete trust, but here was Rika trying, with her raw vegetable juice. Her brow was covered with cold sweat.

That must be Haruko going out onto the veranda of the new room, where Shiro was standing: Mitsue recognized the sound of her heavy footsteps. Haruko's ankles, like those of her mother, were slender and white, and she had delicate feet, but for some reason she made an awful lot of noise when she walked. It was unbecoming. The disapproval Mitsue had felt as a girl when she heard Haruko's footsteps now echoed, unchanged, in her ears. The noise may have gone unnoticed on the expansive floors of the main house, but in this small wing it was much too loud. Suddenly Mitsue ralized that Haruko had always been terribly splayfooted. What a strange thing to discover now, after all these years! Haruko herself must have noticed it long ago, but she hadn't tried to correct it and just kept on walking in her clumsy way, never showing any concern.

Rika's hand stopped its grinding, and without lifting her eyes from the contents of the mortar, she tuned her ears in to the voices of Shiro and Haruko talking out on the veranda. Mitsue felt strangely irritated. After all, Rika was his wife, she could just go on out and join in the conversation if she wanted.

Shiro must have brought up the subject of what to do about Bon this year. Haruko answered quietly that, depending on how things went, they might even get by without observing the ceremonies. Somehow, without ever raising her voice or, with the exception of the noise she made when walking, ever making any assertive gestures, she had become the decision-maker of the household.

Now that Haruko was here, she took over her mother's care. Mitsue, no longer spending her time at her aunt's bedside, put her energy into working in the kitchen. It kept her busy: Shiro was commuting back and forth frequently from Tokyo, so including the invalid there were five people to cook for. Obasan's condition continued to deteriorate and the painful episodes of difficult breathing came more and more frequently. Mitsue couldn't bear to watch her aunt's suffering, and she would flee into the kitchen, but Rika, even with her face drained of color and her teeth clenched tight, would try to keep Obasan company. Everyone took refuge in Haruko's unwavering tranquility.

One evening almost a week into August, taking an opportunity when all four of them were gathered in the kitchen, Haruko, in an unconcerned tone of voice, said, "I wonder if she'll make it until Bon." The day before, Obasan had weakened to the point of being unable to get up, and Haruko had taken on bedpan duty. Obasan seemed to be sleeping, and Haruko's voice was quiet, but the other three panicked and pulled Haruko out into the backyard.

Standing in the shade of the yatsude bushes, Haruko looked calmly around at each of them and, her eyes on her brother, said, "I think she's got less than a week left."

Shiro nodded. Rika's little white face paled even more and stiffened slightly, but she said nothing.

Mitsue was overcome by a strange yearning; as children, the four cousins used to gather like this to plan their fireworks for Bon. She even felt like going over to the house to fetch Kohei, too, pulling him by the hand.

"Well, which doctor should we call?" Rika and Mitsue both looked at Haruko, surprised at the calmness in her voice.

"Which doctor? Why now, suddenly . . . ?"

Haruko answered coolly. "There will have to be a death certificate."

Rika swallowed. Mitsue looked down at the ground. Not far from her foot lay the discarded, translucent brownish shell of a cicada. She shifted her leg slightly and kicked at it. She recalled the time she had counted ten regular steps back from the knothole in the wooden fence that was now gone.

"There will be all kinds of problems if we wait until she dies. We have to get someone to come and examine her and diagnose it while she's still alive."

Shiro nodded his head deeply. "But we ought to get Mother's permission first," he said, looking at his sister's face. She looked back at him and smiled. "I've already talked to her about it," she answered. "She nodded as if she knew this was the end."

Shiro looked as if he had felt a sudden pain in the chest. "She's doing it to fulfill this one social obligation," he said gravely.

"But it's still a good thing." Haruko's brow relaxed. "It's the same in America. They hook you up to machines and then, on top of that, they fill you up with so many painkillers you can't think straight and at the end you might as well not even be a human being. But I think that Mother hasn't felt any pain except in her breathing, and her mind is as clear as ever. I'm happy that she can pass away in dignity, in her own way . . ." Haruko frowned slightly, but calmly continued, ". . . though her physical condition is so terrible."

Then she looked at Mitsue. "Mit-chan, Mother says she wants to say goodbye to Ko-chan; even tonight would be all right."

Mitsue nodded in reply. She wondered whether Obasan would confess to her on her deathbed that she'd been the one who burned her, then felt a sudden anger at herself.

That same evening, after Kohei emerged from the dressing room, his puffy eyes swollen and red, Mitsue nodded off in the corner of the tea room and had a vision.

Several children, joining hands to make a ring around the phoenix tree, were singing, "Little bird in a cage . . ." Though she couldn't distinguish between the clear, high voices of the children, Mitsue knew that Shiro, Haruko, Kohei, and Kazumi, as well as herself, were among them. "Who will be It . . . ?" In the total silence that fell after the song, the ring stopped moving, and all at once the children scattered. The child left crouching directly behind the tree with her hands covering her eyes might have been either Mitsue or Obasan. In the twilight, the cold, dark air pressed down, thick as water, the rich green of the tree deepened even more, and the tree trunk turned pale and as transparent as glass. A huge fish swam up silently and continued on past the dead body that was not quite Obasan or Mitsue. Oh, it's Haruko, she thought, and right then Shiro swam up, weaving his way without a sound through the transparent forest of seaweed. He held a glittering jewel in his lips.

"I want it," thought Mitsue, but she couldn't lift her hand. She started panting for breath, and when she awoke her mouth was wide open like a fish's. There was no way for her to find out whether she had managed to grasp the jewel in her dream and swallow it, but Mitsue strained her eyes in the darkness, trying to remember.

The next day an old doctor who had been working for years in T– came and told them she had four or five days left.

Three days later Obasan breathed her last.

The doctor who examined her was shocked at her condition. He told Shiro that in all his years of practice he had only diagnosed one case like it, and that was long ago. Usually, in treating breast cancer, a mastectomy is performed, followed by cobalt treatments, and then the wound is cleaned up neatly. The doctor said that in a case as unusual as this one, where the ulcer had not been treated, he couldn't positively ascertain whether the cancer had spread to the internal organs, but he thought that it hadn't. Instead, the ulcer had spread from the side of the chest all the way around to the back.

Haruko and Rika had been taking turns attending to Obasan, but because of some sequence of minor events—the telephone or the bathroom—she had been alone at the end. It happened at a perfectly unremarkable time, a little past three in the afternoon— no slanting rays of twilight for her. And the expression on her face fell far short of the beautiful image of serenity that Mitsue had anticipated; the agony of her last painful breaths showed plainly in her face and in the rolled-up whites of her eyes, wide open as if the eyelids had been peeled off.

They called the old doctor again, and he confirmed the death. Rika, weeping, smoothed Obasan's forehead and cheeks, trying her best to soften the dead woman's expression. Mitsue watched Rika's efforts as the face itself, rather than softening, turned cold and seemed to shrink, as if it were caving in on itself. The person who had branded her face and heart with a burning scar was losing her own face, and Mitsue, together with a deep sense of relief, felt a strange redemption.

If, as Obasan herself had once said, at the moment of her last breath she had become a "transparent, nameless spirit" and had flown off to "mount the wind beyond the seas and vanish to some unknown place," then the body that lay here must just be an abandoned vessel, a cast-off chrysalis. Mitsue picked up the cologne bottle that Obasan had kept at her bedside and sprayed a small puff into the air, then took up the fan and waved it gently. She wanted to send a breeze carrying Obasan's own characteristic fragrance to accompany the nameless spirit that had lost all individuality and was now fluttering away.

Obasan had told Haruko that she didn't want her body to be bathed or made up, but would rather have it cremated right away, so they simply put her purple silk gauze yukata on over her nightgown. It was the same one she had worn two months before, when Shiro had brought her, deathly ill, back home.

Now Mitsue understood that what she had awaited so eagerly was ultimately not Shiro or Obasan, or even, as she had once thought, some role that she alone would play out, by herself, on this day, but rather it was something else. And this "something else"—could it have been Obasan's death itself? Of course she had to deny it, but . . . As she sat beside her aunt's corpse, listening to the faraway voices of Shiro and Haruko quietly discussing plans for the vigil, Mitsue felt she could stay here forever, moving her fan back and forth. . . .

Suddenly she opened her eyes. In a corner of the room, darkening now with the early twilight, Kohei and Kazumi were kneeling, their palms together in front of them. Then, in a place that could have been either the vast, whitish expanse of water or the over-grown yard, she saw the other corpse, not Obasan or herself, but the one of her vision, floating again in front of her. She turned her eyes to one side, looking for the tree. There, beyond the veranda, Genji crouched his old, bent body at the foot of the phoenix tree, and behind him stood several of the old townspeople, bunched together in one gray mass, their heads bowed. It was a silent condolence call, offered from the depths of twilight to Obasan, or, rather, to her absence, for she was already gone.

The family would observe the ceremony of the seven-day anniversary of Obasan's death all together, but meanwhile Shiro and his wife went back to Tokyo for a couple of days. The morning they left Mitsue saw them off from the storage gate, then slowly walked back through the grass, her eyes fixed on the house that had lost its mistress. Mitsue hadn't yet returned to her brother's house, but planned to stay in the wing with Haruko until she went back to America.

As they had sat over breakfast, Haruko had said, smiling, "Beginning tonight it's going to be lonely with just the two of us here; let's go ask Ko-chan to let us stay at his place." The suburban houses that now stood beyond the front gate hadn't been there at the time Obasan was living by herself in the wing; it had been much more isolated then. It must have been bad even before that, when Haruko had lived here alone with Obasan. Haruko admitted, laughing, without coming right out and saying so, that she was a real coward in comparison with her mother. She must have assumed that Mitsue was the same way. And now that she thought of it, Mitsue realized that, even knowing that her aunt was terminally ill, she hadn't been afraid in the wing as long as Obasan was with her. But now it was indeed lonely out here alone with just Haruko.

When she got back to the wing there was no sign of Haruko.

Mitsue checked in the ten-mat room, where the altar was set up, but Haruko wasn't there. The framed photograph of Obasan, draped with a black ribbon, showed her with a perplexed smile, and her brow was slightly furrowed.

Although they hadn't made any special announcement of her death, a fair number of people had gathered for the funeral. It was natural that several teachers and graduates from the high school would turn out, but Mitsue, Shiro, and Rika found it strange that the local broadcasting company sent a representative. Haruko thought nothing of it; she said it was because Obasan had been an especially enthusiastic choir director. During the formal funeral at the Sogi family's Buddhist temple, one of the high school graduates had played a tape that had been made several years ago, when the school choir was chosen to represent the Hokuriku district at the national high school choir competition. Mitsue didn't know the song, but the bright, cheerful soprano part recalled for her Obasan's voice singing, long ago, when the main house was still standing. The former student had said that students had been attracted to Obasan not so much for her enthusiasm as for her outstanding musical sense.

The incense that Shiro and his wife had lit as an offering before their departure had burned down, and Mitsue lit another and set it on the stand. She continued on into the dressing room, which had already been cleaned up, and saw Haruko standing outside the veranda. When Haruko saw Mitsue, she touched the phoenix tree's trunk with her hand and said, "This is the *wakagiri* that Mother especially liked, isn't it?"

Mitsue simply nodded.

"It's not much to speak of, is it? Even if we cut it down, we couldn't very well sell it like that big cedar. Shall we just leave it this way?" She seemed to be asking Mitsue's advice.

Haruko's comment was so matter-of-fact that Mitsue knelt on the veranda to take a fresh look at the tree. Indeed, in the flat light of morning, the phoenix tree had become just another tree. Mitsue felt a small shock inside, and she suddenly wanted to know what her cousin, who was so completely candid about everything, thought about her scar. Not knowing how to begin, she devised a little stratagem before speaking.

"I'm worried that I might have left Obasan with some unresolved anxiety at her death when I refused the operation . . . when she made such a point of offering it to me."

"Oh, you mean your scar." Haruko's eyes, looking at Mitsue's face, showed the same simple directness as when they had observed Obasan's illness for the first time. "As for me, I don't think it's so noticeable, but they say that nowadays it's very easy to correct—why don't you just try the operation? Mother often mentioned it."

"Did you know about it?" Mitsue mustered her energy and blurted it out.

"About what?"

"That it was Obasan who spilled the oil . . ."

Haruko's eyes widened a little, but she answered, "No, she's not the one. It was an old housekeeper named Otake."

"That's what I thought too, but Kohei saw it . . ." Mitsue couldn't finish the sentence.

"Well, that's strange," Haruko tipped her head to one side doubtfully, then concluded in her usual flat tone, "No, Ko-chan must have seen it wrong or gotten it mixed up somehow in his memory.

"Mother used to talk about it a lot with me after my first child was born. She said that Otake was an old lady by that time, and, running around underfoot like that, we almost tripped her. When she reached out to the new gas range to steady herself, thinking it was the old kitchen stove, she hit the pot instead. Wait, Mit-chan, don't you remember? Old Otake had this terrible burn mark running all the way across her hand, on her fingers. . . ."

"No, I don't remember ever meeting someone called Otake."

"I guess you wouldn't. I guess I remember because I'm a little older than you.... She used to come over a lot when I was small.... Oh, but then she must have felt awful having to see your face; she must have avoided you."

So Obasan had continually warned Haruko, herself now a mother, never to let small children near when she was cooking with hot oil.

"But then, you know, Mother also said that the moment she realized the oil was spilling, she turned off the burner with one hand and at the same time pushed me out of the way with the other ... actually, you were closer to the stove, and she probably couldn't have gotten you out of the way in time, but if she was going to push anyone away it should have been you. Nevertheless she said she reached out to me, though I wasn't in any danger."

Haruko continued in her indifferent tone, "She always said that it's frightening how selfish the mother's instinct is. Maybe it was something that couldn't be helped in your case, but she warned me to always be conscious of the danger."

"So why did Kohei ... ?" Mitsue swallowed her words.

Haruko tipped her head to one side again, then said thoughtfully, "I wonder ... I guess it was a real shock for him, so young himself and an orphan, and he must have felt some responsibility for you, even at his age. Then, even worse, there was his foster mother showing such blatant partiality, protecting only her own child, even though she wasn't in any danger. It must have been the shock that confused him at the time or made him remember it wrong.... Sometimes it happens with children."

Haruko raised her eyes, then placed her palms in front of her knees and bowed low. "Forgive me. I have to apologize to Ko-chan too; it was because of me that Mother shocked him so." Haruko looked up gravely at Mitsue. "Forgive me."

Maybe it had happened the way Haruko said. In her mind Mitsue gazed at the dark earthen floor of the evening of her accident, and asked vacantly, "Was it raining that day?'"

"I don't know; I don't remember it. But it might have been, especially if we were playing inside. Mother never said anything about the weather."

Mitsue listened absently to Haruko's answer, and remembered something Obasan's brother had said when he came from K– after learning of her death. Though he was an ear-nose-throat doctor, death was nothing new to him, and once he had heard their brief explanation of Obasan's illness he made no effort to probe into the behavior of her immediate family. Instead, he started reminiscing about her: "From the time your mother was a young girl she was known far and wide as a real beauty—though if you took a good look at her, her face wasn't particularly beautiful in itself. You've probably heard about S–, the one who's now in the National Diet and used to be the prefectural governor. Well, he was just one of her admirers. She had her pick of marriage proposals and love letters from them, but she chose your father. The reason she gave was that he was so handsome, but you know of course that he wasn't that good-looking. He was just a simple, unrefined country man, and he had tuberculosis to boot. She must have had her own unique criteria for deciding what was handsome. But the way she died . . ." He broke off a minute, then continued.

"What a barbaric way to die; what an obstinate passivity in facing death . . . it's a rare person who could achieve it. You have to admire her for it."

In that conversation Mitsue learned for the first time what had estranged Obasan from her family. Rather than offering to take care of the young widow and the children at their home, her parents had secretly decided to support Shiro in medical school when the time came. When they finally came out and tried to force Shiro to study to become a doctor and carry on the family tradition, Obasan had refused.

"You know, I ought to have become a doctor after all." Mitsue glanced quickly at Shiro, whose voice was blurred with regret. Perhaps he thought that if he had been a doctor, his mother might have simply turned herself over to western medical science.

Obasan's brother had called it a "barbaric way to die," but it must have taken a brutal courage to carry on that symbiosis with the decaying, stinking flesh of her own body. But her eyes had shown no struggle, only serenity. What could they have been watching?

Mitsue suddenly recalled the glittering jewel of her dream. The corpse at the bottom of the water must have been her own; the green jewel was something her aunt had pulled from deep inside the ulcerating, raw wound in her breast and bequeathed to her.

Maybe Shiro had been nothing but her messenger. Whatever the reason, when Obasan died, Mitsue felt that the evil thing that had possessed her and lurked inside her all this time had at last dropped away, and that her secret attraction to Shiro, too, was gone. . . . Now she could have that operation.

Suddenly Mitsue thought she could.

It was impossible to suspect Obasan of telling Haruko a lie about Mitsue's burn. It must have been the "dark side of Kohei's soul" that had made him see or remember it wrong.

Mitsue raised her head. "Could you give Kohei the tree?"

"What tree? Oh, you mean the *wakagiri*. Of course it would be all right, but how? I suppose we could get a gardener to ball the roots and transplant it, or . . ." Haruko reached over and stroked the trunk, then grimaced. "Ooh! It's covered with ants!" She shook them off her palm and continued, "I heard it from Shiro, but if Ko-chan would take over this place for us we could just leave it here. Of course we can't do anything with the building itself, but perhaps we could leave the tree and let him farm the land around it." The ants that Haruko had shaken off her hand must have landed on her feet, bare except for the sandals she had slipped on; she stamped her small white feet—toes pointing outward as always—loudly on the ground.

"If I have the operation, it will definitely be for someone else's sake, someone I've never even met. . . ."

The translucent little-girl voice struck Mitsue's ear, then, rising along the trunk of the phoenix tree, it disappeared into the sky.

DISCOVER JAPAN, VOLS. 1 AND 2
Words, Customs, and Concepts

The Japan Culture Institute

Essays and photographs illuminate 200 ideas and customs of Japan.

THE UNFETTERED MIND
Writings of the Zen Master to the Sword Master

Takuan Sōhō / Translated by William Scott Wilson

Philosophy as useful to today's corporate warriors as it was to seventeenth century samurai.

THE JAPANESE THROUGH AMERICAN EYES
Sheila K. Johnson

"Cogent...as skeptical of James Clavell's *Shogun* as it is of William Ouchi's *Theory Z.*"—*Publisher's Weekly*

Available only in Japan.

BEYOND NATIONAL BORDERS
Reflections on Japan and the World

Kenichi Ohmae

"[Ohmae is Japan's] only management guru."—*Financial Times*

Available only in Japan.

THE COMPACT CULTURE
The Japanese Tradition of "Smaller is Better"

O-Young Lee / Translated by Robert N. Huey

A long history of skillfully reducing things and concepts to their essentials reveals the essence of the Japanese character and, in part, accounts for Japan's business success.

THE HIDDEN ORDER
Tokyo through the Twentieth Century

Yoshinobu Ashihara

"Mr. Ashihara shows how, without anybody planning it, Japanese architecture has come to express the vitality of Japanese life."
—*Daniel J. Boorstin*

NEIGHBORHOOD TOKYO
Theodore C. Bestor

A glimpse into the everyday lives, commerce, and relationships of some two thousand neighborhood residents living in the heart of Tokyo.

THE BOOK OF TEA
Kazuko Okakura
Foreword and Afterword by Soshitsu Sen XV

A new presentation of the seminal text on the meaning and practice of tea—illustrated with eight historic photographs.

GEISHA, GANGSTER, NEIGHBOR, NUN
Scenes from Japanese Lives

Donald Richie

A collection of highly personal portraits of Japanese men and women—some famous, some obscure—from Mishima and Kawabata to a sushi apprentice and a bar madame.

WOMANSWORD
What Japanese Words Say About Women

Kittredge Cherry

From "cockroach husband" to "daughter-in-a-box"—a mix of provocative and entertaining Japanese words that collectively tell the story of Japanese women.

THE THIRD CENTURY
America's Resurgence in the Asian Era

Joel Kotkin and Yoriko Kishimoto

"Truly powerful public ideas."—*Boston Globe*
Available only in Japan.

THE ANATOMY OF DEPENDENCE
The Key Analysis of Japanese Behavior

Takeo Doi / Translated by John Bester

"Offers profound insights."—*Ezra Vogel*